THIS DARK HEART

ALSO BY CHRISTA LAIRD

Shadow of the Wall
Beyond the Wall
The Forgotten Son
The Dangerous Dream of Ben Maludzi

THIS DARK HEART

Christa Laird

The Book Guild Ltd

First published in Great Britain in 2022 by
The Book Guild Ltd
Unit E2 Airfield Business Park,
Harrison Road, Market Harborough,
Leicestershire. LE16 7UL
Tel: 0116 2792299
www.bookguild.co.uk
Email: info@bookguild.co.uk
Twitter: @bookguild

Copyright © 2022 Christa Laird

The right of Christa Laird to be identified as the author of this
work has been asserted by them in accordance with the
Copyright, Design and Patents Act 1988.

All rights reserved. No part of this publication may be
reproduced, transmitted, or stored in a retrieval system, in any form or by any means,
without permission in writing from the publisher, nor be otherwise circulated in
any form of binding or cover other than that in which it is published and without
a similar condition being imposed on the subsequent purchaser.

Typeset in 11pt Adobe Garamond Pro

Printed and bound in Great Britain by CMP UK

ISBN 978 1915122 735

British Library Cataloguing in Publication Data.
A catalogue record for this book is available from the British Library.

For Giorgia, Alessia, Will, Alexander and Julian – our 'Famous Five'

The Main Characters

Alberic – Simon's officer in the bodyguard.	
Alexander – one of Herod's adult sons.	H
Antipater – half-brother to Alexander and Aristobulus. Appears very briefly but is frequently referred to as their enemy.	H
Aristobulus – Alexander's brother. Appears only once, briefly, but is frequently referred to.	H
Chloe – Simon's sister.	
David and Leah – Chloe's Jewish brother- and sister-in-law, who treat Simon as family.	
Glaphyra – Alexander's wife, daughter of King Archelaus of Cappadocia.	H
King Archelaus – Glaphyra's father, friend of King Herod's.	H
King Herod of Judaea.	H
Lucius Servius Celer, known as Celer – Roman architect and builder, Simon's mentor.	
Nicolas of Damascus – close adviser to King Herod.	H
Philip the Gaul (also called Philip of Nîmes) – Simon's father, a favoured bodyguard of the King.	

Philo – a comrade of Simon's.	
Ptolemy – brother of Nicolas of Damascus, and head of the Treasury.	H
Quintus Marius Severus – a senior Roman architect.	
Salome – King Herod's sister.	H
Salvia – Glaphyra's favourite maidservant, with whom Simon falls in love.	
Saul – another recruit, who becomes an important friend of Simon's.	
Simon – the main character, a reluctant bodyguard, son of Philip the Gaul.	
Theo – a comrade and close friend of Simon's.	
Zamaris – another recruit, who becomes an important friend of Simon's.	

H – Historical. These people actually existed.

The title of the novel is taken from the poem on the following page by Lord Byron. The execution of King Herod's wife Mariamne took place long before my story opens, but it has set the scene for much of what follows in his household. Please note that Mariamne and Mariamme are the same person. In the novel I have spelt the name in the same way as Josephus does, Mariamme.

Herod's Lament for Mariamne

Oh, Mariamne! now for thee
The heart of which thou bled'st is bleeding;
Revenge is lost in agony,
And wild remorse to rage succeeding.
Oh, Mariamne! where art thou?
Thou canst not hear my bitter pleading:
Ah! could'st thou—thou would'st pardon now,
Though Heaven were to my prayer unheeding.
And is she dead?—and did they dare
Obey my frenzy's jealous raving?
My wrath but doom'd my own despair:
The sword that smote her's o'er me waving.—
But thou art cold, my murder'd love!
And this dark heart is vainly craving
For her who soars alone above,
And leaves my soul unworthy saving.

She's gone, who shared my diadem;
She sunk, with her my joys entombing;
I swept that flower from Judah's stem,
Whose leaves for me alone were blooming;
And mine's the guilt, and mine the hell,
This bosom's desolation dooming;
And I have earn'd those tortures well,
Which unconsumed are still consuming!

Chapter 1

"Don't hide your face. Soldiers have to get used to the sight and smell of blood."

I glanced sideways at Father and flinched at the irritation in his voice. I'd planned for those few days together at the opening of King Herod's spectacular port of Caesarea to be the ideal time to confess my secret ambition, to win him over. But now it no longer seemed likely. I'm not sure to this day what it was that gave my father that powerful aura of authority, so that I could never bring myself to argue with him.

We had been allocated preferential seats for the chariot races, near the turn between the two legs of the U-shaped circuit. These bends were the places where the contestants tried to bore their rivals into the wall, or off the track altogether, goading the excitement of the spectators to fever pitch. At one point even I, who knew nothing about the teams, couldn't resist standing up to cheer on the one with white horses, which I liked the look of best. Grooms stood by the turning points, ready to douse the overheated wheel axles with water as the chariots thundered by, their two or three pairs of horses urged on by frenzied drivers wielding wicked-looking whips. During one race, a groom misjudged the distance and was run over before he could get away, but the roars of the crowd continued unabated as if they'd scarcely noticed the poor man being crushed to a bloody pulp. That was when I put a hand over my eyes to shut out what was happening. A wave of nausea rose into my throat and I could smell the sweat which had clamped my short-sleeved tunic to my armpits, but at Father's words I removed my hand from my face and retreated into myself, saying nothing. Then as slaves ran out to cover the arena with fresh sawdust, I reflected that the messy corpse they were dragging away had been someone's son, someone's brother. Amid the shrieking and fist-shaking going on around me, I pursed my lips and felt my chin rise in a surge of silent defiance.

After the final race, as the excited roar of the crowd fell silent, I sensed Father stiffen and straighten up beside me. I caught the harsh whisper, muttered between clenched teeth, "Push your hair back and straighten your cloak," before I looked up to see a large group ascending the nearest gangway, a flash of purple bright in their midst. As the group stopped at the end of our row, I tried without success to swallow. Father was now on his feet, bowing low. I heard him say something like, "Trachonitis… pleases you, Sire?", but it meant nothing to me and all I could think of was how I should behave, face to face, as I now literally was, with the King himself.

Then a voice boomed, "But who is that young man trying to hide behind you? Surely not your son?"

"Indeed it is, Sire. Allow me to present my only son Simon to you." I felt the kingly gaze bore through me as I almost doubled over in my effort to be reverential. It was then that I noticed with a pang of alarm a loose strap in my sandal. I'm embarrassed to admit such an absurdity, but it occurred to me that even this tiny thing might be seen as a mark of disrespect. For a moment I stared down at the strap in dismay for I'd heard what could happen to people who displeased the King. But today at least his mood was genial, and of course he noticed nothing amiss. When I dared to look up, he shook his great head, in which, despite his age, there was not yet a streak of grey.

"It seems but a couple of years since you told me of his birth. You must bring him to court more often now that he is a man." To me the words sounded more threat than invitation. I wished I'd thought to ask Father whether it was permitted to look the King in the eye, so for safety's sake I fixed my gaze on a jewel glinting blood red which fastened the cloak at the royal shoulder. Fortunately the exchange was quickly at an end, and with a nod the King then swept on up the gangway, followed by his large retinue. The bronze cuirasses[1] of several of Father's comrades flashed in the afternoon sun, as the gangway was no longer in the shade of the canopy. A slightly bent but lean and handsome man, whose receding hair, unlike the King's, was greying noticeably at the temples, touched Father on the shoulder as he came level.

"Greetings, Philip, old friend. It's good to see you back safely." Looking at me, he said, "The King is right – you should bring Simon to court more often. Bring him over to the feast shortly. I'll look out for you." I recognised Nicolas of Damascus from the one occasion when Father had taken me to Jerusalem when I was younger. I knew he was an old friend of Father's, and also that he was one of the King's closest advisers. I managed to bow politely, though my knees still felt as if they were filled with water.

Bringing up the rear of the royal procession was a good-looking couple, who seemed to be sharing an intimate joke. I blew out my cheeks when everyone had passed, relieved that my heartbeat seemed to be resuming its normal rate. "Who was that?" I asked Father, who to my surprise was still standing erect and tense, looking up after the royal party.

"King Herod of Judaea, you halfwit!"

"No, Father, the handsome couple at the back."

"That was Alexander, our King's son. And the lady was his wife, the Princess Glaphyra."

"Ahhh! That was Alexander!"

---

1 Piece of armour covering the body from neck to waist.

Father raised his eyebrows in enquiry. As a senior member of the King's personal bodyguard, I knew that he took his obligations of loyalty and discretion very seriously, so perhaps he was surprised by my knowing tone. No doubt he was wondering how much of the gossip I'd heard about Alexander.

After that one visit to Jerusalem, I had begged to be taken back, as I'd been so thrilled by everything I saw there. But to my immense frustration Father had always refused, though he never explained why. My foster father, another soldier in the bodyguard before King Herod pensioned him off, was less discreet than Father.

"It's a human snake pit up there – too many sons, too many wives and mothers competing for the King's favour. Your father wants you to stay well away from the poisonous intrigues there. Till you're ready to follow in his footsteps, that is."

And now that time had come. I was about to start my military training in Jerusalem but first the official opening of the magnificent harbour city of Caesarea, with its lavish spectacles, was the perfect way to introduce me to what was great and glorious in King Herod's Judaea. Or that was Father's idea anyway.

The feast that day was held around a huge freshwater pool on the Lower Terrace of the Promontory Palace. I know what people mean when they say a sight is breathtaking, because as we walked in I literally gasped at the splendour of the place. Colonnades of a stone whiter than swan's wings marched up the seemingly endless length of the courtyard on either side of the great pool, in which fountains splashed, shimmering in the sunlight. Huge urns brimming with flowers stood in the spaces between the columns; portable tables in the shade of the porticos staggered under mounds of food, from all manner of mouth-melting fruit – plump red pomegranates, glistening dates, bruise-purple figs – to entire fishes and roasted poultry. I stared around in wonderment until my gaze came to rest on a semi-circular break in the colonnade, creating a type of loggia. Its vaulted roof was decorated with golden and richly coloured mosaics.

As I lowered my gaze from the opulence of the roof, I suddenly realised that armed and helmeted soldiers were patrolling the back and sides of the loggia. And there, on a raised dais, reclined the King, together with members of his household, waited on by servants balancing trays heaped with food. A harsh gust of laughter rang out from the dais, and I noticed that one of the servants was on his knees, frantically scraping up something that had fallen to the floor. One of the soldiers stood over him, his hand on his sword hilt, so I turned quickly away.

"Impressed? I wanted it to be a surprise. I know you appreciate fine buildings."

So had he guessed? Perhaps, for there was a definite hesitation before Father continued, "Come, follow me. I want to show you something even more remarkable." He guided me through the throng to a spot close to where the musicians were playing. We stood at the end of the terrace and looked down to our left, to where the palace levels fell away in a tiered cascade out into a sea of such intense lapis lazuli blue that it stung my eyes.

"Look over there!"

Reaching out from the shore to embrace a perfect harbour in the curve of their stone arms were two monumental breakwaters, each capped with an enormous tower. "This will be the greatest harbour in the entire Mediterranean sea, Simon, fit for the King's new navy. Greater than Athens. His most ambitious—" Father was whispering in awe when Nicolas of Damascus came up to us and tapped him on the shoulder.

"There you are! Admiring that spectacular view, I see. Philip, the King wants to talk to you. He says he needs to hear what didn't go into the commanders' report about your expedition!"

Father grimaced.

"Don't look so worried – the King's in a happy mood today, and I'll look after Simon," Nicolas reassured him. When Father had gone, he turned to me and said kindly, "Impressive, isn't it? But come, you aren't eating, Simon. Let's see to that right now."

Hungry though I was, there was so much I was bursting to ask about the harbour, but I didn't know how to begin, especially with this important man whom I scarcely knew. I could only gesture towards the view with a sweep of my arm.

"Ah, you probably want to know more about this whole extraordinary project. I like curiosity in a young man. But first things first – let us find some food and then you can ask me whatever you like!" He led the way from the edge of the terrace back into the crowd, before stopping a slave-girl and ordering her to bring us some food and wine.

"So what do you want to know, Simon?" Nicolas asked, when a platter of assorted delicacies had been brought to us by the voluptuous, black-eyed beauty, who appraised me in an uncomfortably blatant way. There were no vacant couches nearby, so Nicolas and I remained standing and while another slave was diluting our wine with warm water he gazed at me with undisguised interest. I felt uneasy under his scrutiny, but then curiosity proved stronger than shyness.

"Well, I'd like to know about everything really. For example, I've heard tell of a tunnel that brings fresh water from as far away as Mount Carmel. Can it be true?"

Nicolas's smile revealed discoloured teeth but brought light to the darting black eyes under bushy brows with which I was to become very familiar in the months ahead. "You know, I am really not the right person to be talking to about all this. I'm an historian, not an engineer or an architect. I wonder… yes, look, over there, talking to my brother Ptolemy. If you can see him behind Ptolemy's platter of food. That's Quintus Marius Severus. He's probably the most celebrated of the King's many architects. He's from Rome. Would you like to talk to him?"

I couldn't imagine anything I'd like more, but before I could reply Nicolas was leading me across and introducing me. "This is Simon, the son of an old friend of mine. It's his first visit to

Caesarea, and he wants to know about the engineering behind it. I wondered if you would be so good as to answer some of his questions, Severus?"

Severus's clean-shaven face was serious and unsmiling. He nodded, perhaps a shade curtly, I thought.

"I-I don't want to be a nuisance, to interrupt." I set down my cup rather shakily, relieved that a tripod stood beside us now as I'd been wondering how to start eating with the platter in one hand and cup in the other.

"That's all right. Ptolemy and I see plenty of each other. Whenever I need more funds for the works."

"Which seems rather frequent these days!" countered Ptolemy, with an edge to his tone.

Severus didn't reply but turned pointedly away from him and addressed me. "Please, finish your meal and we'll go." Flustered by the architect's abrupt manner, I obediently gulped down a mouthful of some sort of fish and almost choked at the unexpectedly salty taste. I looked to Nicolas, who was shaking his head at his brother's heaped plate with clear disapproval, and stammered, "Sir, m-my father?"

"I'll tell him, Simon, don't worry. I imagine he'll be a while with the King. Severus, could you bring him back to the room I'm using as my office? You know the one."

"Very well. We'll be a while." Abandoning my plate with its contents barely touched, I followed Quintus Marius Severus, who used his elbows to burrow through the throng. Once we were outside he seemed to relax.

"I can't bear so much noise – you can't hear yourself think, let alone speak. I don't know how the musicians put up with it." He puffed out his cheeks in relief and then led me down some steps and through a series of walkways and terraces, until once more the sea glittered before us.

"So – what is it you would like to know?" I remember noticing the slow, deliberate way he spoke Greek, and with an accent I assumed to be that of a Latin speaker. Father had told me that nothing so magnificent had ever been built from almost nothing in so short a period – only ten years – so I wasn't sure where to start.

"I'd like to know about everything. How you set about designing such a vast site, about the construction methods, the water—"

"Fine, stop there!" Severus raised his hands. "I can see your interest is serious – I thought just now that Nicolas felt you 'ought' to know about the place, for your education."

"No, no, Sir – I really am interested. Actually not merely interested, I'm fascinated. You see, I..." I stopped. This was not the time nor the place, nor was this obviously distinguished stranger the person to whom I could, or should, divulge my dream.

"Come. We'll sit down over there, on one of those seats on the quay. Then I can tell you a little of what you obviously do desire to know. Normally you'd see hundreds of people busy with building or maintenance work, but King Herod has declared several days of public holiday. It seems eerily quiet."

We settled ourselves on a bench and Severus began. "Well, as you may know, there was a city here before – Strato's Tower – but it was almost completely destroyed in the great earthquake twenty years ago. So King Herod had to start again from nothing. He wanted a port large enough for his growing navy and for trade, because this coast has no other significant harbour due to ferocious southerly winds." As if wishing to corroborate what he was saying, a fresh breeze ruffled and darkened the surface of the harbour waters. I noticed how the imperial standard on a bireme began to flutter in the late afternoon sun.

"The entrance to the port is over there on the northern side, where the winds are quietest. As you can probably see, the whole structure – which eventually will accommodate up to a hundred war galleys – is divided into three, a large outer harbour and two smaller inner ones, again to provide protection against the winds. The southern wall behind us runs out for over 650 feet."

Following the architect's indicating arm, I silently congratulated myself for having more or less correctly estimated the southern wall's measurement. It gave me the confidence to guess others.

"So that one running north-west must be at least a thousand feet?"

I was gratified when Severus regarded me more carefully and said, "Good guess, Simon." Then he continued, "You have to appreciate that impressive though the walls are, it's the foundations which are the real marvel – the foundation stones themselves are massive, about fifty-two by twenty feet. Now, another…"

Severus's pale face had grown flushed with enthusiasm as he settled into his subject. But as he paused to catch his breath, his attention was distracted by a small commotion of people near the huge temple of Augustus, which dominated the harbour from its elevated platform. He went on, though, pride glowing in his voice. "You can see King Herod's desire to use our new Roman technology in the use of concrete. It's imported from the Bay of Naples area – think of that, Simon, a voyage of some 1,250 miles."

"How is it possible to sink such heavy foundations low enough? The water must be many fathoms deep?" I shaded my eyes as I looked across at the walls, marvelling at the enormity of the operation.

"That's exactly the right question to ask. We – by which I mean the King's engineers, most of us from or at least trained in Rome – have devised a new type of wooden…" Then his flow was interrupted by more movement up at the temple.

"What's… ah, I see. Yes, that's Alexander, the King's son and his wife the Princess Glaphyra." Severus sighed. "And the grey-haired man talking to them so animatedly is Sextus Iulius Gamellus – he taught Alexander and his brother Aristobulus, when they were in Rome living with Caesar. I'm related to Gamellus – if he gets hold of you, you may as well forget the next two hours. Let's go and have a look at that big trireme. It returned yesterday with treasure from a pirate ship, which I hear they sank."

But it was too late. A shout rang out across the water, as Gamellus spotted and recognised his relation. "Ah, it's my cousin Quintus Marius Severus! Come up and join us – you can explain things to Alexander far better than I can."

We had no choice after that, but Severus didn't hurry as he led the way up the flight of snow-white steps towards the group. One of the guards moved menacingly towards us as we approached, his hand already on his sword, but Alexander motioned him to step back.

"Thanks be to the gods, cousin, I was hoping I might see you. Alexander keeps asking damnably awkward questions." Gamellus slapped Severus on the back, who flinched and conceded a small nod in return.

"I learnt it at your knee, Gamellus – the art of asking awkward questions!" The King's son inclined his head in the direction of his former tutor. "Severus, *salve*! You and your colleagues have been doing a magnificent job here." He stretched out his hand in greeting, by which I understood something of the respect in which Severus was held. Suddenly Severus was pushing me forward.

"This is Simon, son of Philip the Gaul, one of your father's long-serving bodyguards. He is interested in engineering so I was telling him about the building of the port." I bowed my head respectfully, though not before I'd seen a frown flit across the handsome face. Then to my amazement I felt a genial clap on my shoulder.

"So perhaps we can learn about it together. It's an astonishing project. My father has surpassed himself." His wife, standing to the side of the men, gave a light cough. "Now, dearest, praise where it is due!" A little shoulder shrug told me that she was not inclined to be so generous.

I'd been so emboldened by the events of this extraordinary day that I now dared to look directly at the striking woman whom Alexander addressed as 'dearest'. There was something regal in her bearing, her head with its high cheekbones held erect and proud. I think I would have guessed she was of a royal house even if Father hadn't mentioned it. Behind her stood a small, delicate-featured maidservant. A sudden breath of wind blew a lock of hair across her heart-shaped face, and as she raised a hand to brush it behind her ear, for a few fleeting moments our eyes met. Then she looked down shyly, so different from the brazen stare of the young woman who had brought my food. It may sound strange, but I vividly remember the physical sensation of something falling, or dropping, deep inside me.

Alexander went on talking to his wife as if nothing had happened. "Why don't you go back now that your father has arrived? I'll follow shortly. I want a closer look at this end of the aqueduct with Severus. If I'm too late for the boys, embrace them goodnight from me."

Glaphyra nodded. "As you please, husband," and with that she gathered up the folds of her robe and began to walk away, followed by two guards and her maid, whom I willed in vain to look back. Alexander was not the only one to watch the women as they retreated out of sight, and as I wondered forlornly if I would ever see the maidservant again.

I so badly wanted to know if I had made a good impression but had no time to brood as the King's son then said briskly, "Come, Severus, Simon here and I need some tuition. Let's walk on a bit, and then tell us what you can about the aqueduct at a gallop, please. I must go soon as I can't risk upsetting my father-in-law. He's one of my staunchest allies and these days I need all the allies I can get."

Severus and Alexander led the way along the line of the shore towards the aqueduct's graceful curve. I walked beside Gamellus, who had a pronounced limp, and I saw that he was older and frailer than I'd first realised. I asked him if he'd like me to take his arm, remembering how my sister Chloe used to support our ageing foster father.

"How kind you are! Yes, let me put my arm through yours. I should have brought my stick, but Alexander was in such a hurry to come out and show me the harbour that I forgot about it." As we walked, the gap between us and the other two widened quickly, and Gamellus needed no prompting to start talking as Severus had predicted.

"I used to teach Alexander and his brother. They were quick, intelligent students – fond of sports and having fun, mind you, so they didn't always study very hard. But they were good-humoured boys and we laughed a lot together. I should be careful what I say to you, I suppose, but you have an honest face and to tell you the truth I'm mightily troubled on their account."

Shy as I was in those days and unused to keeping that sort of distinguished company, I was also very curious and well aware that to be talking to Alexander's former tutor was a privilege that was unlikely to come again.

"Troubled?" I prompted gently, though there was little need.

"Well, you probably know, as most people do, that their mother, the first Queen Mariamme, was put to death – murdered would be a truer way of putting it – by their father. Imagine that! The boys were still very small – Alexander about seven or eight, his brother only a year younger. Far too young to lose their mother." Gamellus was staring straight ahead, so he wouldn't have seen me nod in wistful agreement.

"The King believed she'd been unfaithful to him, and though he loved her – passionately, by many accounts – in the end he believed those who plotted against her. Had her killed. Strangled. It's said that afterwards he deeply regretted it, but much good that was. Deed was done. Beautiful woman, too. Bore him five children altogether. It all stemmed from that snake... oh, I must stop for breath."

"Come on, you two – it'll be dark before long!"

Severus was getting impatient, probably guessing that Gamellus was talking too much. After a while we closed the gap and stopped, but as Severus started to explain about the tunnels which carried water between portions of the aqueduct, a sudden burst of cries from the harbour shattered the quiet evening air. Alexander ran across to get a better view.

"It's a liburna leaving port! Pirate patrol most likely. How I'd love to be with them!" I hurried over to where Alexander stood and, glancing sideways, saw how his face had become flushed, his eyes shining with excitement. It was easy to imagine the spirited student Gamellus had described.

Returning to the older men Alexander apologised, "Severus, I think after all I should go. I'm sorry to cut you short – perhaps you'll spare me an hour or two in the next few days. I really don't want to keep my father-in-law waiting for his welcome. He must be very travel weary – we're a long way from Cappadocia."

He touched Gamellus lightly on the arm. "Go carefully, old friend. Come and spend some time with me in Jerusalem when these celebrations are over." After a brief half-frowning hesitation, when it seemed as if there were something else he wanted to say but couldn't find the right words, he raised his hand in a farewell which included us all.

Watching his tall figure recede, shadowed by his guards who had been following us at a respectful distance, Gamellus shook his head. "I am truly fearful for that dear young man – and for his brother. They have powerful enemies, who know how to play the King's suspicions as strings on a lyre." He sighed and held out his arm for me to take again.

"Come, cousin, you're imagining things. It's all that literature you insist on reading. If you stuck to bricks and concrete you'd be on firmer ground. I heard on my visit back to Rome that Alexander and his brother presented their case most eloquently. Caesar exonerated them from conspiracy allegations, so I'm sure you worry unnecessarily." He paused to drop a coin in a dish held out by a one-armed beggar, who peered up with rheumy eyes and thanked him in a way that suggested this wasn't the first time Severus had given him alms.

"Well, perhaps it's my affection speaking," sighed Gamellus, but without conviction. "I hope you're right, Severus. Alexander can be quick-tempered and impulsive, but there's no malice in him. Constant talk of a plot to poison his father – absurd! Well, not absurd – wicked, that's what it is." He shook his head, and I could see that he was far from reassured. I was more intrigued than ever and wished we weren't nearing the end of our walk. With Alexander gone, I could hardly expect any more tuition.

We reached a side entrance to the palace and I took courteous leave of Gamellus. The nice old man and Severus stopped to exchange information about a sick relative back in Rome, so I thought it tactful to go on ahead. While waiting for Severus, I climbed a few steps for a better view back to the harbour and the darkening sea. This had without doubt been the most momentous day of my life. It felt as if a curtain had been ripped back to reveal a whole new world, but it was a world on whose threshold I stood hesitant and unprepared. So much of what I had seen and heard dazzled me with challenge and excitement, tinged, as I pictured the maidservant's exquisite face, with tenderness. But I watched the sun sink below the western horizon, flooding the soft, warm evening with gold, and shivered with a cold and unexpected sense of foreboding.

Chapter 2

"Ah, at last – we were beginning to wonder if you'd set sail for Rome!" This was Nicolas of Damascus, seated at his desk, several maps spread out in front of him. My father was standing behind him pointing at something.

"My apologies. I hope you weren't getting anxious about Simon? My cousin Gamellus appeared with Alexander, who had a lot of questions."

Father looked up sharply. "So Simon met Alexander?"

"Yes, briefly. He had to leave us to go and welcome his father-in-law." A short silence followed, and it wasn't pleasant to feel everyone except Severus scrutinising me.

"If it was brief, then I'm sure there was no harm done," soothed Nicolas, though I noticed that he pursed his lips as if in disapproval. "Severus, will you join us in a cup of wine?" Severus hesitated, then accepted, so Nicolas beckoned to a slave who was standing against a wall holding two jugs and gestured for us to recline.

When we were seated Ptolemy, helping himself to a plump date from a basket beside him, exclaimed in a voice surprisingly high-pitched for so large a man, "Severus, this must be a record!"

"I'm sorry?"

"This is our second meeting in one day and you haven't asked for money once."

Nicolas and Father laughed, but Severus did not even smile.

"I am sorry if you find me demanding, Ptolemy, but the works I have to oversee are enormously expensive. The cost of the materials, not to mention—"

"Come, come, Severus, it was only meant in jest. Relax and enjoy your wine – today is a day of feasting and celebration. We can look at your accounts another day. I'm not accusing you of swindling us, you know!"

"By Hercules, I trust not!"

I felt sorry for the architect. Despite the seemingly jovial manner, there was an aura of menace about this big man who, I now gathered, controlled the King's treasury.

"There is so much work yet to do, and all this feasting and hospitality for crowds of people, the wild beasts, the chariot races and… I don't know what else." Severus raised his arms in a gesture of despair, obviously overwhelmed by the thought of the colossal expense involved.

"Calm yourself, my dear Severus, all is taken care of. The King is solvent – thanks partly to the generosity of our revered Emperor's wife. He also has other plans for helping with the expenses, though those I cannot divulge." He lay back against the cushions on his couch and took a satisfied sip of wine.

"Then I am duly reassured," replied Severus after a pause, in which I noticed a glance pass between the two brothers.

Severus did not delay over his wine and before long took his leave. I stood up out of courtesy, and at the door he turned and addressed me.

"Simon, I am here for another couple of days – at Ptolemy's pleasure, as you've heard – so if you have more questions I or one of my colleagues would be pleased to answer them. We can be contacted at the architects' lodging house – Nicolas knows where that is." I mumbled thanks which were probably far from adequate in view of the time he'd given me, but in that august company I was tongue-tied. Then, with a final bow, he was gone, which was when I realised that Father was looking at me with a puzzled frown. I knew then that our talk about my future had become a matter of urgency, that I couldn't dither and delay much longer. I had to be brave.

Ptolemy gave a hearty chuckle. "I can never resist baiting that man. Why can't he loosen up? Recommended to us by Caesar himself – you can't get much more eminent than that. And King Herod thinks he can do no wrong."

"But you should be more careful about mentioning the King's plans for raising more funds," admonished Nicolas.

Ptolemy, narrowing his eyes so that they became cracks in his wide, fleshy face, snapped, "I am as loyal to the King as you are, Nicolas. Don't tell me what I can say. Brothers, Philip!"

I was too intrigued by the tension between these two illustrious brothers to wonder about the King's plan for raising money. Had I known what far-reaching consequences it would have for my own life, I might have given it more thought.

*

After elbowing our way through the thronged maze of alleyways back to our tavern, Father had news for me.

"Before the chariot races we had a briefing from the senior commander. The King has an *interesting* plan and he needs his most trusted soldiers to carry it out. It means we won't be leaving Caesarea immediately, but you must get back to Jerusalem to prepare for your training. I'll arrange for you to ride with some of the younger men."

I hoped my face didn't betray my relief at the change of arrangement – although I was always shy when meeting new people, I suspected the ride back would be easier without Father keeping a close eye on me, especially if I was with other young men. Father didn't notice for he carried on, "The route should be safe. There's been so much military traffic along it recently that brigands will have had to look elsewhere, but I'll put the money you'll need in two separate purses in case. Go as arranged to David and Leah until you have to report – they'll help you get everything together. I'll join you if I can."

Later we took a cup of wine up onto the roof and sat there quietly, having little need for a lamp under the star-crowded sky. It was then I asked, "Father, why did you look so worried when you heard I'd met the King's son, Alexander?"

"Because, Simon, Alexander is the centre of so much rumour about plots and conspiracies and the gods only know what else. I want you to stay well away from all that. Getting too close can be dangerous."

I was tempted to point out his lack of logic, for I was about to be enrolled in a company of bodyguards that would surely bring me close to *all that*. But instead I exclaimed, no doubt showing my irritation, "Father, I'm no longer a child. I'm old enough to become a soldier, to fight for my King and... " I badly wanted to add 'choose my own profession'. But this was not the time to risk a confrontation. No longer a child perhaps, yet it was reassurance rather than reprimand that I needed at that point. Somehow that sense of urgency to divulge my ambition which I'd felt so keenly in Nicolas of Damascus's rooms had again receded.

"Yes, you are indeed a man now – and it's for that reason I brought you here to Caesarea. But you'd understand my wish to protect you if you knew how... how wicked some of the things are that go on in the royal household." I tried without success to make out the expression on Father's face in the dim starlight.

There was that word again which Gamellus had used. *Wicked!* "But you've always loved the King, been so loyal. I don't understand."

Father put his finger in front of his lips to indicate that I should lower my voice. Then he whispered, "Oh, Simon, there is so much you don't understand. I do love the King, and he has been good to me, very good. I've never forgotten how he granted me personal leave of absence to make arrangements for you and Chloe after your mother died. And I'm convinced my promotion shortly after that was due to his intervention, for in truth I'd done little by then to distinguish myself and the commanders would not have noticed me. No, I don't mean that it's he alone who is wicked, though as the gods know only too well, he is quick to believe in malicious allegations and is prey to murderous rages." Quite an admission from my discreet and circumspect father.

"Is that why he still makes you anxious?" The sense of fear that afternoon in his usually so confident bearing had disturbed me.

"Ye-es, perhaps. One is never quite sure where one stands. But when I talk of wickedness, I mean in the family generally. There's so much hatred, so much jealousy. And I do believe that hate leads to wicked deeds."

"But what has this to do with Alexander? Is it still about his mother being executed when he and his brother were children?"

After a brief silence I prompted gently, "Father?"

"I saw her, Simon. Once." His whisper was almost inaudible.

"You actually saw her? What was she like?" The manner and circumstances of Queen Mariamme's death, together with her renowned beauty, had lent her a lasting fame throughout the land that was almost mythic. Even on our country farm we'd heard of her, so now I bent forward eagerly to hear better, my hands clasped under my chin.

"Not unlike Alexander's wife, the Princess Glaphyra, to look at." At the mention of Glaphyra, I saw again with a warm jolt of pleasure her sweet-faced maidservant. "Both daughters of royal houses, of course, and similar in their features and bearing too. I only had a fleeting glimpse, but I remember her as more beautiful than Glaphyra. But then I saw her at a time of great softness, and… that can make a woman beautiful."

"Softness?"

"Well, I was very new here – it wasn't long after we arrived from Egypt. I was following a senior guard around to learn the duties. He

– we – were ordered to escort the boys' nurse when she took them to their mother to say their farewells." Father paused, as if revisiting the scene he was about to describe.

I waited and I think I was holding my breath. "It then fell to me alone – I can't remember quite why – to accompany the three of them to their mother's apartments. I saw how she knelt down to their height and held out her arms to embrace them both together. It is a scene I will never forget." He paused again and shook his head. "Anyway," he went on, looking down to avoid my gaze, "because of this the King's younger sister Salome is convinced that the two brothers, now that they're grown up, are plotting revenge, against her as well as their father. The part she played in their mother's death is well known."

"Not to me. What happened?"

"Oh, Simon, do you really want to know? It's such an ugly story."

"Please, Father. I surely ought to be aware of these things."

"Well, it was she who – but remember this is only hearsay – persuaded the King's cup-bearer to tell him – the King – that while he was away in Rhodes, Mariamme had asked for help to concoct a love potion." So it was Salome who was old Gamellus's snake!

"The King immediately put Mariamme's eunuch slave to the rack, assuming he'd know what had been going on. He, poor soul, his body breaking under torture, uttered the name of Soemus – the man who'd been charged with looking after the Queen while King Herod was away. The eunuch was probably trying to tell his torturers to go to Soemus for information, but the King leapt to the conclusion that it was Soemus who'd seduced Mariamme. He was put to death without any sort of hearing, but Mariamme was subjected to a mockery of a trial. And it was Salome who was the most outspoken advocate of execution."

We heard shouts and Father peered around nervously. But we were still alone on the roof and it was only another tavern down the street emptying for the night, its customers no doubt under the influence of the free drink the King had ordered to be available throughout the city. A woman screamed, a dog barked and then it was quiet again.

"Simon, I've said far too much – and I've tried over the years to keep you and Chloe shielded from all this."

"Father, don't distress yourself. We never knew the detail, but there were plenty of rumours even in the countryside." I thought of what Gamellus had told me. "But the King has married so many other wives since Queen Mariamme was executed, can it be true that he was as sorry about putting her to death as I've heard tell?"

"Yes, I know for certain it's true. And – well, I'm going to tell you something that I've never told anyone before, as it may explain a lot. But it's a confidence that must remain between us – always. You understand?" He searched my face in the starlight for a sign of agreement.

"You have my word," I whispered.

"Well, the unusual – I can't presume to call it a bond, more perhaps an understanding – which I believe still exists between the King and myself stems from those days. You see, after Queen Mariamme's death, he was desperately ill – in body with terrible head pains, but also in his mind, with a sort of madness of despair. Remorse, perhaps. He was frequently delirious and lost a lot of weight because he wouldn't eat anything. The doctors more or less gave him up because none of the remedies they tried made any difference. One day I was in the passageway outside his sickroom when I heard him calling her, as if she were outside the door with me. He called and called, until it seemed to pierce my very entrails. It was only the year before that we who'd been in Queen Cleopatra's service were given to him by Caesar, so I remember how anxious I was, dithering as to what to do as I stood on guard there outside his door. Then suddenly I knew I couldn't ignore his cries anymore. None of the doctors were around. As I said, people were giving him up for lost by then, and hardly any slaves were in attendance either, so I opened the door carefully and went in, laying my sword on the floor to show my intentions were honourable. The room was dark though it was the middle of the day and scarcely any lamps were burning. I can still remember how stuffy and stale the air was, heavy with the aroma of those herbs and ointments that are used when people are ill – I remembered it from your mother's sickbed. I think of it as the smell of death."

I was leaning further forward to catch what Father was saying in a voice growing smaller and huskier as he went on. I think I must have been stroking the meagre stubble on my chin, for at the mention of my mother I was aware that my hand stopped moving across my face.

"He was no longer an intimidating and powerful king but simply a fellow human being in distress. I remember kneeling by the bed uttering words of comfort. His anguish must have unlocked my own grief for, extraordinary though it may sound, tears ran down my face and my own story – the way I'd watched poor Aziza die, my fears for my two small motherless children – poured out, unchecked, for the first time. Unknown to him, I was also sorrowing for his own two sons, having seen them in their mother's last embrace. Suddenly he propped himself up on his elbow and peered at me in the faint lamplight. Then, perfectly lucidly, he said, 'I don't know your name, soldier from Gaul, but I am sorry for your distress. You have shown me understanding in a way that no one else has since I've been lying here near to death.' I think because of that day he has since – sometimes, anyway – treated me differently from other officers. And yet – well, you were right to pick up my fear today. It never quite leaves me."

I turned away, pretending to be distracted by more shouts and laughter from the street below. My throat was swollen solid. I had never heard Father speak in this way before and knew what it must have cost him to admit to tears of sorrow. He'd often mentioned our mother, and always with affection, but there had never been a hint of the violent grief following her premature death. When I was sure I could speak,

I turned back and looked at him, seeing him, despite the darkness, as never before. I wanted to put out a hand to touch him, yet somehow it didn't happen. Then, as a falling star streaked across the heavens, it occurred to me with the same suddenness that there was one crucial difference between the fates of the two dead mothers. Herod had killed his wife; my father had not. *I* had, though – me, Simon, the son whose birth had brought about the mother's death. The thought hurt, hard and sharp as flint, and I was nowhere near ready to make it more real by putting it into words. We sat in silence for a short while. Then Father asked gently, "I suppose you've missed Chloe?"

I understood full well the sequence of his thoughts but could only shrug. I didn't want to talk about it. It didn't seem very manly, at eighteen, to miss your older sister simply because she had married and moved away from home to have her own family. But Chloe, two, nearly three, years older than me, cheerful, outspoken, protective and always dependable Chloe – converted most unusually to Judaism – had been my substitute mother, often taking on tasks beyond her years to save the strength of our frail foster mother.

I replied gruffly, "Yes, but I'm used to it now," uncomfortably aware that I was missing a unique opportunity to draw closer to Father by offering a confidence of my own. But the gulf was simply too wide.

"Well, once you get started on your training you won't have time to miss anyone – it'll be a whole new life for you." I am sure Father intended the words to be ones of comfort or encouragement, little knowing that each one was a tiny dagger wound. He got up then and, briefly touching my bowed head, yawned wearily. "The companions I have in mind for you are from the Thracian unit and I've known them long enough to trust them – though their manners are a bit rough. Good horsemen too – they'll make sure you have a reliable mount. But now I must to bed."

"I'll stay and finish my wine but I'll be down soon." I couldn't broach the subject then, not after his intimate revelations, for he might have seen my ambitions as disloyalty, either to him or to the King. Surely it could wait for one more day. But I was glad of the feeble light as I smiled at him and then looked quickly down again at my cup, for his affectionate gaze had turned my half-formulated plans for the next day into treachery.

*

Severus had invited me to go and see him if I had more questions. Nicolas knew where the lodging house was, he'd said, as if access to Nicolas was the easiest thing in the world. Even if I were to succeed in getting to talk to such an important member of the royal household, Nicolas would be sure to tell Father. So the problem of how to find Severus in the few hours I'd have to myself the following morning kept sleep at bay, even after I'd joined my now-snoring parent in our shared tavern room and lain down on my scratchy straw mattress. Eventually I remembered the one-armed beggar who'd seemed familiar with the architect. The old man might just know where Severus could be found – it was worth a try, and the thought was enough to summon sleep at last.

In the event I didn't have to approach the beggar, for as I made my way in the direction of the harbour the following morning, I suddenly found myself face to face with Severus himself, in the company of another man who was gesticulating forcefully. When Severus caught sight of me he stopped abruptly, putting up a hand to stop his companion in mid-flow.

"Greetings, Simon. How are you today?"

"I am well, thank you, Sir. I was coming to find you, but... I-I wasn't sure how to. I—"

"How fortunate then. What can I do for you?"

Asked directly in this way, standing in the narrow street with passers-by milling around us and Severus's companion glaring at me, I could only stammer, "W-well, you see, it's not—"

"Well, I can't hang around – I don't want to be late for Paulinus. Where shall I see you?"

Severus calmly answered his companion's brusque enquiry. "I'll see you at the aqueduct – at the place we were discussing. Ask Paulinus to wait for me please."

Severus took my arm and said, "Thank you. That was a convenient way of getting me out of a familiar argument – my colleague's convinced there's something wrong with our chorobates." I must have looked puzzled because he explained, "That's the levelling instrument we use in the construction of aqueducts. Come – let us find a tavern. I've not eaten yet this morning and arguing makes me hungry."

When we were settled, Severus insisted that I share his meal of bread and honey and dates, which in truth was very welcome as Father had left early for his duties and I hadn't yet eaten. As Severus pushed the jugs of wine and water towards me he asked, "So what was it you wanted to ask me about?"

Before long the drink taken unusually early did help to loosen my tongue. Soon I found myself telling Severus about the ambition which had burned within me ever since visiting the Temple years before. About my fear of broaching the subject with Father, my misery at having to start military training as soon as I got back to Jerusalem. Severus nodded occasionally and only looked away from my face when he bit into his bread and honey. I don't think anyone had ever listened to me with such concentration before.

"You see, Sir, I don't know what to do and I don't know who to turn to for advice. My foster father is kind, but he was a soldier himself so he wouldn't understand. Then there's David, my sister's brother-in-law in Jerusalem. He knows, he's the only one I've told. David's a stonecutter – a gifted craftsman – and he could help me if I had any talent in that direction but I haven't. It's the designs and the engineering behind the big structures which really fascinate me. David thinks I should be open with Father and find someone to take me on as an apprentice. But it's not as easy as that. I can't bear the thought of upsetting or disobeying him, my father I mean. And I keep missing the opportunity of talking to him – it's probably too late anyway. Am I being a coward? No, please don't answer that because I know I am. But he's so set on me following him. It's always been his dearest wish for me. Always. And then there's the important matter of loyalty to the King." Without of course mentioning them to Severus, I was only too aware that Father's revelations the night before had made that matter of loyalty all the more relevant.

I must have looked very sorry for myself after that lengthy and, for me, unusual outburst, because I noticed a quiver at the side of his thin lips and a hint of amusement lighting up his brown eyes. But his tone was grave when he replied carefully, "I don't know whether it's cowardly, Simon, but it is understandable. Still, you will have to be frank with your father very soon, and things may not be quite as bad as you paint them. Have you even hinted at any of this to him?"

"Yes, once or twice, but he brushed it aside as childish fantasy. You see, he feels he's favoured in the court, that he can ensure I get a good position, promotions, accommodation – those sorts of things."

"What about Nicolas of Damascus? He and your father are clearly friends. Nicolas would surely approve of your ambition."

Emboldened by the wine, or passion, or both, I blurted out, "Maybe. But I've only met Nicolas once before this, and anyway, he's not exactly accessible to people like me. Father says he's one of the King's closest advisers nowadays and is with him constantly. No, I need someone who really knows about the profession, who would take me on as an apprentice, help me plead my case, convince him that I could one day be a loyal servant to the King as a builder not a soldier." This time Severus actually laughed out loud. "You're not asking much, Simon, are you?"

I felt myself blushing then but had to laugh too. "No, Sir – considering I only met you yesterday!" I felt so much better for having talked openly. And pleased with myself too – this was a tremendous opportunity which I knew would never come again, and I'd conquered my diffidence enough to make use of it. A small but real victory.

Severus then resumed his customary serious expression as he studied me, pinching his lower lip between thumb and index finger as he did so.

"Listen, Simon – you impressed me yesterday, and you've impressed me again today. Yesterday I was glad to oblige Nicolas to escape the crowd, and I didn't realise what a passionate – as well as sharp-eyed – observer you would turn out to be. I like that. But – with the best will in the world I could not take you on as an apprentice. I have to move around too much, often at short notice at the whim of the King, and these days I'm usually assessing and solving problems rather than busy with the actual design and building work. But I may have the solution." I had dipped my last chunk of bread into the honey, mainly to avoid Severus's intense scrutiny, but at the word 'solution' I looked up abruptly, causing the bread to drip some of its golden cargo onto the rough wooden table.

"You do?"

"Yes. The architect in charge of one of the Temple teams in Jerusalem is a former pupil of mine. Lucius Servius Celer must be about thirty now, and doing very well – extremely well – in the profession. I would say in fact that his talent is outstanding. He'd be the ideal teacher for you. He's an admirer of an architect called Vitruvius, and I agree with him that Vitruvius's writings make an excellent grounding for any student of architecture. You might be interested to know that the man himself was a soldier under Julius Caesar before becoming an army engineer. So you see, a military background can be useful for things other than killing people."

I wasn't sure if this was a joke so I ignored it. "So – you think this... this Lucius Servius Celer... would be prepared to have me as, as a sort of apprentice?"

"Only 'sort of', as you put it, in the sense that it wouldn't be official – or not to start with. But you would have to take it very seriously, and then I think he would help you. If I ask him to, that is."

"And you will? But you've only met me twice."

"Enough to know that your interest is intelligent and genuine. The best starting point. And we'll soon find out whether you have the aptitude. That's the point of an apprenticeship. I will write to Celer now and you can take the note with you. I'll put down the place where you'll be sure to find him." As he fumbled in his case for a stylus, I began to thank him profusely.

"Don't thank me yet, Simon. There's still the question of your military service to deal with. That won't be simple, as you're already expected in the army. I think you'll have to continue on that path until you prove you can serve the King in a different way. And there'll be many years of hard work ahead. Have no illusions. This is a difficult and often dangerous business. Celer will guide you well, but he's a young man and still has much to learn himself. Sometimes he needs reminding of that." Severus hesitated, a softer look passing across his features. "But I think you'll like each other. In some ways, you remind me of him."

Severus stopped talking while he wrote his recommendation. Then, handing me the scroll of papyrus, he popped the last date in his mouth and got up.

"Now I must go and settle that argument about the damned levelling instrument. Perhaps your father will be reconciled to your ambitions, Simon, once he sees you have a definite opportunity. And when I'm in Jerusalem I'll hear from Celer how you're getting on. I shall make a point of it."

Unable to find the words to express not simply my gratitude but an overwhelming sense of relief, almost of liberation, I knelt awkwardly down on the straw of the tavern floor till my nose nearly touched his sandals.

"Get up, Simon, don't be absurd," he muttered. But remembering what Ptolemy had said about Severus being recommended by Caesar himself, I didn't think it was an overly extravagant gesture. And perhaps the fleeting valedictory touch on the top of my head indicated that it hadn't in truth been badly received. Severus's suggestion had given me a new thrill of anticipation at the prospect of returning to Jerusalem and of the possibilities that might lie ahead.

Chapter 3

We entered the city by the northern Fish Gate, where I had to screw up my nose at the reek from the nearby fish market. Donkeys arriving at the same time were laden with panniers brimming with the latest catch, the silvery skin of the uppermost fish dry and tired after the journey from the coast, so that I hoped for the sake of the buyers that they'd already been salted. As my companions took leave of me and were riding away, Ziper called back over his horse's hindquarters, "We've worked out where you're staying, Simon – we'll come round and get you one night when we're off duty! Show you some of the pleasures of the city – things you've only ever dreamed of!" He gave one of the loud, infectious laughs I'd grown used to on the long ride from Caesarea and the horse I had ridden, which they were leading away, chose that moment to lift its tail and defecate on the street. Rather apt, I thought, so I chuckled and waved back. I no longer felt shy with the Thracians, and part of me hoped they would honour their promise!

Having only visited David's and Leah's home once, with Father before Caesarea, I soon became completely lost. I wandered through a jumble of narrow alleyways, hearing snatches of conversation or shouts in several languages I didn't recognise and sometimes brushing against washing which hung dejected in the still air. One moment I was swallowing a mouthful of saliva at the aromas of roasting spices and newly baked bread, the next I was screwing up my nostrils to block the stench of open drains and rotting refuse. At one point I had to press myself flat against a rough wall to make room for a flock of sacrificial goats being driven up to the Temple, bleating as if in lament at their imminent fate. I kept hoping, unrealistic though I realised it was, that I might catch a glimpse of the Princess Glaphyra accompanied by her maid. I was nowhere near the royal palace, but the memory of the maidservant brushing back her lock of hair refused to leave me.

It was the stink of decaying vegetables which eventually helped me recognise the right turning, for the house was situated in a courtyard tucked behind a fruit and vegetable stall. Leah gave me a warm if rather harassed welcome. She was in her late twenties, a shock of unruly hair framing a pretty face, small in stature and already well rounded after the birth of three little boys, including twins. She almost always had at least one child on her hip, and today was no exception.

"Simon! I'm so happy to see you back!" she exclaimed, thrusting each of the twins towards me in turn so that they could greet me too. "You look hot and tired – I'll get you some water to wash." I was indeed sweaty and sticky after the long journey so was grateful for the offer. "I want to hear all about it, but perhaps it'd better wait till David is home." Without a pause she went on, "Have you eaten yet today? Well, even if you have I expect you'll be hungry, and the bread's still nice and fresh from yesterday."

We went inside out of the sun and Leah fussed about filling a pot of water and assembling a small tabletop and tripod. She soon placed a slab of creamy goat's cheese and some gleaming black olives in front of me, and I realised how hungry I was. But first there was something I badly wanted to know. "Tell me, Leah – do you have news of Chloe?"

Leah's back was turned as she peered into a storage jar and she hesitated long enough to make my heart miss a beat. Then she said brightly, "Yes, we had a message the other day. They'll be coming for Shavuot, so you'll see them then – if you can get leave, of course."

This was not the news I had wished for as it was well over a year since Chloe had married, but I was delighted all the same. "That's wonderful. How long will they be here?"

"I'm not sure. Several days for sure." Then she changed the subject abruptly. "Are you looking forward to joining the military, Simon?"

I longed to unburden myself, to tell her all that had happened between me and Severus, and was wondering whether I should, when there were shouts and laughter from the courtyard and her eldest boy, Sami, begged permission to join the other children outside. So the opportunity passed and instead I asked, "And how is David?"

Leah shook her head. "To tell you the truth, Simon, I'm worried about him. He seems changed since that accident to his eye. I mean, there's no problem with the sight in his other eye – but I know he has fears for the future. So much work to be done for the Temple and it all seems to be needed the day after it's ordered. Good craftsmanship takes time, time and patience, as David has always said, but I sometimes think he's out of step with the mood of the age. Yet with all these mouths to feed now, we can't afford for him to be out of work."

I was taken aback. "That's not likely to happen – surely? I mean, he's so skilled, so experienced – and there's so much demand for stonework nowadays. Everywhere you look there's building going on."

"Yes, but there are also thousands – I've heard ten thousand but that's probably an exaggeration – of workers ready to work long hours for low wages. They get paid promptly for work on the Temple, so it attracts lots of foreign workers. Jews from all over – Mesopotamia, Greece, Cyprus, Babylonia. No, it's important that David's workshop goes on producing the high-quality work they're known for, but somehow they have to find a way of speeding up – they have to keep on the right side of the architects."

I sat up straighter, bread and cheese poised halfway to my mouth. It hadn't occurred to me before that David might actually know the architect Lucius Servius Celer, which would make introducing myself so much easier. Suddenly I was in a hurry to swallow Leah's generous snack, my wash forgotten. "Perhaps I could go up and see him in the workshop now? I think I remember the way."

"That *is* a good idea, Simon. He needs a break in the worst of the heat. You can take him some of this bread and an extra onion. And oh, how could I have forgotten, biscuits – the locust powder ones you loved before!"

She stood in the doorway waving. "Don't forget to tell him to take a rest!" she called.

How nice to be loved so tenderly, I thought as I set off across the courtyard. In my excitement I didn't look where I was going and collided with one of the twins. After hurriedly checking that the little boy's wails were due more to protest than pain, and a few soothing words, I let myself out through the gate with an eager step, Leah's mention of architects an urgent summons in my ears.

*

David was sitting under an awning outside his workshop. He was twiddling a chisel idly in his hand, the captive audience of a water-seller expounding on some recently discovered underground pool. His face brightened visibly at my unexpected appearance.

"Simon, my friend! Back so soon from Caesarea?" He got up and, after dismissing the water-carrier, gestured for me to follow him inside.

"It's much cooler in there. Good to see you. Have you been home?"

When he inspected the contents of the little bag I handed over, he brightened further. The small interior section of the workshop was dark and cool despite the ferocity of the midday heat outside. He lifted a curtain to show me the yard where the masons were variously engaged in sawing and cutting and chiselling, apparently oblivious to the midday heat and the clouds of grainy dust which made me cough and my eyes water.

"We don't have time to down tools in the heat these days, I'm afraid. So how was Caesarea?"

I started enthusing about some of the things I'd seen, but before I got very far David cut me short.

"Simon, what I really want to know is – did you have a chance to talk to your father?"

I made a wry face. Now, days later, my reticence seemed so cowardly. I could scarcely explain it to myself, let alone to anyone else, but I tried to present it in a positive light.

"No. Well, yes, I did have the chance, but I made the decision not to bring it up. I knew it would distress him, especially after he'd – well, he talked to me about his loyalty to the King." I had to be careful how much I said. David raised his eyebrows eloquently so that I knew my excuse sounded feeble.

"But I met this important Roman architect or engineer – I suppose he's a bit of both – called Quintus Marius Severus. They say he's the mastermind behind the harbour there. He was really kind – talked to me as if he had all the time in the world." I was struck, even as I told David about it, how patient Severus had been with me, an unknown young man with no claims on him at all. "He's given me a letter of recommendation to another architect – one of his old pupils." I patted the pocket holding the well-protected papyrus with Severus's introduction. "He's called Lucius Servius Celer. You don't happen to know him, do you?"

"Know him! Simon, we all know him here. He's one of the best-known figures in Jerusalem these days. In fact, he's the very man overseeing the work we're doing on some crucial tablets for the Temple." I wasn't sure whether to be pleased or daunted by that news.

"So... do you think he'd be prepared... willing... to help me?"

David hesitated. "I'm not sure. He's so busy. He's always in a hurry – it's not for nothing he's called 'Celer'! But then the entire team of master-builders is working under tremendous pressure. The King wants the whole vast undertaking completed impossibly soon and what the King wants, well, you know…" David opened his hands as if to say, "What can one do?" and it was clear to see why Leah was anxious about him. I didn't like to stare too obviously at the damaged eye. Now, even months later, when the splinter had, according to the physician, been completely removed, it looked red and sore and was still half-closed. But my dismay was not wholly for David.

"You don't make this Celer sound at all approachable. I thought – well, from what Quintus Severus said I thought he might be sympathetic."

"I'm not saying he'll refuse to help you, Simon. He's not an unpleasant man, not at all. He always appreciates good work and I must say he keeps his word – about payments and contracts. It's just that – well, I sometimes think he has scant regard for our Jewish ways. He doesn't understand why we can't work through the Sabbath, for example, or festival days, but I suppose that's a measure of the urgency behind the whole project. We're all under immense pressure." He lifted his shoulders in another gesture of resignation.

"So – when are you seeing him again?"

"Soon. He's asked us to put forward a plan for teaching more of the priests about stonecutting. They need the skills to work on the consecrated areas, which we have no access to. We need prestigious commissions like that if we're to survive – the competition is so intense nowadays." Then he brightened. "If you'd like to spend a while here watching the masons at work, I'll take you up to the Temple when it's a bit cooler. How's that?"

*

As we entered the Royal Portico I was robbed of breath, as I had been in the Promontory Palace in Caesarea. The Portico, or Royal Cloister, comprised four rows of columns, with three aisles. There were crowds of people around, but we found a quiet spot where we stopped.

"Notice these exquisite Corinthian capitals – and there are no fewer than 162 of them! Or there will be, when that noisy lot over there have finished their work." I was gazing up at the capitals and the glories of the carved cedar wood ceiling, when David challenged me, "Come on, let's see if we can join hands round one of the pillars!" But the pure white columns were so thick that despite stretching out our arms and hands to their full extent our fingertips didn't even touch. We laughed companionably.

We wove our way through the crowd, for the huge Portico was a public thoroughfare, where stallholders of all sorts proclaimed their wares and moneylenders yelled out their rates to anyone who would listen. Suddenly new high-pitched screams of panic pierced the clamour. Looking around it didn't take long to spot the reason. A youngish man had been arrested by two soldiers, each gripping one of his arms, and he was being dragged, almost carried, towards the gate. A growing group of onlookers made way for them and stood in silence. They passed quite close to where we were standing, and I heard one of the soldiers say roughly, "Stop your shrieking or we'll chuck you over into the Kidron. It's a long way down before you hit the bottom and break into pieces, so shut your mouth." The man went suddenly quiet and limp, and the grim trio carried on their way towards the Double Gate.

"It wouldn't be the first time," muttered David. "A hint of what's in store for you, I'm afraid."

Looking around me, I suddenly noticed plumed helmets punctuating the crowds. I recognised from Father's descriptions that these particular soldiers were the Roman Temple guards, but before long it could be me dragging someone away for punishment or execution. One of the main purposes of King Herod's bodyguard was after all to ensure his safety by removing all possible threats. Would I, could I, obey an order to throw someone to their death on the rocks far below? Had Father ever done such a thing?

David touched my elbow. "Come. I want to show you the tablets we're working on," and he led me into the quieter Outer Court towards the balustrade encircling the Court of Women. The balustrade was carved in exquisite lattice work and was pierced by gates at regular intervals. I saw that at each gate an engraved tablet warned that no foreigner was permitted to cross this barrier on pain of death. I was taken aback by the severity of the wording, inscribed in both Latin and Greek. Perversely, it provoked an unexpected yet intense desire to gain admittance to the forbidden Inner Courts. Above those raised inner enclosures shone the Sanctuary. I found that looking up at it was like trying to gaze at the sun with unshaded eyes.

David again interrupted my thoughts to bring my attention back to the tablets. "The ones you saw the men working on earlier are for the gates on the other sides of the Court," he said with pride. "It was one of these which… well, never mind." His hand went involuntarily to his bad eye, and I guessed the rest.

"They are beautifully done, David. But you paid a high price, I think." David nodded and sighed. It struck me how unfair it was that this devout Jew should have been injured in the very process of protecting his religion's most holy place from desecration by non-believers.

As we descended the great staircase leading down from the bustling Royal Portico, David turned to me. "I have a surprise for you. Before we came out, I had a message to expect Lucius Servius Celer tomorrow. That will be your chance to meet him."

I felt my mouth go dry. My one great opportunity, but it was perhaps already too late. I hadn't yet had the courage to talk to Father and I had no way of knowing if I'd see him again before the training started. Looking down at my new military sandals with their conical hobnails, which Father had proudly bought me in Caesarea, I thought fondly of my old comfortable ones with the unreliable strap. Perhaps these new ones were a sort of augury, a pointer to the direction my life must now take, whatever I wished. The worst of it was the suspicion that things might have been different if I'd been braver. I turned back to look up at the four-towered Antonia Fortress, housing the barracks which were to be my home for the foreseeable future. Sitting atop its huge rock dominating the northwest corner of the Enclosure, its sombre bulk seemed to condemn any attempt to deviate from the future which had been decided for me without my consent.

But when I thought of the next day's meeting with the Roman architect my despondency faded in a flare of excitement. Perhaps – despite everything – he might be able to help me. I wasn't to know that the next morning would bring a development of a very different kind.

Chapter 4

It was still early when, on my way back from the well where I'd fetched water for Leah, I heard a hoarse yet familiar voice call my name. I turned quickly, sloshing water from one brimming jar over my leg. There, limping towards me, tunic awry at the shoulder, one sandal thong dragging in the dust, was none other than Father.

"Father! What... what can this mean? What's happened?" Depositing the jars on the ground, I reached out an arm in support and could only repeat, "What's happened?"

"Something dreadful – and I fear something worse may follow."

I had never seen him so distraught. He kept running his hands through his thinning hair, looking distractedly around him as if terrified of being followed. His hand and wrist were tightly bandaged, and his breathing was laboured as if he'd been running hard.

All I could say was, "Come, let's go in and see Leah. You need some rest and refreshment. Where... what...?"

"No, Simon – I can't tell you. Or not here. I do need to rest, yes, but I had to come... come and see you... before you report tomorrow. I'm not... not ready to face anyone else."

I made a lightning-quick assessment of the situation. "Father, stay here while I take these jars inside. Then we'll go and sit in a quiet place a few streets away, where we won't be overheard. I'll be quick."

When I returned I took his arm and led him to a place I'd seen where some building work had been started and then abandoned. Several large stone slabs were left lying in the shade of two pomegranate trees, and they made convenient seats.

"Now, please tell me what happened."

"First you must swear on your mother's grave not to breathe a word to anyone. The King would have me executed if he knew I'd given away his secret."

"Of course, Father, of course. I swear – on... on my mother's grave, may her spirit forever be in peace." Gooseflesh stippled my bare arms. Never before had Father spoken to me in this desperate way, not even when he confided in me on the tavern roof in Caesarea.

"As I told you, several of the King's most trusted guards, me included, were selected for a special mission. He wanted us to return to Jerusalem together – that's why I couldn't come with you. During the journey he constantly reminded us of the need for secrecy about what we were about to do. I feared..." – he paused for breath and coughed – "I feared it might be some bloodthirsty act of revenge against one of his enemies, for as the gods know he has enough of those. I love the King, Simon, but he's a man of towering rages. In such dark moods he... well, I cannot bring myself to utter words which would amount to treason." He once again looked fearfully over his shoulder and all around us. I found myself doing the same thing, infected by his fear.

Then I had to prompt, "No one's around. So then?"

Father's cough came again, a hard, rasping sound. He continued, "Well, we reached Jerusalem as it was getting dark, but he wouldn't allow us to go back to our billets or into the palace. Instead we had to wait in complete silence outside the city walls. Then, when the darkness was total, because..." – more coughing – "there was no moon last night, the order came – in a whisper, mind you – that we were to go down into the sepulchre of David and Solomon, as King Hyrcanus had done years ago. That was when it's said he found three thousand silver talents." I sat back, rigid with shock.

As Father went on, his voice became still more hoarse so that I had to lean towards him to hear properly. "You must remember, Simon, the King has spent fortunes on his great projects and new cities – he needs money not for himself but for the people of Judaea." Unbelievably he was trying hard to remain loyal.

The sun's heat was beginning to intensify. Father, who had taken off his helmet, kept wiping moisture from his brow and temples with his un-bandaged hand. When he coughed again, it was for what seemed like a long time. In front of us a couple of bright green lizards darted over a honey-coloured stone slab. A mangy cat slunk across the ground, giving us a wary glance before disappearing over the edge of the terrace to the level below.

"Let's get out of the glare." I placed my hand under Father's elbow and edged him sideways into deeper shade under the pomegranate trees. "And then?"

"Then the King ordered several of our comrades to start moving out the items of gold furniture and precious ornaments, which we found almost immediately, though there was no money to be seen anywhere." I saw how his chest heaved so told him to take his time.

"I think King Hyrcanus must have removed all the coins, but from the entrance the King seemed to have forgotten about secrecy because he was shouting commands to carry on searching, to go further into the tunnel. He insisted we go even as far as the bodies themselves – of King David and King Solomon, you realise. Simon, I admit there are times when I've mocked the Jews for some of their beliefs and taboos, how they worry about what's pure and impure, but in my very bones I knew this thing we were doing was wrong, very wrong. A sort of sacrilege. The dead should be allowed to rest, and especially the royal dead." He shook his head, as if reflecting on the enormity of what had taken place. "I almost wonder…"

"You wonder?"

"Well, I've heard the King is mindful of the ancient prophecies and there's that famous one about a child being born who'll reign on

David's throne and over his kingdom forever. Something like that. Isaiah, I think. Maybe because of that the King wanted to find the actual throne – who knows? It's only just struck me."

I was puzzled, not knowing the prophecy. "So what happened next?"

"Hard to say because it all happened so fast. But suddenly there was a great sheet of flame in front of me and two of my comrades, one of them my friend Paul, screamed in terror – I couldn't see them, they were obscured by flames though they were only a short distance in front of me. There was an overwhelming smell of burning, the tunnel was filled with smoke. I'm afraid I had only one thought and that was to get out. I didn't even try to save my friend Paul, may the goddess Eleos have mercy on me. The breath was crushed out of my chest… it felt as if people were pushing me against the tunnel wall. There was complete panic. I hate underground places anyway, and I… I don't know how I didn't die in…" He stopped and coughed violently again in an effort to bring up phlegm from deep inside, but nothing came. Clutching at the gold torque around his neck as though that might give him some relief, he managed to resume, though his breathing was laboured.

"There've been times before when I thought I might die. Fighting. Attacks by brigands, enemy soldiers. This was quite different – this was wrong, I knew it was wrong. If I'd died then I don't think my spirit would ever have been at rest… how I fear for those poor comrades who perished down there. Their screams will stay with me forever. Maybe the spirits of King David and King Solomon will protect them – I pray so, for after all they were acting under orders. Terrible orders." He shuddered, and went on. "That fire. It's not easy to explain. Punishment from the gods cannot be ruled out."

He wiped his temples again, and I waited, aware of a hammering in my own chest. Then he turned once more towards me and pleaded, "Simon, can you see why it's so important to keep this all completely secret?"

I had begun to notice how the sun's shadows were moving and I confess to a sneaking worry that I would be late for the architect – or might even miss him altogether. Quickly ashamed of these thoughts at such a time I pulled myself together and assured him of my assent.

"And your hand?"

"I must have put it out to steady myself in the panic and the sides of the tunnel were burning hot. I felt a stab of acute pain, and when I got out I saw it was very red, and looked badly burnt. The physician in the barracks thinks it will heal – I told him I was clumsy with a cooking fire. But it's still painful, very." He touched the bandage gingerly as if to soothe the wound underneath.

The thought of the poor guards who had died such a terrifying death, the sight of Father's distress and painful hand were upsetting enough, but there was something else that was troubling me about the story.

"Father, have you often had to follow orders that you knew… well, that were terrible, wrong?"

Silence. Then, "Oh yes, my son. But not like these."

A shiver crawled down my back as I remembered the wailing prisoner threatened with being thrown to his death over a cliff. "So – have you ever tried… to refuse?" I was aware of the question's impertinence, that it lacked my usual respect for Father's authority, but I had to ask it.

Father answered slowly in his new rasping voice. "It's a good question, Simon. A very good question. But you know the King cannot tolerate disloyalty and to disobey him is in his view to be disloyal. And the penalty for that, I don't think I have to…" – he broke here for another cough – "to spell it out. Yes, sometimes we're ordered to do things which we should not do. Bad things. But to refuse takes courage, more courage than I have." He paused. "This time, though, I did dare to… well… at least to… hesitate. At the entrance. This was a royal sepulchre – a place that's almost holy amongst the Jews. But that was when I knew it was an order I couldn't refuse."

"So how exactly did he threaten you?" Something in me made me persist. I had to know.

He put the good hand to his chest, which was clearly hurting him. In a speech punctuated now by longer pauses for he was exhausted, he gave me my answer.

"Then I'll tell you – though I didn't want to. He said to me, 'Philip of Gaul, I have trusted you for over eighteen long years. And I was looking forward to welcoming… your son… into my service. Don't… disappoint me now.' So – do you think I had a choice?"

So that was it, the bitter, bitter irony. I now knew without a doubt that after such a revelation, I had lost all chance of being open with him about my great ambition, whatever the outcome of my meeting with Celer. It was as if those warning words of the King, uttered in thinly veiled threat to his loyal guard, had finally sealed my fate. There could now be no escape from military service.

But there was something else, something I have been loath to admit to myself, let alone to set down in writing. However, as this account is primarily for my own record – and at the most for a limited number of readers – here it is. The problem was not only that my dream of contributing in some small way to the architectural wonders of our age was now fading away. No, it was something less honourable, shameful even. I was afraid, fearful. Afraid of all that being in the bodyguard would mean. Afraid of inflicting punishment and pain and death, afraid of having to obey dreadful orders, afraid of being captured or wounded, afraid of dying in combat with a sword through my entrails. I was, when all is said and done, nothing but a coward with a dream.

Chapter 5

A little later I gazed after Father's bowed figure as he retreated into the crowded street. He said he felt calmer after he'd unburdened himself and insisted he should go back alone. He believed I would be in danger if spies saw us together in the city so soon after what had happened and was worried in case they had already done so.

Despite all that he had told me, I can't have banished all expectation because very soon I was hastening towards David's workshop for my meeting with Lucius Servius Celer, of whom I had formed a mental picture. I'd imagined him to be a big man, taller and broader than me, with a dark complexion. I was taken aback when we came face to face, for Celer was nothing like that. He was slightly shorter than me but powerfully built. More surprising, though, was his colouring. The curtain of David's workshop entrance had been left slightly open and the shaft of light that entered the dim interior revealed a fair complexion, with blue-green eyes and dark blond hair, a lock or two of which strayed across his forehead.

Whether it was due to David's mention of Quintus Severus as he introduced me, or natural courtesy, Celer stood up and greeted me in a most friendly manner. I fumbled in my tunic and produced the rather crumpled scroll of papyrus whose presence I'd checked several times a day since leaving Caesarea. Celer held the document without reading it. Instead he put his head on one side and looked at me enquiringly. I tried to appear calm and confident, though feeling anything but.

"So how do you know Severus?"

"I-I met him in Caesarea. My father took me there for the opening, you see, and I was introduced to him – Severus, that is – by Nicolas of Damascus."

"You certainly have some important friends! May I ask who your father is?"

"No, I mean, yes, of course you may. What I meant was, no, my father's not very important. He's an officer in the King's bodyguard. But he knew Nicolas of Damascus back in Egypt, before I was born."

Celer's face cracked into a grin, which immediately melted some of my shyness. "Simon, in my view, being a senior member of the King's bodyguard is a very important position. Especially if he happens to be a friend of Nicolas of Damascus." And he added, "The King needs all the protection he can get." Then he clapped me on the shoulder. "Come, let's sit down and I'll read what my mentor has to say. I assume he's recommending you for something?"

"I'll get us all a cup of wine. We should seal our contract, Celer!" I could tell David was pleased and when he came back with the wine and some of Leah's biscuits, we all toasted whatever arrangement had been concluded. Then David tactfully said he would share the good news with his assistant Reuben and their other colleagues working out at the back.

Soon Celer stopped reading. "My mentor obviously formed a favourable opinion of you, Simon. But tell me now in your own words what it is you want me to do for you."

I'd imagined feeling shy and awkward at this crucial first meeting, but having overcome my diffidence with the older and more celebrated Severus in Caesarea, it wasn't so difficult to find the words to explain. "My problem is that I'm about to start training, so that I can join King Herod's bodyguard and follow the career my father has chosen for me. But I've absolutely no interest in the military and… you see, unfortunately my father doesn't yet know this."

"So what is it you wish to do with your life, if you had the choice, that is? Which of course most people don't." Celer spoke faster than Severus, but with the same Latin accent, and he seemed not to blink as he appraised me with his striking blue-green eyes.

I hesitated, and then, as with Severus in the tavern, it all came tumbling out. "I want to understand the principles behind all these wonderful buildings I see everywhere and… I don't know how to describe it but I want to… well, make stone come alive. Like it has up at the Temple, which makes me think of a giant woken from sleep inside its hill." I stopped there, surprised by the passion which had flowed into words I'd never thought of, let alone used before. Celer hadn't taken his eyes off my face, but a slow smile spread now across his own.

"That's well put, Simon." He pinched his lower lip, in a gesture which reminded me of Severus, and his response was slow and pensive. "I think I can help you, but we have to tread carefully. If your father is a friend of Nicolas of Damascus, it's clear that he, and therefore by association you yourself, are well-known in palace circles. The King himself is probably aware you're about to take up your duties. So – it's probably not only a matter of getting your father's agreement, though that's important too. You can't simply decide to opt out of the obligation, even if it's not one you have chosen. That could – conceivably – be called desertion. And I don't have to tell you what the penalty is for that." I stared at him, wide-eyed, for I had never considered that particular consequence. *And I was looking forward to welcoming your son into my service. Don't disappoint me now.* I realised that Celer's caution was well-founded.

Celer held up his hand. "But, despite all that, I don't think you need be too despondent. The master himself was in the army and became Julius Caesar's chief engineer, so there's a noble precedent."

"Master?" I asked, acutely aware of my own ignorance.

"Why, Marcus Vitruvius Pollio, of course. His ten books on architecture are our most valuable source of instruction on almost every aspect of building, to my mind, anyway. They'll be the first thing you should become familiar with – but never fear, I think I can lay my hands on a Greek translation for you. I attended his classes on several occasions – an unforgettable and not altogether comfortable experience!" Between his thumb and forefinger he stroked the sides of his chin, which was clean-shaven.

"Simon, I will give this some more thought, a lot more, because I can see this ambition of yours is serious. Obviously no temporary whim."

I nodded in vigorous agreement. "No, indeed! I've wanted this ever since my father brought me on a visit to Jerusalem years ago."

"I like that – in fact it reminds me of myself. But I was lucky, because I didn't have a predetermined path laid down for me. On the contrary, my father was only too pleased I wanted a career that didn't involve leaving Rome – ironically, as it turned out, as I now spend so much of my time here in Judaea. So perhaps I can do for you what Quintus Severus did for me – I suspect that was in his mind when he wrote. Where will you be based for your training?"

"To start with in the Antonia Fortress, but I don't know for how long."

"I see. Well, for the time being the only option is for you to study in your spare time. Every hour when you're not on duty, that is. And I mean every hour. Eventually – who knows? But one thing I *do* know is that the King is passionate about building and has many of his own reasons to show that his constructions are the finest and most technically advanced in the Roman world. That, one day, could be your salvation. But let's not run on ahead – you've a great deal of work to do first, my young friend. A great deal. And it won't be easy combining it with the other duties."

Celer got up then to walk around – I had the sense of a man full of pent-up energy. He picked up one or two of David's tools and swapped them from one hand to the other, distractedly, his brow creased. "Yes, indeed. I will help you," he said eventually. "The first thing I'll do is get hold of a precious translation of Vitruvius's first book for you. Then you must work through them systematically, all ten of them. And at each stage you'll need to see examples of the theory, both finished and in the process of construction. I like this, Simon – it'll be a project for me, too. I must learn to teach. I'll be in contact."

Then all at once he gave his thigh a sharp slap. "But now I must go – there's a mountain of things to see to." With a cheery farewell out to David at the back, Celer was suddenly gone, leaving me to bask in a sunrise of hope.

Later David and I walked home together. As we passed a cluster of workshops and stalls selling jewellery, David pointed one out. "That one there's noted for its fine craftsmanship. It's expensive and it's where some of the ladies of the royal household come to buy ornaments and gemstones."

Remembering the silver and turquoise adornments worn by Alexander's wife Glaphyra, I peered with immediate interest into the cave-like interior, half hoping for a glimpse of the Princess and particularly of her maid, whose sweet face still lingered in my memory. There was no one there but I kept my disappointment to myself, and if David noticed a sudden slouch of my shoulders he didn't remark on it. As I wondered if I would ever see her again, I also wondered if she ever thought of me and what sort of impression I had made on her as we exchanged that – for me – fateful glance at the port in Caesarea.

Chapter 6

Long before I entered the main courtyard of the Antonia Fortress the next morning, I could hear the commotion and buzz of excited voices. The place was teeming with young men. Every so often shouts could be heard above the general din, as senior soldiers bellowed instructions from where they sat at little tables under the colonnades. It wasn't at all clear where I had to go to report and I silently cursed myself for not arriving earlier. I shouldn't have allowed motherly Leah to repack my bundle several times so that it sat comfortably on its pole over my shoulder. I was wandering around this way and that until eventually I bumped physically into another fellow who looked as confused and lost as I felt.

"I'm sorry," we each spluttered simultaneously. "I'm trying to find out where to go," I confessed.

"Me too," said the stranger in heavily accented Greek. "It's all so chaotic – and I'm a bit deaf, so I can't hear what the soldiers are yelling out above all the noise!"

Then I spotted a smaller queue. "Shall we try that one over there?" I suggested, pleased to have an ally.

My new companion was small and slight of build, with almost golden-brown eyes and protruding ears. "My name is Zamaris and I'm from Babylon. I've been drafted." He pulled a face, clearly unhappy with the situation. "And you?"

There was something disarming about him, so although usually reluctant to confide in strangers, I explained, "My name is Simon. I haven't been drafted exactly, but I'm here because my father's in the King's bodyguard."

"That sounds important! So have you volunteered for that?" If only he knew!

"Not exactly. But it's expected that I'll follow him into the King's personal service, so I have to do some of the same training as the regular army. I need to know how to use weapons, of course."

"Will you have to go on these forced marches we hear about, carrying heavy loads and stuff? They sound dreadful."

"You don't seem too keen on the army!" I chuckled sympathetically.

"I'm certainly not. I hear you can be exempted for a year if you're engaged, which was almost enough to make me ask my cousin to marry me. She's the only young woman I know."

"So what stopped you?"

"You haven't met my cousin!" We both laughed.

"So are you from Jerusalem?"

"No. My father has to move around with the King, so I was brought up by foster parents – we lived near Sebaste, me and my sister."

"I see. And your mother?"

"Next!" The soldier at the registration table barked at us – we had suddenly got to the head of the line.

Zamaris gave me a little push. "You go ahead!" he hissed.

The registration officer held a huge scroll of papyrus attached to two pieces of wood and kept winding it from side to side in an effort to find the names in the many columns.

"Simon, son of Philip of Nîmes, you say." He studied his list for what seemed like an hour, boredom and irritation evident in his frequent heavy sighs. Suddenly his manner became more amenable.

"Ah, yes, here it is. I see. All right, young man, you can wait over there under the eastern colonnade. Your commander will be there soon to give you all your instructions." He made a clumsy move to get to his feet and point me in the right direction, but the papyrus roll began to unravel itself so fast that he had to sit down again in a hurry to rewind it. Suppressing a snigger, Zamaris managed to give me a conspiratorial wink before he was called to give his name and the soldier's curt, gruff manner was resumed.

I waited for my new acquaintance to see where he had to go. "You were obviously in favour! My company's quartered over there in the north-east tower, so I'll walk with you as far as your billet. You were saying – about your mother?"

"She died. When I was born."

"That's tough. Sorry to hear it. How were they – the people who brought you up, I mean?"

"Nice. Bit old. But they were kind to us – and keen on education, which is why my father chose them. I had lessons in arithmetic and reading, and I read Homer with a man who'd been a slave and later became part of the household. He loved history."

"You were lucky. My father came to Jerusalem as a pilgrim some years ago and stayed – his business paid better here than at home. He's much more interested in making money than in education, which means I didn't get much. Still, I did teach myself to read."

"Yes, I suppose I *was* lucky. And I had my sister – she's a couple of years older than me so she was a bit like a mother sometimes."

"You mean she ordered you around! No need to tell me – I have three of them."

"And a cousin!" I reminded him, and we both laughed again. We had walked slowly but had now arrived at my assembly point. "I suppose this is goodbye then – perhaps we'll bump into each other again. Good fortune!" I regretted having to take leave so soon of this friendly fellow with the protruding ears.

"May God grant it so. Good fortune to you too!"

A number of other young men were already waiting around; a few were sitting quietly on the steps, sharing some bread and olives; one pair was testing wooden training swords in mock fights, punctuated by loud expletives in some language I didn't recognise; another was grunting loudly in a wrestling match. I'd always enjoyed wrestling with the boys around the farm at home, and I wouldn't have minded having a go myself, but no one took any notice of me and I was pleased not to have to introduce myself. As I stood watching, I suddenly heard my name called out.

"Simon, son of Philip the Gaul!" I felt myself cringe as I had no wish to be singled out, and several of the others looked at me curiously as I owned to the name. It was an older man with several striking scars, one of which ran from the top of his cheek beside his nose down to behind his ear, who approached me holding a small package.

"A messenger delivered this for you." He studied my face and as he handed it over he said, "I know your father, I think. Philip the Gaul? You resemble him a bit. We fought in Trachonitis and Batanea together. It left me a memory or two." And he ran a finger down the scar.

"Yes. Philip the Gaul is my father," I whispered.

By contrast the officer's voice was raised deliberately. "Well, young man, you needn't think you'll have any privileges because of your father – good, brave soldier though he is. Everyone is treated the same in my unit."

I stopped cringing then and found the confidence to say, "I would never have expected to be treated any differently, Sir."

The officer's scar puckered as his face registered approval. "Good answer. And worthy of Philip the Gaul." He looked around at the others. "Now, everyone – gather round and I'll tell you the drill. I'm to be your commander for the period of the training and my name is Cyrus. There aren't many of you this time, so we'll get to know each other well. Remember always that it's a great privilege to be training for royal bodyguard duties, and I expect you to earn it. Now listen to me carefully."

Not a man used to being disobeyed, I thought, but the package which Cyrus had handed over demanded my urgent attention. A piece of linen was folded around a leather pouch. I couldn't unwrap it openly when I was meant to be listening to the briefing, but I surreptitiously prised it open wide enough to see what it contained. To my amazed delight, the first words I saw at the top of a small scroll of papyrus were 'Vitruvius. Book 1. Preface.' So Celer had been true to his word.

Later, when I at last had time to myself, I read the accompanying note.

Simon,

I am confident this will reach you safely, as I have discovered there is only one training unit to which you could be attached. Read the Preface and first book of the master's work. Read and learn, take notes and commit as much as possible of it to memory. When you have finished please return it, for translations are very scarce, and then I will obtain the second book for you. I don't know when you will be free, but I – or my assistant Tertius Sabinus or another colleague – can be found most days at my office. You will find it at the corner of the Temple Enclosure where the western and northern walls meet.

Study carefully.
Celer

Perhaps, after all, my dream for the future was not irrevocably doomed. Reluctantly I tucked the letter back in the package, wondering how I would ever find the time and space to study. And the privacy. For the present at least my ambition had to remain secret. But find the time and space I was determined to do. So, at the first opportunity, I took myself off on my own to explore the rest of the unit's quarters, and to my delight I came across a small, half-concealed recess at the top of the steps leading directly down to the Temple colonnades. On that occasion the light was already failing, but I resolved to return to this quiet spot with my precious reading material as soon as the routine permitted some privacy and solitude.

Very early in the morning turned out to be the best time, so I planned to rise at dawn on the third day. The night before was almost sleepless. I thought of Father and wondered whether his wound and cough were getting better and whether I would soon receive a message. I thought perhaps I should write to him but his insistence on secrecy made me hesitate in case I wrote anything incriminating. But it was more the noises of my comrades that kept me awake – the snoring, the farting, the murmuring, the occasional moan or cry – and because of my intention to rise long before the others, I was half aware throughout the night that I might sleep too late.

As soon as the first grey fingers of light prised their way through the narrow slits high up in the walls, I was wide awake and neatly arranging my belongings on the mat according to instructions. I crept like a cat out of the dormitory and up the various flights of steps to the alcove, from where I could look directly across the north side of the Outer Court towards the holy precincts of the Temple itself. As the silver trumpet calls rang out across the city marking the dawn sacrifice of a lamb on the Temple altar, invisible of course to me, I sat down on the low parapet and gazed in amazement at the spectacle before me, trying to absorb every detail. I savoured the unusual quiet, the day's contingent of sacrificial animals not yet having arrived at the Sheep Gate, and only a few merchants already out preparing their stalls. Then, with a pleasurable sense of anticipation, I undid the scrolls and started to read. It did not take long for my eagerness to turn to dismay.

It wasn't the Preface which disheartened me, for that simply contained words addressed directly to Caesar. It was the first chapter, 'The Education of the Architect', that filled me with something close to despair. Expecting to read about the need for skill in drawing and a sound knowledge of arithmetic and geometry, I was horrified to find a long list of other requirements before arithmetic was even mentioned! "*The architect,*" I read with some difficulty, for the scribe who had translated the original Latin seemed to have been in a hurry and there were smudges over some of the words, "*must be educated in many areas of study and diverse types of knowledge, because it is his judgments that put the other arts to the test.*" It got worse. "*Let him be skilled with a pencil, knowledgeable in geometry, be familiar with a good deal of history, have considered the thoughts of the philosophers, comprehend music, have some understanding of medicine, and be acquainted with the views of jurists and astronomers as well as with the doctrine of the heavens.*"

To think I had actually boasted to Zamaris the Babylonian that I had been educated! All those hours reading Homer and listening to stories about the Greek gods – a fine help they would be to me now. There was no way I could ever acquire all this learning. The whole thing was an empty dream, an arrogant ambition. I'd aimed too high, like a Judaean Icarus – and we all know what happened to him. I couldn't even finish the chapter because progress was laborious due to the quality of the copy and I couldn't afford to be late for Cyrus's morning roll-call.

Stuffing it back in its pouch with rather less care than when I'd taken it out, I fought back tears hot with rage and disappointment and made my way back to the refectory, only to find I was too late for the first meal of the day. Saul, a recruit of diminutive stature from Galilee, who slept on the next bed mat and with whom I had had several friendly conversations, had assumed I'd been in the latrines and taken pity on me, so he'd broken off some of his own bread with a crumbly piece of goat's cheese to share. I did manage to mutter some thanks before I became aware of Big Peter, already established as the unit's loudmouth and bully, calling out, "See how you're looked after by your devoted little friend, Simon. He'll be making your bed next, in more ways than one!"

Hilarity from some of the others standing around did the rest. Fury and frustration over Vitruvius found focus in Big Peter's great grinning mouth which dissolved in a blur, and the next thing I saw was a red trickle running down the man's chin. A bolt of pain at my temple told me I'd received a blow in retaliation. Scarcely aware of what I was doing, only of a rhythmic chorus from the onlookers, my arm was already raised in readiness for the next punch, when I felt myself dragged back by my tunic.

"It's not worth it, Simon, leave it," came Saul's anxious voice. The pull unsteadied me and I had to lower my arm. My adversary, also being restrained by another recruit, was spitting blood and froth into the palm of his hand and inspecting the contents.

"If I've lost a tooth you'll pay for it, you bastard," he was shouting.

But then came a roar from Cyrus. "What's going on down there? I said there was to be no fighting. Get out to the yard now and if I catch any of you fighting again you'll feel the vine saplings on your backs."

I exchanged murderous looks with Big Peter, and as we all obediently filed outside one or two of the others muttered in my ear that they were glad I'd made a stand against him. I gingerly felt the side of my head, wondering whether I'd develop a black eye, and nodded in acknowledgement of Saul's whispered thanks.

The next night I slept no better, for now I had the texts to worry about with their formidable demands. *Why didn't either Quintus Severus or Lucius Servius warn me?* The resentful question kept returning. I couldn't get comfortable on the thinly padded mat, and only drifted into a fitful sleep after mentally redesigning the dormitory to minimise the drafts. But, mindful that Celer had instructed me to commit as much as possible of the Vitruvius text to memory, I once again got up at first light and crept out to my reading place halfway up the tower. If possible, things were even worse that second morning.

"*...since this area of learning is so wide and so diverse, I do not think that anyone has the right to call themselves an architect until they have from boyhood climbed through the various levels of knowledge in the* *arts and sciences, and only thus reached the heights of the architectural profession."* I slammed the document down onto the low wall of the parapet, not really caring if I damaged it. *That's it – finished!* It wasn't the end of the book by any means, but for me it was the final blow, the crushing end to my dreams. Still just nineteen, and already too late. Well, this morning at least I wouldn't be late for the meal – and I thumped my way down the narrow steps, as loudly as my sandals would permit. As soon as there was some free time, I would take the cursed book back to Celer and tell him the whole idea had been utter nonsense.

Chapter 7

The next day brought news that changed my plan, and for a while caused me to forget both anger and disappointment. Our instructor for the morning's session on military ethics was a Roman officer, who harangued us on soldierly discipline. "Never be violent among yourselves, never accuse anyone wrongfully, never…" But I never heard the rest for Cyrus Scarface suddenly appeared and whispered in the Roman's ear, as he did so pointing at me in the back row. I got up quickly in answer to Cyrus's beckoning, thanking the gods that my still-smouldering anger had stopped me opening Celer's precious scroll, which would surely have been confiscated.

Cyrus led me into the sparsely furnished room he used as an office. A tall, fair man in shining half-body armour and a red cloak like Father's was waiting for me. I thought he looked familiar.

"This is Alberic, a comrade of your father's. I am afraid he has come with bad news."

"Your father is very sick, Simon. If we hurry, there is perhaps time." He spoke in clipped, staccato Greek.

Cyrus's tone was grave as we parted. "If there is a chance, Simon, remember me to your father. He was a good comrade." As I followed Alberic towards the vast complex of the royal palace, it came to me where I'd seen him before. He had been with Father on some errand for the King, and they'd stopped on their way back to Jerusalem to visit Chloe and me. It must have been about five years earlier, but Alberic the German, as Father had called him, was strikingly different to look at from most of the men I knew. His straw-coloured hair – much blonder than Celer's – made him easy to recognise.

After a while, Alberic slowed his pace and said, "We have met before. Did you realise?"

I didn't want to talk, only to concentrate on lifting one suddenly heavy foot in front of the other as quickly as possible, but was mindful of my manners. "Yes, when I was a boy. You came to the farm with Father."

"I remember the occasion well. We were returning from Jericho. Your father brought some of their famous date wine as a gift, but your sister said you were too young to try it!" Perhaps it was the mention of Chloe, but dazed though I was the shared memory was oddly comforting, and I said I remembered it too. At the palace gates, we were quickly waved through by the sentries who knew Alberic and we made our way across a courtyard towards one of the three great towers overlooking the compound. The one Alberic made for stood high on a plinth and had three tapering storeys. Like the other two it was constructed of blocks of creamy stone, and despite the gravity of the occasion I noticed how perfectly they fitted together, so that they looked like a single rock, pale as milk.

"This is the Mariamme Tower, the most beautiful of the three. There are comfortable rooms on the first floor. We had to carry your father up the steps inside, but the King ordered us to bring him here. He said Philip would know why. I myself cannot explain that to you."

After the conversation in Caesarea, I had no need of explanation, and it confirmed for me how much of a valued servant Father had been to the King. As we reached the top of the steps, a curtain was drawn aside from the doorway opposite and a young woman emerged holding a bowl covered with a cloth. It was the very slave-girl I had thought about every day since our fleeting and wordless encounter in Caesarea. And here she was, right in front of me. Her long-lashed eyes were even brighter than I remembered, her raven hair even silkier.

"Is there any change, Salvia?" asked Alberic.

"His breathing is more difficult, I fear, Sir." Then she looked straight at me and whispered, "I am sorry." She stood aside for us to go into the sickroom before descending the steps and I had to stop myself from turning round to watch her go. Entering the room I recoiled at the powerful herbal smell and remembered how Father had described it as the smell of death. There were several people in attendance – a couple of soldiers, dressed in red cloaks and tunics similar to Alberic's, a man in an ordinary civilian tunic and cloak, and two older slave-women. One of them was leaning over Father's inert figure, wiping his forehead with a cloth. When she saw us she stepped back and allowed me to approach the bed. The soldiers, perhaps tactfully, seemed to be concentrating on something outside on the ground below, while the man in the cloak took a seat at the side of the room and examined his fingernails.

Dropping to my knees, I grasped Father's limp hand. "Father, it's me, Simon. Press my hand if you can hear me." But there was no answering pressure. His face was the colour of cinders and his chest heaved with the effort of a harsh, laborious breathing. "Please, Father, press my hand. I'm here, Simon, your son." Still nothing. Then, not caring whether the others heard, I managed to whisper something which only the imminence of death made possible.

"We love and honour you, Father, Chloe and I. Your two grateful children." I knelt beside him in silence, and then suddenly there was a loud gurgling noise from deep in his throat. In a panic I leapt to my feet and looked frantically around the room. "Can someone not do anything? Help him? Please!" The man on the bench was up and instantly by the bed.

"I am sorry, Simon – there is nothing more to be done. I am Hicesius, one of the King's physicians, and I have been asked to attend to your father. If I could save him, believe me I would."

We both looked down at the bed, where the ghastly noise had ceased. Father lay still. It was as I jumped up and away from the bedside, that he had departed this life.

I stared at the physician and, raising my arms in a gesture of helplessness, mouthed the word, "Why?" How could this be, when only a week ago we had sat under the pomegranate trees holding a lucid if difficult conversation? Father had been distraught, fearful too, in discomfort from his burnt hand and coughing painfully, but he could walk and talk and there had been no indication he was near to death. In the days since I had thought of him often, wondering whether his wounds and cough were improving – I hope it is not merely my conscience claiming that – but I should have found a way to contact him, to send him a message of concern, and remorse at my neglect for a long while obscured my grief.

The doctor laid his hand on my shoulder. "I'm afraid we don't understand it, Simon. In all my experience, both in Alexandria and here, I have never come across the like. But two of his comrades have fallen very sick with similar symptoms. One of them has severe burns, like the one on your father's arm but worse. The King could tell us doctors only that they were in a fire. So maybe they breathed in some sort of poisonous smoke or fume which took time to work its evil. Maybe it is something we mortals will never know. I am so sorry." The implication was that perhaps this strange sickness was a message from the gods.

There followed a prolonged silence in the room before I realised that everyone was looking at me expectantly. Of course, as the eldest – or in this case only – son, I had certain duties to perform. What were they? This was all such a shock, so completely unexpected that I had had no time to prepare myself. I remembered something about closing the eyes of the deceased, but they were already closed. What I would have given to see those sad grey eyes once more while there was still life in them. I remembered then that I was expected to kiss the body, so I leant over and planted a tender kiss on the damp forehead. The two Jewish slave-women began keening as they tore at their clothes, but Alberic came forward and said gently, "Let us go. I will now help you with the funeral arrangements."

As we left I looked back at the bed, almost expecting to see Father rise up and tell me he hadn't really died. The women were already lighting lamps and placing them at his head and feet, and we left them to lift his body onto the floor where they would prepare it for burial. As we walked down the steps Alberic explained, "There are people in the city who take care of the arrangements. I received a royal order through Nicolas of Damascus that we should not skimp on your father's funeral. So we know what to do."

On the contrary, I had absolutely no idea what to do or where to go and was immensely grateful to have his guidance. We were making our way towards the main gate, when the slave-girl Salvia passed us carrying two large water jars and heading back to the entrance of the Mariamme Tower. Still unaware of Father's death, she inclined her head in renewed greeting. I noticed that a few strands of hair had escaped from one of her plaits and imagined myself arranging them back on top of her head. I turned to gaze after her until she disappeared into the tower and then, realising that Alberic was watching me, felt my face go hot with shame. I knew that Alberic had read my thoughts, and at such a time. But surely Father couldn't really be dead! It must all be some nightmare, the business with the fire and the burnt hand and the cough, too. My head was light and dizzy with confusion; sorrow was biding its time.

"Simon, I saw how you looked at that slave-girl. Earlier and now. Remember she is a slave and you are to be a member of the King's special bodyguard. There is a big difference. That is one reason to stay away." I nodded meekly but then looked down at my feet, unsure whether my face would betray my real reaction to this stern warning.

"But there is another more important reason. She serves a household that is under much suspicion here at the palace. The physician requested her presence at your father's bedside because she is thought to have skill as a nurse. She once helped him when her mistress the Princess Glaphyra was sick with fever. And when the Princess is in Jerusalem, Salvia is her favourite. I tell you this for your father's sake, may the gods look kindly on his soul. It is better for both reasons that you stay away from her."

I knew that Alberic spoke in good faith, and that he had held Father in high esteem, but he couldn't have chosen words more likely to stimulate my interest in the girl. An aura of intrigue and danger now enhanced her delicate beauty. I have sometimes wondered since if it was that alone which postponed my grief.

Chapter 8

I was granted leave to attend Father's funeral and the following day was a Sabbath, when the recruits in our unit, some of whom were Jewish, were given a rest day. Assuming that Celer would be working anyway, I decided to see if he was in his office and return the Vitruvius without further delay. Father's death still didn't seem real. Although I would have given anything to bring back the previous few days so as to send him even one small message of comfort while there was still time, the impact of his loss had not yet hit me. It was as if I had grown an outer layer of protective skin.

"Simon, young friend, it's good to see you. But so soon?" Celer got up and greeted me cordially, apparently unconcerned at being diverted from the bewildering array of calculations which littered his table.

"I didn't want to waste any more of your time." Drawing the pouch out of its secret place in my tunic, I almost threw it down in front of him – with hindsight rather rudely, I suppose. "It was kind of you to send me this, but… well, it's too much. It's all beyond me. How can I possibly aspire to all that knowledge? I'm only a farm boy, with a basic education. I can't hope to understand astronomy and music and philosophy and history and all the rest of it. I should have thought of that before and I'm truly sorry I wasted your time."

"Now, now, you stop right there, Simon!" Celer gestured peremptorily for me to sit down. He was not a tall man, but he exuded an air of command, and as he stood there in front of me, blue-green eyes flashing, he did not spare my feelings.

"What do you mean – 'it's too much'? You knew all along there'd be a huge amount to study, but I thought you were prepared for that. This was your cherished ambition – or so it sounded when we met the other day. That's why my busy mentor Quintus Severus took the time and trouble to recommend you to me. He clearly believed in your sincerity. And I did too. That's why I lent you our precious translation of the master's work. But here I see you fall at the first obstacle. Simon, what is the matter with you?" It was the verbal equivalent of a sound shaking. If I had expected sympathy or understanding, I was clearly not going to get it from Celer. And he hadn't finished.

"Do you think I got where I am today, sent from Rome to take charge of some of King Herod's most important projects, without years of study and hard work? Do you think I started off with knowledge and understanding of all the arts and sciences which the master mentions? Do you think I didn't have to sacrifice hours of leisure time, that I didn't have to watch my friends go to the baths or the stadium without me? Simon, I am frankly disappointed." Celer went back to his desk and sat down hard, making a show of sorting the jumble of tablets and scrolls in front of him. There was a long silence, in which I could only look down at the ground, unable, or unwilling, to face him.

After a while I ventured, in a half-whisper, "I am really sorry. But it all feels too much. I know so little – you have to remember where I'm starting from." I opened my arms in a gesture of helplessness. Celer's angry outburst almost succeeded in releasing delayed tears of grief for Father, which I was determined to stem at all costs.

When I dared to look up, Celer's lips were still pursed tight and he gave a heavy sigh. Eventually he acknowledged, "Perhaps I should have warned you more carefully. And perhaps I would have done if I hadn't had to send the book by messenger. If you think his written word is daunting, you should see and hear the man himself. Still, you're overlooking something crucial, Simon. He doesn't say that an architect has to achieve perfection in all these subjects, he's very clear on that. Only that he needs an awareness of them, a grasp of their principles."

"But there's so much, across such a wide range. And how am I supposed to acquire it when I've got to spend most of my time practising how to cut an enemy in two with a stupid wooden sword?" I didn't even try to conceal my bitterness.

Celer's tone softened. "Now, now, my boy – self-pity never got anyone anywhere. You don't have to do it all at once, you know. There's no date by which you have to prove you're ready – it all happens gradually. Why, Vitruvius himself started off in the army. You take – and make – your chances where you can. And you learn as you work – I'm learning all the time. Even Quintus Severus probably is, too, despite all his experience. Take one small example. I had no knowledge at all of astronomy even as recently as two years ago, but I applied myself to reading enough about the equinox and the solstice and the courses of the stars, and then I was able to design a large sundial for one of the palace courtyards only last year. Cheer up now, all is not lost!"

I wished Celer had said some of this before, when we first met, as I now began to feel silly, childish. Perhaps he read my thoughts, for he suddenly leapt to his feet, pushing back the errant lock of hair.

"Come on, Simon. Maybe all this is partly my fault – I should have realised it would alarm you and taken more care to prepare you. Let me put that right now. We'll go outside the Enclosure – it's too noisy and crowded here today with everyone coming to worship, not to mention smelly from all those animals. I'll show you some of our stockpiles of different types of stone and other materials – then you can take the second book away with you, which is all about them so it'll mean more when you read it. I'll introduce you to the watchmen, too. Then if you come back to take another look they won't suspect you of being one of the thousand thieves they have to deal with! You won't want any more black eyes!"

"Oh, that – small difference of opinion!" I had forgotten about my bruise, which was no longer sore, and I jumped to my feet, flooded by a rush of relief and gratitude. As we left the office and emerged into the crowd, Celer put a fraternal hand on my back, his disapproval seemingly forgotten. Almost immediately we found ourselves surrounded by several bleating goats, one of whom butted Celer in the stomach. "Ouch! Steady on, old fellow – it's not me you should blame for what's going to happen to you!" He laughed as he gestured an acceptance of the child goatherd's apology.

Later, on returning to Celer's office to collect the next book, we found a slave pacing up and down outside. "Rufus, what brings you here?"

"My master needs to speak to you urgently. He begs you to come quickly." The slave spoke behind his hand, glancing warily at me as he did so.

"Your discretion is commendable, Rufus, but there's no need to be quite so secretive. So what's happened?" Then he added quickly, "No, don't tell me. I'll hear it directly from Alexander. Tell him I'll come very shortly, but first I must close up here." The slave bowed and lost no time in departing with his message.

Celer looked at me as if weighing up how much to say, but in the end offered only, "Alexander, the King's son, has been my friend for years – since his days at Caesar's court in Rome. I will not, cannot say more – except that I love and fear for him." There it was again, that sense of unease, of foreboding, which I had felt so strongly in talking to the old tutor Gamellus. It was as if I had an almost personal connection with the threatened Prince now, having met and been greeted by him in so friendly a manner. And hadn't Father been haunted by the sad farewell between Alexander as a little boy and his condemned mother? Then another cause for alarm struck me.

"If… if you're his friend, might you be in danger too?" If there was self-interest mixed with my concern, Celer chose to ignore it.

"Simon, you look gratifyingly anxious! Don't be. It's true that the King has a habit of putting Alexander's friends and servants on the rack to extract confessions. Spurred on, of course, by… well, that aunt and half-brother of his. But the King won't touch me – I'm not one of his eunuchs to be replaced at the flick of a knife. I'm too useful to him, and besides, he knows very well that I have friends in high places in Rome."

I did wonder if Celer's confidence might be misplaced. After all, it occurred to me that Alexander too must have friends in high places in Rome, given what I'd heard Severus say. We were by now in the office and Celer went to a recess in the corner, shut off by a small wooden door. As he took out a key from his tunic and opened it, he explained apologetically, "I'm afraid the script is too precious to allow more than one book out of safekeeping at once. Not that I don't trust you, but I certainly don't trust all those young men you're billeted with. And you may have to go off on marches at short notice, so there's always a risk of loss or damage."

"I shall guard it with my life," I vowed, and I meant it, profoundly relieved that my outburst had been forgiven. I was being granted a second chance which I knew I didn't deserve.

"Well, let's hope that won't be necessary! Don't look so solemn!" Celer gave me one of his winning grins, as he locked the little door and then blew some dust off the scroll before putting it in a protective pouch.

"Read it, Simon, read it slowly several times, only a small piece each day so that it sticks in your mind. Don't try and memorise too much at once. But above all, do *not* despair – try and remember or note down the things you don't understand and I'll help you with them when we meet next. Tertius Sabinus would like to help too, I'm sure. Poor Sabinus – he's the site manager, I suppose you'd call him, but he's much more besides. He had a son he was training to follow him but he died of typhus last year. You can trust him with your secret."

*

Walking back through the first of the great courtyards in the Antonia, I was surprised to be passed by a hunched and hurrying figure, encumbered by what seemed like a double load of equipment. Pausing to take a better look, I recognised Zamaris, the nice Babylonian I'd talked to on registration day. His face, half hidden by an enormous shield, which at first all of us recruits struggled to carry effectively, glistened with sweat.

"Zamaris!" I cried in greeting, genuinely pleased to see him again. "What in the name of Herakles are you doing?"

Zamaris stopped but looked around him nervously. "Well, I'm not doing this for fun, you may be sure! I was caught going home for the Sabbath last night without permission and this is my punishment – I have to spend three hours running round this accursed courtyard, loaded up like a bloody mule. I can't even wipe the sweat off my face, let alone get to my accursed water bag."

He looked so comical that I had to make an effort to ask seriously, "But I thought Jews were allowed to go home for the Sabbath – if they live in the city."

"We are – but we have to get permission and I couldn't find the officer I was meant to ask, so I risked it. And of course our commander is the worst bloody tyrant in King Herod's entire army, so there was no question of being let off for the first offence. He's already made it clear he dislikes me anyway – humiliates me and the only other Jew in the unit at every opportunity." Zamaris paused to get his breath. "And of course I often don't hear the orders because of my bad ears, so I get things wrong all the time. He's a Gentile and he's got no time for Jewish rules. I shouldn't be doing this today – I'll probably go to hell for it."

"I'm sure you won't – your God will know it isn't your fault." That probably sounded a bit glib from a non-Jew, so I added hurriedly, "All the same, it's shocking to treat you like that. Let me help you rearrange the load to make it more comfortable."

"Thanks, but I think the whole lot'll come tumbling down if you try."

"Well, at least let me give you some water." I untied my own bag from my waist and held it to his mouth until his thirst was quenched.

"Thank you, friend, that's saved my life. It's hellishly hot under this lot." He managed the same sort of mischievous grin that I remembered from the first day. "Let me know if I can ever return the favour."

Chapter 9

I didn't have to wait long to find out how Father's death would change my life.

"You won't be joining us on cavalry training," Cyrus told me one morning. "You've been summoned to the palace. The order came from no less a person than Nicolas of Damascus." I didn't know what to say. "You've gone quite pale, young man. Make no mistake, this is an honour. If I didn't know better I'd think you were less than pleased!"

No wonder I'd gone pale. Joining the King's bodyguard was a daunting enough prospect in itself, but to hear that I'd been personally summoned, singled out while still untrained, was terrifying. "When?" My voice was almost a croak.

"Well, you can have one last day with us – we're learning how to look after the horses today, so that'll be useful for you. Shortly before sundown, you will be met at the main palace gate." The now-familiar scar puckered briefly, the only sign of benediction.

I'd been too preoccupied during my brief time in the Antonia to forge strong bonds, so making my farewells was not hard. Big Peter, who'd made a point of avoiding me since our exchange of blows, trumpeted loudly for all to hear that 'little Saul will be very sorry to see him go'. I resisted the urge to swipe him round the mouth again and make sure of knocking out a tooth this time.

Saul was indeed sorry. "I was hoping to ride with you on the cavalry training – to show you I can handle a horse if not much else," he admitted when we were out of earshot of the others.

"Well, at least you'll have a chance to impress that lot." I tossed my head in the direction of Big Peter and a group of his hangers-on, and wondered how the little Galilean would fare once I was gone, as I know I gave him at least a measure of protection. I'd have liked to say farewell to Zamaris but heard that his company was out on one of the poor fellow's dreaded marches.

So that evening, as the sinking sun cast its golden glow over the city, I found myself once more picking my way through the crowded – and by this time of day filthy – streets towards the huge complex of the royal palace. The last time it had been to Father's deathbed and my legs had felt heavy with dread, but I'd kept up with Alberic, for speed had been of the essence. This time an onlooker might have thought I was searching for something I'd lost, as I walked slowly, head bowed, staring at the ground. But I wasn't looking for anything tangible. What dragged at my footsteps like dung on my sandals were anxious questions. When would I now have time to read and digest the remainder of Vitruvius's second book, safely wrapped in a spare tunic in my bundle? How would I manage to keep in contact with Celer now that I'd be so much further away from his office? Above all, what awaited me at the palace in the service of the mercurial King?

At the palace gates, I waited a little distance away from the fierce-looking sentries, their unsheathed swords glinting in the dying rays of the sun. I was reluctant to approach them on my own, especially as I had no proof of my summons. Cyrus had assured me I'd be met, but he had no idea by whom, so I was mightily relieved when Alberic himself appeared.

"Come, we are to report to Nicolas of Damascus first. Then someone will show you to your quarters. I will be there later myself, when the men in the hunting party return." I detected a brisker tone now that I was a subordinate soldier rather than the bereaved son of a comrade-in-arms.

Nicolas of Damascus was sitting at his desk, stroking his beard and deep in thought, as a slave announced our arrival. I noticed that his table, quite unlike Celer's, was tidily arranged with piles of documents carefully positioned at right angles from one another and labelled with letters of the Greek alphabet. Nicolas welcomed me affably.

"Thank you, Alberic. You may go now – I'll have a slave show Simon where to report when we've talked." His words were polite enough, but his manner was dismissive. Despite our former association, I felt very timid left alone in the presence of the great scholar, renowned because of his closeness to the King as one of the most powerful men in the land.

"Simon, I didn't have a chance at the funeral to offer you my sincere condolences on your father's death. It is a matter of great sadness. But I will come straight to the point. You have probably wondered why you've been summoned to the palace so soon, when your training has barely begun. And as you will know from your time up at the Antonia, there is no shortage of men who would give much for the same distinction. The fact is that one of the soldiers who was with your father when he was injured has been making strange allegations and we need to know what Philip told you before he died – before the rumours get out of hand. Do you follow me?"

I may have been young and inexperienced, but I was old enough to sense danger, and something told me to be very careful indeed what I said next. "I... I'm afraid I don't think I do." I frowned to underline the impression of perplexity. "Rumours about what?"

Nicolas's features visibly relaxed. "I am glad to see that you are puzzled. But I must ask you, did you see your father in the last week of his life?"

I knew I mustn't lie. I'd heard about the many spies in town and anyway, Nicolas might be able to check. "Yes, yes, I did. He came to see me when I was staying with Chloe's brother-in-law. The children always make a lot of noise in the house, so we went for a little walk on our own to be able to talk in peace." Was that already saying too much? Would Nicolas want to know why we needed to be alone? What we had to talk about? This was not going to be easy.

Sure enough Nicolas came back sharply. "Talk about what?" I shrugged and was deliberately hesitant. I certainly couldn't mention the distressed state Father had been in. "Er… I don't really remember. He did say he wasn't feeling well and had hurt his hand – there had been some sort of accident the day before. I asked him what had happened and he said something about a cooking fire, but that it wasn't serious so we talked of other things." In order to sound completely plausible I made myself recall earlier conversations I'd had with Father about my training. If pressed, I would simply transpose them. I had sworn on my mother's grave never to divulge what Father had told me, and I never would.

But Nicolas seemed convinced. "Good. An absurd claim has been made about how your father's injuries – and those of a few other soldiers – were sustained, and how two others actually died. It is of course natural that you should want to know how he met his death, and as Philip himself told you, it was an unpleasant accident with a campfire on the return journey to Jerusalem. He was clearly injured more than he realised. I strongly advise you, Simon, not to ask any further questions about it. These rumours are pernicious and must be stamped out. Together with those who circulate them."

I felt my arms go rough with gooseflesh. If I had confessed to knowing what had happened, some excuse would surely have been made to gag me. No doubt forever. That oath of silence had indeed been necessary. This was my first direct experience of how dangerous life in King Herod's court could become – even for someone as lowly as myself.

But then almost immediately I became aware of a rage rising up like a flame inside me. Did Nicolas not think I had a right to know exactly what had brought about Father's horrible and untimely death? How dare he tell me not to ask more questions! How dare he lie to me! A campfire indeed! He might be the most revered scholar in the whole of the known world, for all I cared, but he had no right to say what he had said, to take that threatening tone with me. And the less so because of his former friendly association with Father. I had no doubt whatsoever that the hapless soldier, whoever he was, who had dared to raise his voice would have been most effectively silenced. But I kept my counsel. Of course I had no choice. I simply nodded acquiescence and sat there quietly, awaiting further instructions, so that Nicolas, sitting across the table from me, would have had no idea of the drumming in my chest.

"Before I call a slave to take you to the barracks," he continued, "let me give you a word or two more of advice. You may find the palace a confusing place, perhaps not always a peaceful one, but never forget that your first duty is to the King. Do not allow yourself to be tempted into taking sides with any members of his family against him – and that includes his sons and their wives. There are times, Simon, when there are unnatural feelings of enmity between sons and parents – fortunately that is not something you have experienced. Never allow yourself to be deflected from your loyal duty to King Herod. Do you understand me?"

"I'm not sure that I do understand entirely, Sir, but I will try and do as you say." Playing innocent was probably the safest policy. To my surprise, I was beginning to discover that I had a bit of a talent for deception.

But Nicolas seemed satisfied. "Very well. And remember, your father was my good friend and I would not wish any harm to come to you. So if you are in doubt about anything, anything at all, if you hear rumours or information that you think might mean danger to the King, come straight to me. I am *your* friend too."

"Thank you, Sir." I recognised the veiled menace in his words and now felt truly out of my depth. I could not ignore the chilling suspicion that had I confessed to knowing about the opening of the sepulchre, then for all those protestations of friendship, Nicolas would surely have had such a potentially dangerous witness disposed of.

"And most of all, beware the sons of the first Queen Mariamme. I strongly advise you to keep your distance from both princes, Alexander and Aristobulus, and from those who serve them. Should it arise, do not volunteer for any duties under their command. Now I will let you go and unpack your belongings." With that Nicolas rose to his feet, and came round to me, placing his hand on my shoulder in his former avuncular way.

"Good fortune, Simon. May the gods smile on you in your new life with us here."

*

From his immediate appearance when summoned, I felt sure the slave had been listening behind the door. He put out a hand to take my bundle with its precious contents, but I politely declined and clutched it tighter to my side.

"As you please. Then follow me." Which I did, staring in amazement at the sheer splendour of the complex as it unfolded, courtyard by courtyard. There were colonnades on every side, each one flaunting pillars of different-coloured stone; lawns of an almost mineral green were punctuated by pools into which fountains poured continuous streams of water; roses and hibiscus and other blooms which I couldn't name tumbled out of great clay pitchers. The many cotes were full of the pigeons which the King was known to breed, making soft cooing noises which seemed to complement the burbling of water. I delighted in the sheer drama of the spectacle. Suddenly the slave stopped abruptly in his tracks, throwing out an arm to make me do the same. It was a rough gesture that landed on my stomach like a blow. Caught unawares I was about to complain when he hissed, "Let that lot over there go. Don't want to get tied up with *her*." I looked around and spotted several women walking down the central walkway of the compound in our direction, visible over the low hedges of the section where we stood. One was taller, altogether larger, than the others and her hair was elaborately piled on top of her head. She was twiddling a flower in her hand and was talking animatedly to the companion next to her, the other two trailing behind.

"The King's sister, Salome. Keep your distance is my advice." As the women passed on beyond us, he looked me up and down impertinently. "She'll seduce a handsome youth like you as soon as look at him." I wasn't sure whether to be afraid or flattered but decided as the slave then spat voluminously onto the path that flattery had not been intended. Soon he stopped outside the double doors of a long, low building, which ran alongside the high wall surrounding the whole palace complex. I had invented a new game with myself in which I had to guess the dimensions of walls and other structures, to be checked with Celer later, and I estimated the exterior wall to be at least forty-five feet tall.

"I expect someone'll come and meet you soon. They don't usually lock the door so you can go in and dump your things – I have to get back now."

The slave turned away, leaving me hesitating on the threshold. After a little while, I took a deep breath and pushed the door open to find myself in a sort of antechamber, contemplating through another doorway the huge space which was to be my home for the foreseeable future. I screwed up my nose at the sour smell of stale urine and sweat and old lamp oil, though it was a combination already familiar from the Antonia. The room was gloomy, with only a few small windows high up in the walls on one side, and it must have accommodated about a hundred beds, all lined up identically with only the space of about half a man's height in between each one. A blanket was neatly folded on every bed, red, blue or green, each colour being grouped into sections. I looked around while I became accustomed to the gloom. Then, as I stood wondering if someone would soon come and tell me what to do, I caught the soft sound of musical notes coming from the far end of the dormitory. I do not have a musical ear, but there was something about the sad melody floating down the length of the room that made me want to listen. Then, suddenly, it stopped, and I saw a figure moving towards me. As he drew closer, I saw that it was a man of roughly my own age, with a long, narrow face.

"I'm sorry – I thought I was alone. I don't know you – so you must be new. Greetings!"

"I'm sorry to disturb you." I gestured at the lyre which he was holding. "I was told to report here but there doesn't seem to be anyone around – except you, I mean."

"And I'm the last person to tell you the drill! Don't worry – the place will be seething before long now that it's getting dark. Enjoy the peace while you can. I'm Theo, by the way." Fading light from the outer doorway showed up slanting, almond-shaped eyes and his grin of welcome revealed remarkably white teeth.

"And I'm Simon. Pleased to meet you." I meant it, for I was relieved to have found someone to talk to.

"I can't show you to your bed as I've no idea which it is, but you're welcome to put your bundle down on mine till you know." I thanked him, and, not wishing to appear rude, decided to do that. I reckoned I'd be able to keep it in sight.

Theo explained, "I'm here on my own, unusually. The others are either out hunting with the King – there was a big one on today – or they've got so-called security duties, which means spying, of course. Also Salome is back today from Caesarea and she usually manages to lure a few of her brother's soldiers over to her wing. That's to be avoided at all costs, by the way – she's known to have an eye for a nice young man."

By now we were sitting side by side on Theo's bedding, and, taken aback by his candour, I thought I'd ignore the remarks about Salome.

I was becoming familiar with the reputation of the King's sister but this warning was the second similar one in quick succession, and I would have loved to know more. Instead I asked, "So why aren't you out hunting too?"

"If I tell you, you must swear to keep it a secret. You look the sort of person who can be trusted. Well, I made out my neck and shoulder were giving me trouble so was given a day off duties. I injured them slightly a few weeks ago in a riding accident, and it comes in useful now. I hate riding and I hate hunting even more, you see. Absolutely loathe it. The last time I went out I happened by mischance to be one of the first in at the kill, and I almost vomited as the poor beast – it was a stag – went into its death throes. Had to control myself as the King was in the company. There – now you know what a fine brave soldier I am!" He spread out his arms in a theatrical gesture of surrender. "I have nothing more to hide!"

I regarded him with curiosity. I'd been brought up in the country and the death throes of an animal had never really affected me – they were what happened in the natural order of things.

"So, so, well, this may sound a bit rude considering I've only just met you, but why—"

"I know exactly what you're going to say. Why am I here? A soldier? And in the King's bodyguard, at that? Well, in life one doesn't always have a choice, you see."

Can't disagree with that, I thought.

"The truth is I'm not really cut out to be a soldier, but a year or two ago Antipater – that's the King's eldest son, in case you didn't know – came back to court after a long estrangement from his father. He and his mother brought their soldiers with them, which included my brother Andreas. They – that's Antipater and his mother – needed to stay in favour with the King so they handed all the men over to be part of his bodyguard, under his command."

"I see. Actually, I'm not sure that I do. Why does all that mean you had to be a soldier too?"

"Well, our parents had died of typhus, you see, and I was a bit young to fend for myself, so the easiest thing was for my brother to bring me with him. And Antipater agreed. I don't think he cared either way, but he *really* likes my brother so was happy to do him the favour." Theo raised his eyebrows to convey his meaning.

"What would you have preferred to be?" I thought I knew the answer already and suspected a potential ally.

"A musician. Definitely. And I haven't given up hope because the King loves his entertainments. Anyway, tell me what you're doing here? Usually the new recruits come in groups, not singly."

"My father died, and I've been summoned to replace him."

"I'm sorry to hear that. Who was he, your father? Would I have known him? There are hundreds of us, but you never know."

"He was an officer, known as Philip the Gaul – he'd been with the King for at least eighteen years."

Theo exclaimed, "Philip the Gaul! I did know him, of course I did. Quite senior, wasn't he? Oh, but in the name of Apollo the healer, I hadn't realised he'd died. He was the senior officer in charge when I had that riding accident and was kind to me. Made sure I wasn't badly hurt and then persuaded me to get back on the damned horse, said I'd never have the courage if I didn't do it straightaway. I'm sure he was right, too. Hate the creatures. But that's terrible. What exactly happened?"

"I'm not really sure. He had some sort of accident." I realised this might be the first of many awkward questions about Father's death and wished I'd asked Nicolas to give me an 'official' story. I fancied Theo looked at me searchingly after my evasive answer.

"Well, whatever it was, I'm very sorry." He changed the subject. "Shall I show you round a bit? Where we eat and spend our off-duty time?" With a quick glance back at my bundle, I allowed myself to be led round the huge dormitory. Theo proceeded to point out certain beds as belonging to men who were pleasant or useful to know or who, because of deplorable habits, were best avoided.

"Timon here's a nice fellow and gets sent cakes from his mother which he always shares. Still, he snores like a camel so I hope your bed won't be near his!" I decided I rather liked my new friend and his irreverent manner. And he'd been nice about Father, which was a distinct point in his favour. But it wasn't long before our quiet conversation was interrupted by the din heralding a general return, and then a crowd of noisy men burst into the building, all shouting at once – or so it seemed to me. My usual shyness, which had been partially dispelled by Theo's friendliness, returned.

"Ah, there's Alberic the German. He's one of the better officers in charge so he'll tell you what to do and where to go." I was relieved to see Alberic, but then I realised I'd left my bundle on Theo's bed and darted back down the long aisle without another word.

"You must have something valuable in there. I've never seen anyone move so fast!" I mumbled a few words about something precious that had been lent to me.

"I've got to go now. My brother has wangled me duty for Antipater again tonight. I wonder what he has lined up for me this time!" Theo looked around quickly, and then murmured in my ear, "Last night he had me creeping around outside the apartments of Aristobulus trying to eavesdrop. Bit of marital tension there, I'd say. Interesting." I thought of the affectionate way the old Roman tutor had talked about Alexander and his brother Aristobulus, and I tried to remember who it was that Aristobulus was married to.

But with no further explanation and a quick wave, Theo was gone. I was beginning to suspect that now I was garrisoned in the palace complex itself, and despite the dark warnings delivered in – was it *really* friendship? – by Nicolas of Damascus, it would not be easy to remain distant from the intrigues and dangers of the royal household.

Chapter 10

Life in the palace complex was to have some compensations. I had only caught sight of Salvia three times, each one all too brief, yet that was enough to make me long to see her again. Once I thought I glimpsed her disappearing at the end of one of the plant-lined paths, but when I reached the junction with the main central avenue there was no further sign of her among the throng of servants and tradesmen. Then one afternoon I was walking back to the barracks when some soldiers ahead of me started to whistle. To my surprise and delight, there was Salvia herself hurrying towards them. She was ignoring the whistles by appearing to study the ground but happened to glance up as I drew level with her. I stopped, unsure what to say and all too aware that the men ahead had turned round to watch.

It was she who spoke first, hesitantly. "I… I was very sorry about your father."

"Thank you. It was a great shock. I believe your name is Salvia?"

She started, surprised. "Yes, how did you know?"

"The officer, Alberic, used it – that day when… well, you know." We stood in silence, while I wondered desperately how to prolong the exchange.

"Where are you going?" I ventured.

"To buy ointment for one of my mistress's sons – he has a skin rash which bothers him sometimes. I… I should hurry, before the shop closes for the day."

"Of course. Don't let me detain you." I bowed, quite unnecessarily given her slave status, but it felt the right thing to do. As she gathered her skirts, I managed to add, "I hope I will see you again." She said nothing but lowered her eyelashes and gave me a little smile which suggested she wouldn't be sorry to see me again either. Or that's what I chose to believe. It was only as I walked on, forbidding myself to look back, that I realised I should have thanked her for attending Father as he lay dying. How silly – that was the obvious thing to say. I wondered miserably how long I'd have to wait for another opportunity. Then the grim warning came back to me, "*I strongly advise you to keep your distance from both princes, Alexander and Aristobulus, and from those who serve them.*"

A couple of the men had waited for me. "Not bad, not bad, Simon. Not really our type, though – needs a bit more up here!" One of them made a gesture pushing up his chest and they both roared with laughter. It was meant in good humour so I could hardly take offence, but I said nothing. When talk turned to women as it often did, I never mentioned her. It was usually lewd stuff or about where to go for the next brothel visit. My burgeoning feelings for Salvia were my precious secret, of which their bawdy laughter would have been a violation. In any case, nothing had happened to talk about and after Alberic's warning it was unlikely that a relationship between a guard and a slave – even if it were to develop – would be condoned. Instead I had invented a fictitious girl, from a farm next to the one where I grew up, to keep the others happy and to avoid unwelcome advances as an assumed boy-lover.

*

When our off-duty times coincided Theo and I sat together, and Theo would treat me to gossip he gleaned through his brother. "Antipater's once again desperate to find enough evidence to accuse his half-brothers of plotting to kill their father, so he and that dangerous schemer Salome have forged a new alliance. Believe it or not she's even stooped to using her own daughter Berenice to spy on her husband, Aristobulus, to try and find out exactly what's going on. Poor thing – Berenice, I mean – she won't know which camp she belongs to, no wonder she always looks so miserable!" Due to my growing sympathy for Alexander and members of his household, these reports disturbed me.

"But there's something else. Something that might be of more interest to you." I thought Theo looked at me meaningfully.

"Go on."

"Well, rumour has it that the King tried to penetrate the royal sepulchre, I suppose to look for treasure, and I hear he now regrets what he did. His misfortunes have increased since then and it's said he believes the God of the Jews is punishing him for his impiety. One of the Jews who works for Antipater, though I've no idea how he knows, told me the King is scared of some ancient prophecies. Apparently there's one that says a child will be born 'who will inherit the throne of David forever' and lots more that I can't remember."

I realised this must be the one Father had mentioned in that conversation under the pomegranate trees. The memory was so vivid that it brought a lump to my throat. But Theo was in full flow and carried on, oblivious.

"Then there's another by a prophet called Jeremiah, so this old man told me, which says the days are coming when the Lord will raise up for David a righteous King, who will reign wisely and do what is right in the land. Not surprising Herod's got the wind-up. Anyway, he's commissioned a monument in white stone to be erected by the entrance to the sepulchre – a sort of propitiation, I suppose."

Sounding as casual as I could, I asked why he thought this news would be of interest to me.

"Because I strongly suspect that your father's death had something to do with it. That day when you arrived and I asked how he'd died, you were very careful what you said. The whole place was gossiping about that mysterious fire in which some soldiers had been killed and others injured – there was plenty of speculation as to how it happened. You didn't realise?"

"No, I didn't." I ached to tell him more, but, remembering both my oath and Nicolas's warning, could say nothing.

Theo continued in what was for him rare seriousness. "You don't have to tell me if you don't want to, Simon, and I won't ask the reasons. But if he did meet an unexpected death because of that fire, then – if it were me – I'd want to see this monument as a memorial to a father who was sacrificed to King Herod's greed. Never mind King David."

I hadn't thought of Father as having been sacrificed in that way, but now I realised that despite his efforts to defend the King's motives, it was exactly what had happened. After pausing to let his words sink in, Theo went on. "He's using a Roman architect who's been taken off his duties at the Temple to do this work in haste."

"Do you know his name?"

"Lucius Something or Other Celer, I think. A disciple of Quintus Severus, the great mind, they say, behind the harbour at Caesarea."

I let out an exclamation of surprise. "I know them both. That's to say, I met Quintus Severus in Caesarea at the opening, and Celer… er… well…"

Theo's widened eyes registered astonishment, and I realised that if I said any more my secret would be out. But what did it matter? After all, I knew Theo wanted to be a musician rather than a soldier, so why keep my own secret from him? Only the commanders mustn't know. So I explained everything. "He's lending me some books on architecture, which is very trusting of him as they're worth a lot. One at a time, of course. I'm only on the second one now!"

Theo clapped me vigorously on the back. "So *that* was the precious thing you didn't want to let out of your sight on the first day! And I thought it was at least a bundle of love letters. Now I understand everything, you sly creature!"

It was a relief to have someone to confide in at last. "Actually, I'm very worried about how to stay in contact with him, get the books back to him and things. Easy enough from the Antonia, but here... I don't know how it's going to work, when we're not supposed to leave the palace without permission. Suggestions welcome."

The day after this conversation gave me something else to worry about. Another soldier and I were sent outside the compound to arrange delivery of some equipment, and as the errand was informal we didn't have to wear our full uniform or helmets. We were about to return to the palace through the main gate when one of the sentries barked at us to stop and stand to attention as the King's sister and other members of the royal family were on their way out. Very soon a large, imposing lady appeared, a great deal of hair pinned on top of her head by an array of jewels. I recognised her not only from descriptions but also from the fleeting glimpse I'd had of her on the day I arrived. The famous – or infamous – Salome, younger sister of the King. She had heavily made-up and striking green eyes, which rested fleetingly on me as she passed. At that instant I knew with certainty that I had been noticed and, brief though the glance was, that it would have repercussions. *That dangerous schemer*, Theo had called her. How I wished for once that I'd been wearing my itchy helmet which made me less recognisable.

Salome was flanked by a couple of slave-women, and after she'd passed me, I saw her bend down to whisper a few words to one of them. Behind her was a thin young woman, pretty in a pale sort of way, and much more simply dressed. I assumed this must be her daughter, Berenice, the go-between, the spy. She looked weary and miserable, as Theo had observed, and the reddish rims round her eyes suggested she'd been crying. Near the back of this little procession was another woman, tall and gaunt with greying hair pulled severely back from her lined face. I deduced from one of Theo's descriptions that she must be the so-called Two Times Doris, divorced first wife of the King brought back to court after an absence of thirty years. The fleshy man with the definite double chin on whose arm she walked was surely her son Antipater. So this was the King's eldest son and scheming, hostile half-brother to Alexander and Aristobulus!

Although pleased at last to be able to put faces to the oft-heard names of these powerful people, it was Salome's piercing glance which accompanied me back to barracks that day, causing me prickles of unease.

Chapter 11

One night my patrol group was on its way back after the second watch outside the palace walls, when we were startled by a shrill, prolonged scream. We stopped in our tracks. The blood-chilling sound came from a tall, narrow building tucked against the outer wall of the complex and almost concealed by trees. It was mainly bricked in except for some slits near the top, just visible in the faint moonlight.

"That must be the torture chamber. I wonder which poor sods are getting it tonight," muttered Philo, another relative newcomer like me. The ghastly sounds stopped, leaving a sinister silence to swell the darkness, but then, as if they had paused only to gather strength, the screams started again with renewed force. I felt fear, cold and reptilian, creep up inside me and shivered. "Can we go back now?" I asked the officer in charge.

He was firm, though not unkind. "Simon, you've much to learn about the ways here. You need to harden yourself, young man." Philo and I exchanged a glance of understanding in the flickering torchlight, and we were all silent for the rest of the walk back to barracks.

"That building is well known as one of the torture chambers," explained Theo matter-of-factly the following day. "It's bricked up for the first two floors to keep the noise out, but as you discovered it doesn't. And sooner or later we'll probably have to work in there ourselves. I believe that's sometimes one of our duties – as *loyal* bodyguards." He almost spat the word 'loyal' and I stared at him. What did he mean, *work in there ourselves?* I wondered what, exactly, we would be required to do, and whether it was work Father had had to do sometimes to earn his preferential treatment.

Theo saw my reaction and took me by the arm. More gently he said, "Come – let's go outside to somewhere quiet. I need to tell you something." We walked to a courtyard which was becoming a favourite because of its seclusion in a quiet corner not far from the barracks. A steady sparkle of water cascaded into a pool from the mouth of a marble fish and water lilies crowded round its base, carved with a tracery of vine leaves and grapes. I thought of David, whose workshop produced beautiful things like that, and felt a twinge of nostalgia for the safe, well-ordered home which he and Leah ran. I'd sent a note to tell them of my move to the palace, and telling them that I would seek leave to visit them while Chloe was in town.

"Simon, this isn't what I wanted to tell you, but first you should know something about those screams you heard last night. I'm sorry to say, they were almost definitely caused by my own brother."

"Your brother?" The scent of the jasmine tumbling down the wall behind us became suddenly sickly.

"Yes, Andreas. I'm not blaming him – and neither should you," Theo added defiantly. "He has no choice, Simon. He has to obey orders if he wants to keep not only his position but also his life. And mine too, probably. Who knows what they might threaten him with if he resisted? That would take the sort of courage which not a lot of us have."

Theo's words were an eerie echo of Father's in that last conversation. I bent down to adjust a sandal to hide my scowl of pain.

"Go on."

"Well, as I told you, although Andreas is now officially under the King's commanders, in day-to-day practice he still works for Antipater. Not sure how he wangles it, but he does. And Antipater tells him things. He's convinced his half-brothers are still planning their father's death."

"On what evidence?"

"Berenice – that's Aristobulus's spy-wife, remember? – overheard her husband and his brother Alexander making a plan to kill their father while out hunting. Salome of course went straight to the King and he's now gone mad. He's imprisoning everyone he can think of and torturing them to try and find out what's going on. But people say all sorts of things when their bodies are being stretched like so much papyrus and end up blurting out what they think the King wants to hear. Last night, according to Andreas, was the turn of the three eunuchs who are close to the King – the ones who bring him his supper and put him to bed and all that. Antipater is alleging that Alexander bribed the eunuchs to transfer their allegiances to him. It'll be them you'll have heard." He paused for breath.

"So why Andreas?"

"It was men in Antipater's camp, people like my brother, with no personal loyalty to either Alexander or Aristobulus, who were instructed to torture the eunuchs to get a full confession."

"And did they? Get a confession?"

"Well, Andreas was very tired this morning – apparently it's exhausting work turning the heavy screws which stretch the rack." I wasn't sure whether the remark was ironic – I did wonder sometimes whether Theo ever took anything seriously.

"Anyway, he was up doing it all night. I did glean between his yawns that he got the eunuchs to admit quite a lot."

"Such as?"

"That Alexander still deeply resents his father for putting his mother to death and that he ridicules him for dyeing his hair black to conceal his age. According to the eunuchs he has predicted the

King won't live much longer and claims to be ready to take over the kingdom. Says he has friends in high places who'll support him when the time comes."

"So what happens now?"

"Well, the King now fears for his life, as well as for his power and his throne. That's dangerous, highly dangerous, for anyone he even remotely suspects. And he suspects anyone who has links with or affection for Alexander and Aristobulus. Those poor wretches last night are by no means the only ones being tortured – probably as we speak."

Links with or affection for... I recalled what Celer had said when Alexander's slave had summoned him. "I love and fear for him." The long-standing friendship between the two men was no secret. Surely this meant that, despite his confidence, Celer himself could now be a suspect, in danger. And I heard again in my head Nicolas's warning, *keep your distance from both princes, Alexander and Aristobulus, and from those who serve them.* This was all beginning to come uncomfortably close to home.

*

"I have some brighter news and something more relevant to you. But we need to get going to the baths with the others. I'll tell you there!" Once sitting side by side in the hot steam, Theo challenged me. "Guess who I saw today?"

I was still preoccupied with the news he'd given me earlier, so I just shrugged.

"Well, you might look a bit more interested! Our orders were changed and we were sent to guard the sepulchre. The King's afraid the new memorial will attract thieves. Your friend Celer was supervising the work there and I managed to have a word with him! So he knows where you are now. How about that!" He turned a glistening wet face towards me in triumph.

"That is good news – though I'm not sure Celer would recognise the description of me as his friend."

"On the contrary, he seemed very keen to know how you were getting on. I assured him I'm the only one who knows about the architect's books, so he suggested sending you the next one via me and getting me to bring back the one you've got. He thinks he'll have to be at the monument for the next couple of days till he's sure the builders know exactly what to do – the King's taking a great personal interest in it."

So he should, I thought bitterly, *so he should*. "But Theo – I'm not nearly ready. I'm trying to copy out as much as I can so I have a record – it's all so hard to memorise."

"Be as quick as you can. I might not... oh no!" Ziper – the Thracian who'd brought me back from Caesarea and who'd recently been moved to our unit – had thrown a wet sponge at us which landed squarely in Theo's right eye.

"Come on, you two, liven up. Who are you talking about so seriously? A woman – or a boy?"

"None of your damned business!" I shouted genially, retrieving the sponge and chucking it back, hitting the target of Ziper's nose. This was a cue for the outbreak of a general fight with sponges as ammunition, and then several bystanders joined in by throwing sandals and other items of clothing into the fray. There was general shouting and laughter, the din magnified by the low roof and the steamy atmosphere. Then someone threw a metal strigil, which landed on a Thracian shoulder and drew blood. This changed the mood immediately and Theo breathed, "Oh, oh – I can see some old scores being settled now – let's get out." All the noise must have alerted the duty officer, because he came striding in, blowing a trumpet and threatening reduced rations for days if order were not restored at once. That quietened things down, but instead of being allowed to cool off in the frigidarium, we were all made to vacate the baths immediately. There was no more chance for private conversation before Theo's next shift, though he did manage to mutter that he'd see if Celer would part with the next book before I'd finished with the present one.

My rota at that time consisted of duties in the morning and the first two watches of the night, leaving the afternoons free for me to study. The next afternoon, driven by a new sense of urgency, I hid myself away in the little courtyard where the stone fish continued to regurgitate its watery insides. There, resting the documents on a stone bench, I knelt beside them and scratched away feverishly with my stylus, until my calves and feet felt as if they'd been invaded by a whole legion wielding miniature blades. I had to limp round the pool twice to alleviate the discomfort before settling down to another section. As I rolled the precious copies and tucked them away into my tunic, I felt a thrill of anticipation at the prospect of the next book, which, according to the promise at the end of Book 2, would focus on the temples of the immortal gods. This, truly, was what I had been born to do.

Catching sight of Theo coming towards me on the way back to barracks, I quickened my step. But when Theo opened his arms to show he'd brought nothing back, I felt my shoulders sag in dismay. "Sorry to have raised your hopes, Simon. Celer wasn't there after all. He'd been called away to sort out some problem up at the Temple." That's how it always was: one step forward and two back. I was dependent on so many things beyond my control, and sometimes that earlier despondency invaded me again.

*

But the disappointment was eclipsed the following day by an unwelcome summons. Ever since Salome's retinue had passed me several days before, I had feared – intuitively I'd known – that I would soon receive an order to attend the King's sister. And so it proved.

"Simon, you've got to report to the Lady Salome's apartments –

now. She wants a couple of strong men to help move some furniture and she particularly asked for you to be one of them. How she knows you is a mystery to me, but it's not for me to ask questions." The officer who conveyed the message stared at me suspiciously. "Can't think why she needs soldiers to move furniture – it's a job for her slaves, if you ask me. Philo, you go too, you've got the brute strength. You're to report without helmets and cuirasses, by the way. Just tunics, prepared for heavy work."

I recalled Theo's words the day I arrived – *that's to be avoided at all costs*. But now it seemed I had no choice in the matter.

"Ah there you are." The King's sister met us herself in the antechamber to her private apartments. "I'm glad to see you've come dressed for hot work. Now, I want the chests in here moved to my reception rooms. They will be useful for storing my grandchildren's playthings. They'll enjoy digging around in them. Then, the couches which I'll show you need…" and so the instructions went on.

I tried to take them in, but it was hard to concentrate with those penetrating green eyes fixed – or so it felt – mainly on me. I was surprised to hear that she not only entertained but also wanted to please her grandchildren. It somehow didn't fit with her demonic reputation, especially when I reflected that some of her grandchildren were also the children of Aristobulus, allegedly her deadly enemy. Maybe after all she had a softer side. As she turned to explain something to an attendant, I risked studying her profile. Her black – probably dyed – hair was piled on top of her head as usual and secured with gem-encrusted clasps. She was a big woman, though not fat, with an obvious taste for brightly coloured clothes and liberal make-up, and there was something undeniably striking, even elegant, about her.

She hovered around, watching our exertions and calling out instructions – but not rudely – in a deep, husky voice. Then, directed to move a large chest, Philo took one end and I the other. It was much heavier than we anticipated and, stepping back, I was caught slightly off balance. Letting go of my end of the chest, I tripped over a pottery vase which we should have moved beforehand. Horrified, I stared down at the shattered vessel.

Turning to Salome, I bit my lip and stammered, "I… I…"

"Don't worry, young man. There are plenty more of those. I hope you haven't hurt yourself?" Momentarily speechless at this unexpected concern, I became aware of a bejewelled hand patting my arm. Fleetingly my eyes met hers, and, absurd and conceited though it might sound given the chasm between us in status and age, there was something flirtatious in her glance. Then she turned and, clicking her fingers at a female slave standing against the wall, gestured to her to clear up the fragments.

"Thank you, my… lady. I do apologise," I mumbled. Philo, whose puffed cheeks and curled lips betrayed a stifled desire to burst out laughing, saved the situation as soon as he could speak. "Let's try again. I'll count to three this time."

When we eventually finished the work to her satisfaction, Salome called another slave to bring fruit and water for our refreshment. As we left, she said, "You've worked well, young men – I will probably call on you again." To me this sounded more like threat than approval and once more I was aware that her gaze rested on me in particular. Then, as I reached the door, she called me back, and I was afraid she was going to mention the vase again.

"Simon, isn't it? I believe you're the son of Philip of Nîmes." She'd obviously made enquiries, and I remembered how she'd whispered something to her slave after they passed me by the gate.

"Yes, my lady!" I replied, wishing I'd checked beforehand on the right way to address her.

She nodded. "I thought so. I knew him a little – he attended my brother, the King, for many years. A sad business, his… er… accidental death."

There was a question implicit in her remark, and it suggested she didn't know exactly how Father had met his death. Or did she?

Perhaps she was testing me, but I didn't wait to find out. I muttered another apology for the broken vase, bowed respectfully, low enough to avoid meeting her gaze again, then hurried to catch up with Philo.

"Well, she didn't seem all that bad – whatever people say," he exclaimed. It was true she had been very decent to us but I was all too aware of her threat to call on us again and wondered what her real reasons were.

Chapter 12

At the start of our meal that evening Alberic banged on a dish for silence, his already florid complexion even more flushed than usual. He had an important announcement to make.

"The King of Cappadocia will soon arrive in Jerusalem. He has urgent business with the King. I need eight of you to act as his bodyguard. As this is an unusual opportunity, I am prepared to take volunteers. I insist only that some of the eight should have at least a year's experience as a guard."

There was a brief silence while we all weighed up whether it would be to our advantage to volunteer. Theo, the only one I had told of my interest in Salvia, gave me a smart nudge in the ribs. I didn't need a second one, for I had quickly worked out that as the King of Cappadocia was Princess Glaphyra's father, acting as his bodyguard would be more than likely to bring me into contact with Glaphyra's preferred slave. *Should it arise, do not volunteer for any duties under their command.* But surely this was different, exceptional, and I wouldn't be strictly under *their* command. I raised my arm, forgetting that I had been about to ask for leave to visit Chloe while she was in town. Glancing around I realised with dismay that I was one of about a dozen volunteers.

"Thank you. We will draw lots later." I noticed with irritation that as Alberic sat down, one of the other volunteers was quick to offer him the untouched dish of lentils.

Later Theo, true to form, filled me in on the background. King Archelaus had come to Jerusalem to punish his daughter and son-in-law for plotting against his friend King Herod. "One of Alexander's friends has confessed under torture that the Prince has had some deadly poison made up," Theo whispered. "I hear King Archelaus has threatened to have both his son-in-law and daughter executed if their plotting can be proved. They say he's reproached Herod for being too lenient." Then, typically sceptical, he added, "It all sounds most unlikely for a father. I suspect it's tactics to make King Herod calm down a bit. I may be wrong but time will tell."

Time did tell. Before long it was common knowledge that Alexander and Glaphyra were once again in the clear. "Clever old man, I told you it was tactics!" Theo chuckled. With family relations improving, a date was now set for a lavish entertainment in honour of the royal guest. Theo was granted time off to practise his lyre and pipes, for his brother had used his influence to ensure he'd be one of the performers, and I was delighted when Alberic drew my name out of the lots to guard the foreign King.

*

The first duty session provided not even a glimpse of Salvia, let alone a meeting. I walked back to barracks in a sulk, ignoring the chatter of my comrades and kicking a broken piece of pottery ahead of me. But the prospect of the entertainment which before long was to take place in the new theatre, some seven furlongs south of the city walls, cheered me up. Surely I would see her there.

For two whole days we guards – including those of us watching over King Archelaus – were required to check all the comings and goings of actors, singers, acrobats and other performers to ensure that no weapons or people of a suspicious nature found their way into the theatre. Easier said than done, for all sorts of packages were brought in which could potentially spell danger – equipment for the acrobats, musical instruments and piles of costumes which were deposited in rooms behind the stage. On the day itself slaves came and went with covered jugs of water and wine, trays of delicacies and pots of aromatic spices, some of which were smoking gently and filling the whole space with a heady scent. As the first members of the invited audience started to arrive, Alberic sent me and several others to stand flat against the wall with a clear view of the rows which would accommodate the royal household.

The first to arrive were the non-royal prestigious guests, most of whom were unknown to me, but before long Nicolas of Damascus appeared, together with his brother Ptolemy. Then came a group of the King's younger children, around nine to eleven years of age, attended by nursemaids. Soon after that the royal wives entered, singly, each attended by their own servants, and were so close to me as they passed that had I so wished I could have put out my hand and stroked the silky splendour of their robes. But I only wanted to watch the entrances, anxious not to miss Salvia's arrival, although for a long time there was no sign of her.

When a man entered with a strong resemblance to the King, though shorter and much stouter, I guessed this must be his brother, Pheroras. I recalled one of the Thracian brothers remarking that it was a long time since Pheroras had seen his own toes, and I could see now what they meant. Still, I had my own reason to feel sympathy for the King's brother, for it was well-known that he was in love with a slave woman. When Salome finally appeared the hubbub of conversation fell briefly silent as she made her commanding way, with much rustling of skirts and cursory nodding to the royal wives, to the seat next to the one reserved for the two kings.

With so much going on, my attention was briefly distracted from the entrances so I did not immediately notice that Salvia had arrived. But suddenly there she was, behind the Princess Glaphyra, who had come in almost simultaneously with Salome through the entrance on the other side of the theatre, her arm tucked into her husband's, her proud dark head held high. It was as if the entrances had been carefully choreographed by someone with a keen eye for dramatic effect, but it was not the regal Glaphyra who quickened my pulse – it was the sweet-faced maiden who followed her.

Next came Aristobulus, or so I assumed, for as far as I could tell from where I stood he was a smaller, fairer version of his brother. His wife, Berenice, was at his side, though her arm was not linked through his and she soon joined some ladies in a row further forward, while he took a seat next to Alexander and I saw how their heads bowed together in a quiet exchange. In quick succession, through the entrance nearer to me, came Antipater, apparently deep in conversation with his mother. I was close enough to notice that every finger of his pudgy hands glittered with rings. A brief trumpet blast from somewhere in the background announced the imminent arrival of the two kings, and an expectant silence fell on the auditorium. I looked across at Salvia, who stood at the end of the row where her mistress sat with Alexander. I willed her to look over in my direction, though I realised she might not recognise me under my helmet, but she was concentrating on the opening through which the two kings were expected to emerge.

The men in the auditorium rose to their feet as the monarchs entered, until King Herod made a signal with his hand and everyone sat down again. He seemed to me even larger than when I'd seen him at Caesarea, his striking head of hair even blacker. Though by all accounts a little younger, the more bent and white-haired King Archelaus appeared older. He turned and looked around the auditorium as he took his seat, smiling in silent acknowledgment of the assembled company, but his glance rested eventually on his daughter, to whom he raised his hand in greeting. It was a dignified and benevolent performance, and I could understand why he was said to be popular.

The entertainment was a Greek play, which was supposed to be humorous. I found it boring – in fact, I couldn't find anything funny in it at all. Anyway, I couldn't concentrate, as we guards had had strict instructions to scan the audience at frequent intervals for any signs of disruption or disturbance, anything at all which could conceivably become a threat to the kings. It was a long time to remain standing completely still and my back began to ache, but the pain was forgotten every time my eyes came to rest on Salvia. She seemed to be following the action on stage with enthusiasm, though once, as clouds passed over the sun and a little breeze stirred the air, she crept along the row of seats and leant across Alexander to pass her mistress the cloak she'd carried in over her arm.

Unsure at what point Theo would be performing, I felt a flutter of anxiety on his behalf. Between each act of the play there was a brief intermezzo, with music and dancing, during which members of the audience got up and went to speak to others and slaves passed trays of nuts and fruit down the rows. During the first interlude I noticed that Philo was conducting a body search of a newcomer in the far entrance; as I watched, I realised that the late arrival was Celer, who, once he'd passed the inspection, hurried down the steps two at a time, until he reached the row where Alexander and his entourage were seated. Aristobulus got up to make way for him next to Alexander, but before sitting down, Celer bowed respectfully in the direction of the two kings. They both inclined their heads, and Archelaus smiled briefly at him in return. King Herod was almost simultaneously distracted by Salome whispering something in his ear, and I wondered whether her timing was deliberate. Theo would be proud of me, I reflected.

Celer immediately began in his quick, observant way, to look around him, nodding in greeting to various people in the audience. Aware that my helmet would probably prevent him from recognising me, I tried surreptitiously to push it further back on my head. This must have worked, because as one of the performers came on stage to announce the next act, Celer spotted me and raised his hand – it was a small, spontaneous gesture of recognition, but under the circumstances perhaps an unwise one. I was unable to reciprocate, though I did raise my eyebrows which he would almost certainly not have seen, but I still caught myself glancing guiltily towards King Herod, as if already accused of the crime of greeting one of Alexander's friends. The King of course was unaware of me, but someone else had noticed. Sitting a few places behind the King was Nicolas of Damascus, who had obviously recognised me despite the helmet. He nodded in my direction. Was it a rather curt, disapproving gesture or was I imagining things?

Trying to ignore the twist of anxiety in my stomach, I turned to the stage. I didn't want to miss Theo. I'd not been to a theatre performance before and was surprised at the way the audience kept up its chatter, punctuated by louder shouts of laughter. Several of the actors were young men in white masks acting as women. Some of the audience threw flowers at them, calling out lewd suggestions. A glance in the direction of the kings showed that all this was quite in order, as they were both smiling. Theo appeared in the second intermezzo and was the very image of concentration. With eyes narrowed, presumably against the glare of the sun for the stage faced due south, and beads of sweat visible on his brow even from my distance, he seemed oblivious to everything around him, especially when the tempo grew fast and he and his fellow musicians played as if their lives depended on it. Perhaps, in a way, they did, for a poor performance in front of such an important guest would surely incur the King's wrath. Theo appeared again at the end of the play, which culminated in much singing and dancing, and this time he was playing the double pipes. I watched with trepidation, remembering the problems he'd had fitting the double reed into the instrument. But the response from the audience was as reassuringly raucous as before, and I was fairly confident that the toll of two broken reeds and a litany of swear words had been worth the effort.

At the end of the whole performance I waited, stock still as previously instructed, while all the members of the royal family left.

While wondering if I could somehow contrive to get to the other side of the theatre to make contact with either Salvia or Celer, or both, to my horror I was accosted by none other than Salome. Suddenly she was there towering over me on the step above yet leaning down close enough that I could smell the onions on her breath.

"Ah, Simon, my young friend, son of Philip the Gaul, I was pleased with your work the other day. Will you come to my apartments later today? I have an errand I'd like you to run. Don't worry, my brother won't object."

"My lady, I must attend on King Archelaus today. I have strict orders while he is here." To my relief the words came out firm and decisive, though I cringed inside, hating the idea of being addressed as her 'young friend', dismayed that I should be seen talking to her at all.

"That's of no consequence. I can wait until he departs. Unless of course I get your orders changed." With that threat and an eloquent rise of a blackened eyebrow, she swept on up the steps. Immediately I looked across to where Salvia had been and was in time to see her following her master and mistress through the exit. I dreaded the conclusions they would draw if any of them had recognised me and witnessed the exchange. And Celer, had he seen? Everyone else was now getting up from their seats and milling around, either greeting acquaintances or making their way to the exits, and I had completely lost sight of Celer in the confusion. Absorbed in self-pity for letting another opportunity slip away, I didn't notice the architect coming up the steps towards me, again two at a time, from the direction of the proscenium. When I did catch sight of him, I was immediately cheered.

"Simon! We meet again at last! I'm glad you got rid of *her*! What did she want?"

"We had to move some furniture for her a few days ago, and now she says she wants me to run an errand for her."

"That's not good. But you can hardly refuse – I can see that."

"Well, I did tell her my orders are to attend King Archelaus while he is here."

Celer's brow cleared. "Good fellow! Still, perhaps only a temporary reprieve. But be careful of her. Now, I have the next few books for you. I'm going to let you have several at once after all – I saw your friend Theo so I realise it's become much harder for us to meet. As you're attending King Archelaus at present, perhaps you can find a pretext to come to Alexander's apartments to collect them?" I made a dubious face.

"It's all right, Simon. Thanks to his father-in-law, poor Alexander's no longer a persona non grata, you know – for the time being at least." *Perhaps*, I thought, *perhaps it would after all be safe.* But I wished I didn't feel so exposed talking openly to Celer in this way, wondering who was watching us, remembering Nicolas's warnings and that earlier stern admonition.

"All right. If it's going to be difficult, I'll keep them with me. Come and find me when you can. I have to supervise some difficult repair work on the city wall near the northern boundary of the palace complex over the next few days. If you need an excuse, say I have something for you from Quintus Severus, who knew your father. Sometimes a small lie is necessary. By the way, I was extremely sorry to hear about your father – from Theo. You should have told me when you came to my office – I might not have been so fierce." He touched my arm lightly and then, tossing back the familiar lock of rebel hair, turned away, almost immediately greeting someone else in the thinning crowd. He was on the point of leaving the theatre when he hurried back down the steps to where I had to remain standing until the auditorium was completely cleared. "An afterthought, Simon – try and find out when you'll have some leave, then maybe we can make a plan. Oh – and once again, be careful with *that woman*."

He bounded back up the steps, leaving me with decidedly mixed feelings. The distinguished and influential Lucius Servius Celer, so important for the future I longed for, was taking me seriously.

And Celer at least seemed more concerned than suspicious at seeing Salome talk to me. Yet the misgivings, – yes, I had to call it by its true name – the old enemy fear, still sat heavy in my entrails. The fact that the infamous Salome, having taken note of my existence, did not seem inclined to leave me alone made me feel very vulnerable indeed. How could a lowly bodyguard *be careful* in the face of orders – or threats – from someone so powerful?

Chapter 13

A day or two after the performance King Archelaus called us volunteer bodyguards together and graciously thanked us for our services, not that they had been onerous given that he'd also brought some of his own soldiers with him. He told us that his business with his old friend King Herod was now concluded and so he was preparing to leave Jerusalem. Of course he made no mention of the nature of that business, though by now we were all in the know. Maddeningly, the new duties hadn't brought me into contact with Salvia, but I had glimpsed Glaphyra and Alexander strolling in the gardens with him and on another occasion he'd been hand in hand with his two grandsons. It did seem as if he'd succeeded in calming the situation.

"King Herod wishes to accompany King Archelaus as far as Antioch, leaving early tomorrow. They will need a large escort, so I need to send a contingent of my men to go with the cavalry. I will have more information this evening." Alberic's characteristically clipped announcement could not have come at a worse time for me, as that very morning I'd received a note from David to say that Chloe was preparing to leave for home and was disappointed not to have seen me. I could no longer put off requesting leave of absence, but now even half a day looked impossible and I had so wanted to see my sister, for the first time in nearly two years. Antioch was many days' march away, and if I were selected to go with the escort not only would I certainly miss Chloe, but I would also be unable to meet and make a plan with Celer while he was working nearby on the perimeter wall.

I decided I must approach Alberic, telling myself I had nothing to lose. "I had decided to include you, Simon. Don't look so miserable. This is not a disaster! We will be back in about two weeks. I am sure you can get word to your sister, who will understand that your royal duties come first."

I felt a hot rush of irritation. It certainly was a disaster – a double one. And I couldn't believe there'd be a shortage of men keen for the privilege of accompanying the royal procession to Antioch.

"When we return you may have some leave. It will be due to you anyway."

"Thank you, Sir," but I made sure my tone conveyed my disappointment.

On the way back to the dormitory, I bumped into Theo, who was feeling despondent about the way the entertainment had gone. There had been no messages from anyone, not even from his brother. He was beginning to wonder whether he was in some sort of disgrace. "And I thought it had gone well enough – even on the pipes – despite that idiot next to me playing the wrong note about six times. And the audience noise drowning out the lyre." I saw that this was not the right time to talk about my own worries.

"I thought you played really well. I could hear it and I was at least halfway back."

"No, you weren't, you liar! I saw you – you were on the level with the two kings. And thanks for the encouragement, but I know you have about as much musical discernment as a cavalry horse."

"Oh, thanks – given how you feel about horses!"

*

The next morning while we were preparing for departure, I was called to the entrance where a slave had appeared with a summons. "You are to report directly to Nicolas of Damascus."

This was surely a reprimand, or worse. Nicolas had doubtless observed me talking to Celer and had considered it disloyal. Alberic readily gave me permission to absent myself when he heard who had summoned me and Theo grimaced, indicating that like me he suspected bad news. I'd told him about the conversation with Celer in the auditorium.

"Good luck, old man!"

I followed the slave through the compound, oblivious for once to the elaborate wonders of the palace gardens, convinced I was being taken at best to be disciplined, at worst – well, I couldn't help thinking back to those cries in the night. I told myself not to be absurd, that only slaves were legally allowed to be tortured, but my throat had other ideas and had gone bone dry. To my astonishment, as we reached the door of Nicolas's office, the great man himself came out to welcome me affably.

"Ah, Simon – I have a surprise for you. A visitor! Come!" Taken aback, I followed him into the dim interior where, to my delight and amazement, stood my sister Chloe.

"Don't look so astonished – it *is* me, not a ghost!" She darted forward to embrace me fondly, so I was glad I wasn't yet wearing my hard cuirass ready for departure. I looked round at Nicolas, who, before explaining, sat down behind his table covered with its neat piles of documents and scrolls.

"Chloe wrote me a polite message to say that she has to leave Jerusalem soon and was anxious to see you before she goes. I was pleased to have the opportunity of meeting my late friend's daughter again, now she is an old married lady, so I readily agreed." He looked at us standing side by side and smiled, a different man from the one who had cautioned me so severely on my arrival.

"I have had a nice talk to your sister, but now I must go and attend to some business for the King – I'll leave you two alone for a while and will ask Amyntas to bring you some refreshments."

"I have to leave shortly for Antioch in the King's party, Sir," I explained.

"If you have to leave before I get back, Chloe will be safe here in my office until her brother-in-law collects her later. Chloe – in that case use the time well. You'll find some Homer over there, so make yourself at home."

"Thank you, Sir, thank you very much indeed." My gratitude was indeed sincere, all the more so for being mixed with relief. But the great scholar had not finished with me.

"And Simon. Another word of warning. There is nothing wrong in principle in your talking to Lucius Servius Celer, though I don't know how you came to be acquainted. After Severus, he is probably the most gifted architect we have here in Judaea at this time, and much valued by the King. However, he is also an old friend of Alexander's from his boyhood years in Rome, and these days no one, I repeat no one, is beyond suspicion. Be very careful."

I watched the slightly stooped figure retreat through the doorway, his warning a slingshot in my stomach. *He may be famous for his knowledge of history*, I thought, *but those little black eyes miss nothing of what's going on around him in the present.*

Chloe frowned in puzzlement. "What was all that about?"

After I'd recovered I explained, choosing my words carefully. "He saw me speaking to an architect who is a friend of the King's son, Alexander. He'd warned me on my first day here to steer clear of Alexander's friends because of all the rumours about plots and conspiracies. But Alexander's father-in-law, the King of Cappadocia, has been here – we're escorting him part of the way home which is why I have to leave for Antioch very soon. They say he's brought about a reconciliation, so I'm not sure why Nicolas is still being so fierce about it."

Chloe was not unduly interested. "I see. Well, anyway, I've come with much more important news! See if you can guess!"

Turning my attention back to her I studied her face, which was alight with happiness – even the dimness of the room could not obscure the shine in her eyes. I did guess, immediately, but hesitated to put it into words, in case I was wrong.

"Simon, I'm with child!"

"Oh, that is wonderful news!" We embraced again, and I felt a great lump in my throat as I held the back of her head to my shoulder. I truly rejoiced for her, yet the joy was tinged with sadness for it had come too late to share with Father. And the memory that the gods had not permitted my own mother to see her baby son, let alone any grandchildren, crept unbidden into the heart of my delight.

"I know it was a bit bold writing to Nicolas of Damascus – he's so important nowadays, they say. But I remembered he and Father were friends so I took a chance – and it worked!"

"You never were lacking in self-confidence!" I had often envied her the quality, the shield behind which I'd often hidden my reticence, my shyness. Chloe had been the rock of my childhood.

"So, isn't it exciting! We've certainly had to wait a while – I think we were all beginning to give up hope." I recalled Leah's hesitation and sudden change of subject when I enquired after Chloe. "Anyway, the baby's due in mid-December by my reckoning. You will absolutely have to get leave and come and see me as soon as it's born. Meanwhile, you must help us think of names!" I chuckled in my pleasure at seeing her again, and so radiant. But then her expression grew suddenly sombre. "But it will be too late for Father. I am so sad he'll never see the baby, never even know about it. Simon, you must tell me about his last days. I still don't really understand why he died. David took me to the burial chamber so that I could leave my offerings, but I would rather have gone with you." I noticed for the first time that her skirt was torn at the hem and stained with dirt marks in fitting respect. It always surprised and impressed me, the way she had embraced the traditions of the faith she had, so unusually as a Gentile, married into.

"I was about to request leave to come and take you there myself, but then we had this damned order to escort King Archelaus to Antioch." I gave her an account of the last time I saw him and of the funeral, mentioning only his bad cough, hoping that she wouldn't ask more searching questions into the circumstances of his death. Even – perhaps especially – to Chloe, I couldn't admit to all those dagger-like reproaches that still kept sticking their points into me when I was least expecting them. *I didn't ask permission to go and see him when I knew he was unwell. I didn't make any effort. I didn't even send him a message.*

*

Back at the barracks, I was met by a beaming Alberic – or as near beaming as the reserved, correct German ever allowed himself to be. He didn't enquire why I'd been summoned by such an important personage but came immediately to the point.

"Simon, I have found someone to take your place. One of your comrades has made a special request to be included. His family live near Antioch and he hopes to visit them. So you can have your leave now, as there will be fewer duties while some of the royal household are away. You have three days from tomorrow – you must report to Walcaud before you go and again on your return." Walcaud was a spiteful, humourless officer, but it didn't matter because this was splendid news.

I did wonder if I should confess that I had seen Chloe, so the reason for needing early leave no longer applied. But at that very moment Alberic was called away by several of the men who'd almost come to blows arguing about items of kit for the journey. Relieved, I thought of the other, covert, reason for my request and wanted to shout out loud with the thrill of anticipation – three whole days! At last this would be a chance to observe some of the building work in progress, to see the theory I was trying so hard to learn translated into practice. And perhaps I would at last meet Salvia again, for I'd heard that Glaphyra was not included in her father's escort. With all this going through my mind, by the time I reported to Walcaud before leaving the premises next morning, my excitement was almost at fever pitch.

Chapter 14

"I don't know how Alberic thinks I'm going to cover all the posts with only half the men. Be gone then, but one blink of an eye late back on Thursday, you'll be in trouble." I had no doubt that Walcaud's threat was real, but Thursday evening seemed a luxuriously long way away and nothing could cast a shadow over my sunny mood. I knew exactly where I was going, and, without helmet and full uniform, my step was as light as my humour.

It was clear from the wooden scaffolding and the number of workmen where the repairs were taking place, though there was no sign of Celer when I arrived. I watched the men for a while, envying the rippling muscles of their bare brown backs. Then I walked eastwards along the inside of the old city wall, looking for a bench or any place to sit where I could read again the pages I'd laboriously copied. I so wanted to impress Celer with all that I'd absorbed and to have sensible questions at the ready. But the quest for a quiet spot was fruitless, the whole place resounding with the morning shouts of goatherds, the clatter of hooves and the bleating of sacrificial animals being beaten along their final journey. The few little alcoves which would have served my purpose had been ruined by use as urinals, their rank stink mingling with that of the fresh piles of manure steaming in the early sun and already attracting clouds of flies. Soon I gave up and retraced my steps towards the site of the renovations. This time Celer had arrived. He was standing on top of the wooden scaffolding, absorbed in discussion with two of the workmen. When he eventually looked round he spotted me standing below, waiting shyly to announce my presence.

"Ah, Simon – so you've managed to come! Excellent timing – I have something to show you. A perfect demonstration of a technique described by the master. Come, come," he added impatiently, putting out his hand to steady me as I reached the rickety top of the installation. I drew in my breath at the unexpected view which unfolded across the lush gardens of the steep-sided valley towards the Hill of Gareb to the north, and to the south-west, where the dusty road to Bethlehem and Hebron snaked away through barren slopes, into the blue distance. Celer did not give me time to admire the panorama but launched straight in.

"Do you see these charred olive wood ties? Now you've read the part of the book that deals with city walls, so you'll appreciate these. They're there to bind the two faces of the huge stones of the wall, to ensure endurance. This wood doesn't decay, you see – neither water nor weather can harm it. All substructures that require a thickness like a city wall will last much longer if they're tied in this way." He turned to the two builders. "Good work, men. Keep going – you must be about halfway!"

When we got back to the ground, he carried on, "Good. I'm pleased to have been able to show you an excellent example of theory carried into practice. Now let's go and have a look at some other things. These towers, for instance. Note that these are all round, though polygonal are also acceptable. Can you remember why the master says square towers are not practical?"

I was entranced. For the next two or three hours I followed Celer around as he carried out his inspection of works in progress, and peered fascinated over his shoulder at the plans of various foremen. I answered Celer's questions carefully and was gratified to get most of them right. I'd have liked to take notes, but there was no time, so

I resolved to write it all up that evening at David's and Leah's house, where I planned to spend the next two nights.

Suddenly, Celer stopped. "You've been concentrating hard, and I can see you've been doing your reading. I'm hungry after all that and I expect you are – let's go and get something to eat." We were packing up the measuring instruments when there was a shout and, looking up, I was taken aback to see none other than the King's son Alexander sauntering towards us.

"There you are, Celer. I wondered where you'd been hiding. Anything to avoid coming hunting with me!"

"Hardly hiding! I've been around here close to the palace perimeter all morning – a man does have work to do you know, or *some* do anyway."

"Celer, surely you can spare a few hours to come hunting with me," wheedled Alexander. Then, more brightly, "I need to celebrate. My father-in-law, true friend that he is, has managed to bring some sort of peace – however temporary it may be – to the royal house of Judaea, and my own beloved father has left today for Antioch. He'll be gone for at least two weeks. And I, with all Jerusalem, am the happier for it!" Celer raised his eyebrows and glanced at me, clearly surprised at his royal friend's lack of discretion.

"Please!" Alexander leant back against one of Celer's prized walls, pulling a pleading face like a child's, taking no notice of me.

Celer ignored his plea. "This young man is Simon, son of Philip the Gaul, who was one of your father's favoured bodyguards. He has an ambition to be an architect, and I am tutoring him – at the request of Quintus Severus." He delivered the last sentence almost defiantly, as if expecting a reproach.

Alexander turned then to study me. "Haven't I seen you somewhere before? You seem somehow familiar." There was an edge of suspicion in his tone.

"Yes, Sir – it was at the harbour in Caesarea. I was with Quintus Severus and you were—"

"Ah yes, yes, I remember you – and the occasion now. Poor Gamellus was with us. I wonder if he's home safely. He does so hate sea voyages." His voice had become quiet with concern.

"We were going to get something to eat. Perhaps you could invite us to your apartments where the offerings are undoubtedly superior to anything we can find in the town. And I think we should get out of the open air as soon as possible now that the wind has started to blow from the east." Celer screwed up his nose in distaste as an acrid smell of burning flesh mingled with incense wafted towards us from the direction of the Temple.

"Come on then! But only if you promise to come hunting with me tomorrow!"

"Not tomorrow, Alexander. I'm expecting Quintus Severus to arrive in Jerusalem tomorrow or the next day and I have so much to show him and ask his advice about."

Alexander grimaced. "I confess I was pleased when poor Glaphyra went down with one of her headaches, and my father-in-law suggested I stay here with her instead of joining his escort. *Aha*, I thought – *an opportunity to go hunting and enjoy myself, without having to pretend I'm less skilled than you-know-who!* And now *you*, one of my oldest and dearest friends, are denying me my pleasure! Some friendship!"

We had passed through the main gate into the complex, where the guards had saluted respectfully, when Alexander suddenly stopped.

"We'll wait here – let them pass." In an eerie repetition of my first day at the palace, there was Salome, a couple of other women and a few attendants walking in the direction of her apartments, about a hundred yards away from us on a parallel path. Silently I beseeched the gods, *please don't let her look in this direction, please don't let her see and acknowledge me.* At one point a harsh peal of laughter rang out, and glancing at Alexander standing still as a statue beside me, I saw how his lips had all but disappeared in a grim straight line.

"She may well laugh, the scheming bitch," he hissed. I had heaved a surreptitious sigh of relief as the group of women passed on their way without looking round, when something made Salome turn. Immediately she spotted us three men watching them. She stopped, her companions following her lead, and stared intently across the rose beds and lawn between us. I was quite certain that she recognised me, for I was off duty and wore no helmet that would partially have concealed my face. Would she acknowledge me? Give some sign that we were acquainted? Eventually, with a haughty nod of her finely dressed head, she continued on her way.

"I fancy she looked at you particularly as if she knew you," said Alexander, undisguised suspicion in his voice.

Celer came to the rescue. "She does. She spotted him one day and made a special request for him to come and help move some furniture in her apartments. We can all guess why!"

Alexander nodded, grimly. "Yes indeed." He searched my face. "Have you had any other contact with her?"

"No. But after that entertainment in the theatre she came up to me and said she wanted me to run an errand for her. I told her I was ordered to attend King Archelaus while he was here, and she said she might try and get the orders changed. But now he's gone so… if… if she summons me again, I wouldn't… really… be able to refuse." I wasn't sure if that would be enough to reassure Alexander that I had no wish to be associated with the enemy camp, but his features relaxed and he clapped me on the back.

"I understand that. But be careful, that's all. Believe me, no nephew ever had more cause to mistrust his own aunt. She'll be best friends with you while it suits her and then she wouldn't think twice before dropping poison in your wine." It was all very well for Alexander and Celer to keep telling me to be careful – as Nicolas did for different reasons – but I was no Heracles and what was I supposed to do if given an order by the King's sister herself?

As the women moved off, Celer addressed Alexander. "It may have been a bad move on your part – not going with the escort, I mean. Your lovable half-brother will have plenty of opportunity to sour your name behind your back – while constantly claiming that he is your staunchest ally, of course."

"I thought of that but decided to risk it. And after all, Aristobulus has gone with them."

A distinctly uncomfortable witness of such talk, I followed them at a respectful distance until Alexander turned back to me. "I rather like the look of this young man here. What did you say his name was? Perhaps he'll come hunting with me instead!" I was relieved to hear his friendly tone.

"I-I'm afraid I've never hunted, Sir." I faltered.

"No matter. I'll soon teach you. You look athletic enough – I'm sure you'll learn quickly."

"Alexander, please. Simon has very little leave from duty, and what time he has he must devote to study. It's not fair of you to try and distract him." Celer's irritation was clear, his jaw set firm. I couldn't but admire the way he stood up to the demands of a king's son. I'd already had occasion to observe that he was quick to laughter and quick to anger, but now I could see that a chip of flint lodged in his nature as well.

Alexander returned his friend's steady gaze, his face flushed. There was a brief tense silence, during which I thought of what the old tutor had said, back at the harbour in Caesarea. *Alexander can certainly be quick-tempered – he's hot-headed and impulsive*, and wondered anxiously what would happen next. Then Alexander relaxed into a chuckle, as if bearing out Gamellus's other words, *but there is no malice in him.*

"All right, Celer, you win – as always. But I shall hold you to that hunting trip before they all get back. Now come in, let's see what there is to eat." As he turned to lead the way, Celer and I exchanged the briefest of glances, but it was enough to convey a sense of complicity. I could no longer doubt that Lucius Servius Celer, according to Nicolas of Damascus possibly the second most gifted architect working in Judaea, was my ally. Surely my dream was now, despite everything, within reach.

I was dazzled by the sumptuous decoration of the apartments. The mosaic floor of the room we were invited into was one large hunting scene and frescoes covered the walls, against which leant couches draped with richly coloured textiles. In a shallow pool in the centre of the floor stood a statue of a stag, one leg raised as if about to flee. I was looking up at one of the pictures trying to work out which scene it depicted from the life of Dionysos, always a favourite from childhood because his mother had died in pregnancy, so that I didn't at first notice Salvia as she entered the room in answer to Alexander's summons by bell. When I caught sight of her, I gave an involuntary start and felt my face begin to burn. Salvia bowed briefly to Alexander and replied, in answer to his enquiry, that her mistress was feeling rather better and had managed to eat something. At that point a little curly head peered round the door, and Alexander called out, "Hallo, little man, you can come in, you know!" But the small boy, probably not more than three or four years old, grabbed Salvia's skirt and disappeared almost immediately. I saw how the father's face had softened. "Pity, he'd have liked to see you, Celer." And to me he explained, "Celer plays the fool with my sons and they love him for it. Whirls them round and round till they are quite dizzy!"

Alexander invited us to recline on one of the gorgeous couches. I was conscious of the layer of building dust that had accumulated on me during the morning's lessons, but as Celer sat down without attempting to brush his off I did the same. More slaves entered with folding tables and platters of appetising food – salt fish and eggs, and pieces of spiced chicken surrounded by chicory and pepperwort, dandelion and lettuce, accompanied by a basket piled high with round loaves of warm bread. "I bet this is better than what you get in the barracks, eh, Simon? I can almost see you salivating!" Celer grinned at me. "And look, eggs! I've not had eggs since the last time I was in Rome," he added, reaching forward to help himself with boyish eagerness. "And I must say, the vegetables in this city are surprisingly good given the climate."

"Well, you know why they're so good, don't you?" Alexander gestured at me to help myself.

"Of course I do. You're speaking to one of the architects of the Temple, my boy." I frowned, not understanding the connection, but Celer had not forgotten his teaching obligations for the day. "Now don't tell me you've never wondered what happens to all the blood from the sacrifices? You disappoint me, Simon. The Temple floor slopes in different directions, you see, so blood from the sacrifices can be easily rinsed away. There's a drainage channel which starts near the altar and then leads underground to the Kidron Valley where many of the gardens are. It makes them wonderfully fertile."

"Anyway, have some more of them – the snakeroot is particularly good this season," and Alexander indicated the platter. But my mind was only temporarily distracted by the food. Alexander had been so unexpectedly welcoming and hospitable, treating me like another guest, a friend of Celer's, rather than a servant or a soldier, that it gave me courage to voice an idea that Salvia's brief appearance had given me. "Sir, I would really like the chance to thank your maidservant for nursing my father in his last days. Would that be possible?"

To my dismay, Alexander stopped still in the middle of handing a cup of wine to Celer. He stared at me strangely, his brows furrowed in what I can only describe as amazement mingled with sorrow. There was a silence, and I felt very uncomfortable, assuming I had somehow been discourteous. Celer said nothing but was watching us intently. Eventually Alexander responded, "Of course you may. I'll call her back shortly." Then he asked, his voice barely audible, "So you loved your father?"

What manner of question was this? "Yes, Sir. Very much." And only now, in the affirmation of it, did I realise how true that was. "His death from a mysterious illness was very sudden and came as a terrible shock."

More loudly now Alexander went on, "Believe me, you were fortunate. It is better to have loved and lost a parent than to have one whom you hate and fear. I am in a unique position to compare the two – my younger brother Aristobulus and I, that is." I didn't know what to say. Celer, with a fig stopped halfway to his lips, raised his eyebrows and blew out his cheeks, so that Alexander realised he'd spoken too personally for the occasion.

"By Herakles, I've only just met you, and listen to how indiscreet I am. I hope Celer is right, for he obviously thinks you can be trusted."

"Indeed I can, Sir," I assured him emphatically, moved by the passion in his outburst.

"Come, let us drink another cup and be happy. Then I should go and attend to my wife."

"And we must get back to work. I have to teach Simon three weeks' worth of lessons in three days." Thus Celer let me know that the rest of my precious leave would be used constructively.

"I thought you said you were busy preparing for Quintus Severus?"

"So I am. But it's a wonderful opportunity for our apprentice here. He could never meet a better authority on the building of large structures – given that he won't be able to meet the late master himself!"

"You and that Vitruvius." Alexander laughed.

I was summoning up the courage to remind Alexander of his promise to call Salvia, when Celer, who must have noticed my reaction when she had appeared, did it for me. "Don't disappoint the fellow – have that girl brought in, Alexander, or he'll be moping all afternoon and he won't absorb a thing I tell him!"

"Certainly. But before I do, let me tell you, Simon, that if you've taken a liking to Salvia you have chosen well. She is one of our most trusted and competent servants, and I know my wife would like to grant her her freedom in due course. She has some education too. Treat her kindly." I was delighted to hear her spoken of with such respect by no less a person than the King's son, her master. Competence and education could only add to her charms, though my affection was not in need of them. Nor did I need the admonition to treat her well, but I was glad he showed no hint of disapproval that a soldier should have feelings for a slave.

"Alexander, come on, let's go and say hallo to the boys before you attend to Glaphyra. Then Simon can say what he has to say in private." They both stopped at the door and looked back at me, each with a boyish, conspiratorial grin on their face, which I was to have grim cause to remember.

Thus it was that when Salvia returned, carrying more wine and water, having mistaken the reason for fresh summons, I met her alone. Shy and often diffident, on this occasion I surprised himself by approaching her with a calmness which belied the pounding in my chest. Gently I took the jugs from her and explained.

"Your master called you for me. I wanted to thank you for nursing my father when he was taken ill. I should have thanked you the other day when we met on the path, but…" I tailed off, savouring the close-up detail of the heart-shaped face I had so often pictured in my mind. The neat but very slightly crooked nose, the eyelashes which curled up at the ends, the tiny lines at the sides of luminous, dark eyes, the smooth olive complexion.

"There is no need to thank me, Sir," she replied in a soft voice. The Greek was perfect, but I couldn't place the slightly sing-song accent. "Your father was a pleasure to nurse – so courteous, even though…" She stopped, as if afraid she might be saying too much.

"Go on, please." Something seemed to have muffled my voice but I made an effort to remain straight and calm.

"Even though I knew he was in a lot of pain. I'm so sorry."

I hesitated, not sure how to ask what Father had said to her as he lay dying, but then suddenly the words were there. "Did… did he say anything that I might be glad to know?"

"Mostly he thanked me for dressing his burns and changing his linen." She paused and frowned slightly, perhaps from concentration, perhaps unsure whether to say more. Then she added, "Yes, there was one thing that would be good for you – or your sister – to know. He said, probably on the day he died, I am not entirely sure, 'I have a daughter a little like you – you are caring for me as she would have done.'" Then she said again, "I'm sorry."

I wasn't immediately able to speak. I didn't think that Salvia looked at all like Chloe, but I was deeply touched by Father's comment and knew that Chloe would be too. In a curious way it seemed to bind the three of us together. I was loath to break the intimacy of the silence, in which the memory of Father's last day united us. But then, to prolong the conversation, I found myself asking her where she'd learnt her nursing skills.

"I nursed my brother when he was sick back home in Syria. He recovered so I gained a sort of reputation which wasn't in truth deserved – I'm sure he would have recovered anyway."

"So your home was in Syria. How did you come to end up – if that doesn't sound impertinent – in the King's court in Jerusalem?" Salvia raised her chin lightly and tucked a loose strand of hair behind her ear, a mannerism I recognised from our previous meeting and which I found entrancing.

"My father was in some trouble and couldn't pay his debts. So my brother and I were taken to the slave market in Tyre." She paused and swallowed hard at that point, perhaps trying to force down an unwelcome memory. "Princess Glaphyra was in need of servants and I was bought on her behalf – I think they thought my nursing reputation, deserved or not, made me suitable for the royal household here."

I was horrified. It all made Salvia sound like a piece of merchandise – which, I realised, was exactly what she had been.

"I am very sorry," I breathed.

"Please don't be. In the end I was lucky, and so was my brother. We weren't sold to Rome, which would have been different – the rumours in Tyre about what often happened to those poor people were terrible. No, my mistress has a temper but it never lasts long, and she's almost always good to me." She gestured down at the skirts of her robe, a pretty deep green. "She passes on her clothes to me, which I have to alter because she's taller, but I always have nice things to wear. And she lets me visit my brother sometimes." Then she added, tossing her head in pride and meeting my gaze for the first time, "He's bought his freedom and works on the olive presses. He makes a good living now, so he's able to send money home to our father."

Much more than the father deserves, I thought to myself. I wanted so badly to gather her to my breast and hold her there, to stroke her plait of shining hair and kiss the curve of her lips, but I could only gaze at her, grateful for having learnt so much about her in such a short space of time. That was how Celer found me when he returned.

"Come on, Simon – we have work to do!" Then, an idea occurring to him, he turned to Salvia. "Can you be trusted to keep a secret?" I wondered in trepidation what he was about to say. I had begun to recognise that Celer could be rash.

"I sincerely hope so, Sir," she replied with an almost haughty dignity which brought a smile to both our faces.

"Good. I ask because from time to time this student of mine will have documents to send to me, and me to him – only architectural texts, nothing of a treasonable nature, I assure you. Your master will testify that I can be trusted. Would you be willing to act as messenger?"

Turning to me he said firmly, "I think the situation has changed sufficiently, thanks to King Archelaus, for this to be safe."

I wanted to drop to the ground and kiss his feet. But would Salvia agree to do this? Then the tiny play at the side of her mouth and the dance in her dark eyes were answer enough.

Chapter 15

Celer arranged to meet me with Quintus Severus at the Triple Gate the next day. I set out in good time, anxious not to keep them waiting. I wondered how much Quintus Severus would remember about me, whether he would be pleased with my progress and whether Celer would tell him how discouraged I'd been at the beginning. But as I approached the little jewellery shop which David had pointed out as a favourite of the royal ladies, such questions were chased out of my head. There, right in front of me, was a small group of women, in the centre of which stood none other than the King's sister. There was no escape.

"Ah, the son of Philip of Nîmes! We meet again. What a coincidence – I was going to send for you later today." I bowed, partly in deference, partly to avoid the green, unblinking scrutiny. She went on, in an accusing tone. "I noticed you yesterday in the company of my nephew, Alexander, and his friend the architect."

I had to look up. She had inclined her head to one side, awaiting an explanation. "Yes, I… er… well…" I must have looked and sounded pathetic. She let me sweat for a while, before continuing coldly, "Strange friends for you to have, young man. I doubt whether my brother the King would approve. But perhaps we can turn the friendship to good use. Come to my apartments at sundown today.

And whatever other duties you have, that is an order." Then, gesturing to her attendants to follow, she swept on down the sloping street, without another glance at me. Certainly nothing remotely flirtatious in her manner now. I remembered what Alexander had said the day before and concluded that she had already dropped poison into my wine. Metaphorically so far but I knew that wouldn't be the end of the story. I stood still as stone, staring after the retreating figures. It was a while before I could move my legs in the direction of the Temple, my head now a whirlpool of worry. For I had little doubt what the summons meant. *Perhaps we can turn the friendship to good use.* Salome wanted to recruit me as a spy.

As I approached the agreed meeting place, I heard my name called and there was Celer hurrying towards me. Before I could open my mouth to tell him what had happened, he announced, "Change of plan. Quintus Severus wants to inspect the drainage system from the Temple court into the Kidron Valley. Because of the stink," he wrinkled up his nose to illustrate the point, "it can't be working properly and since Temple funds are being used for its maintenance, people at the Treasury are asking questions." I knew a pang of disappointment – important though the drainage channels were for the life of the city, they were not what principally interested me. More urgently, I needed somehow to warn Celer of Salome's intervention, and now Severus himself was coming towards us.

"I was very sorry to hear about your father, Simon – I saw Nicolas of Damascus briefly yesterday and he informed me."

"Thank you, Sir." I inclined my head respectfully, wondering what story Nicolas had concocted.

"Celer tells me you are a promising student, Simon. Keep it up."

Celer laughed. "Don't look so surprised! I like enthusiasm and I like a sharp eye. You've demonstrated both with your intelligent questions – that's all. No need for a swollen head!"

"And today I'm pleased you're joining us to see what repairs are needed to these vital water channels. You can read up about it later – Book VIII deals with it all." The great Severus could not have been more gracious, but I was simply too anxious that morning to appreciate my good fortune.

"Celer, I have to speak to you – something awful has happened." My whisper, as we followed Severus with one of his engineers to the first of the suspect sluices, was fast and frantic.

"Can it wait till we've finished here? There'll be an opportunity on the way back to the office. Severus will have other people to see."

"Only as long as it's before sundown." At that point Quintus Severus stopped to wait for us and there was no more opportunity for private talk. For me the day's tuition, which was to have been so thrilling, so stimulating, had lost all its lustre, and as the hours went by fear and foreboding gave way to resentment and rancour. She – Salome the serpent – had spoilt everything.

When eventually Quintus Severus had gone off on other business and Celer heard what had happened, he reacted more calmly than I'd expected. "Simon, there's no need for panic. Pretend to go along with whatever she demands, but make sure you don't give her any information she couldn't get another way. Give her useless bits of gossip. You can tell her anything you like about me, for example. She can't touch me. Tell her I see Alexander regularly and we laugh a lot – even about her, and the clothes and make-up she wears. That'll infuriate her but it's not something she'll want to repeat to the King! She's too damn vain."

I swallowed to help the dryness in my throat, wishing I could be sure it would all be as easy as Celer made out. "But you will tell Alexander – in case he sees me with her? Or hears something. I couldn't bear—"

"I'll tell him, but he knows how she operates so won't be surprised. And he won't blame you, so don't worry. You'll still be able to see that pretty slave-girl you seem to like so much! I'll send over the next book with her in a day or two – someone else has it today. Go on, the sun'll be going down soon – you'd better obey that order. And stop looking so worried!" He gave me a friendly slap on the back to propel me on my reluctant way.

*

Arriving at Salome's apartments, I was surprised to find the doors open, and a slave-girl, obviously waiting for me, asked me to follow her. She ushered me through the rooms in which Philo and I had moved the furniture, to a small space behind a heavy curtain, where Salome was seated at a table sorting through samples of fabric. She looked up, nodded her recognition and dismissed the servant.

When the girl had disappeared Salome stared at me, in no hurry to put me at my ease, and she did not invite me to be seated. Eventually she said, "Simon, son of Philip of Nîmes, I like you and I would not want you to come to any harm. But I don't think my brother would be happy to see you consorting with Alexander or with any of his friends. I wonder how that came about?" The pleasant, mildly coy tone she had used when Philo and I were in her apartments had vanished completely. She raised her blackened eyebrows, demanding an explanation.

I had had time to think about this, lending only half my concentration to Severus's lesson about the water sluices. I made my voice firm and clear to belie the turmoil inside. "When I was in Caesarea, I was introduced to Quintus Severus by Nicolas of Damascus, because I asked questions about the engineering there. He suggested that as I was interested in such things, I should speak to his former student, Lucius Servius Celer, back here in Jerusalem. And Lucius Celer" – I was careful to refer to him formally – "has been kind enough to show me some of the structures." Salome's stare was unblinking, but her scrutiny, far from intimidating me this time as I'd anticipated, brought back the burning rush of anger I'd felt when Nicolas lied to me about Father's death. I raised my chin, returning her gaze as if I had nothing to hide.

But Salome was not that easily satisfied. "And Alexander?"

"He came to talk to Celer while I was with him – I think he wanted him to go hunting with him."

Please, please don't let her know that we went back to Alexander's apartments to eat. I prayed in silent fervour to Zeus or whichever of the gods might be listening.

At long last she said, "Very well. I see. But since you have become acquainted, let us put it to good use. I want you to continue to see Lucius Celer and whenever possible his old friend Alexander, and keep me informed of any plans they have, where they go, who they meet – that sort of thing." Then her voice grew softer, less menacing. "Anything they say or do which might affect the welfare of my brother the King. His safety is my paramount concern, especially in view of certain ancient prophecies, which his enemies may try to use to their advantage. By keeping me informed in this way you can prove your unswerving loyalty to him."

I was almost beginning to accept a more benign motivation, when she added in her former tone, "Loyalty which I happen to know was what my brother so valued in your father." The honeyed cunning of this statement was not lost on me. But I was learning.

"My lady, I will do my best for the King, of course – but my period of leave is very brief and then I will be back on duty, with little time at my disposal." I omitted to mention that I still had one day of leave left, relieved that Celer's plan for the following day was to give me tuition related to drawings, costings and tools, in his office which would be safely away from prying eyes.

"I understand. But you will take every opportunity that presents itself. I am sure you have many architectural questions you would like to ask our talented Roman builder. And then your questions can – or will – probe a little further. I stress the *will*. You may go now. But come back as soon as you have any information to report – however little it may seem. I shall be waiting." She gave me a curt wave of dismissal, as she would to a slave.

As I turned to leave she called after me, "And Simon, son of Philip the Gaul, you should know that it never pays to cross me or disregard my orders." It was hard to imagine her playing with her grandchildren after that.

*

It was Ziper, the jolly Thracian, who brought the welcome tidings after I'd been back on boring duty for a while, my three days' leave already a golden memory. "Simon, my lad, there is the prettiest little thing you've ever seen asking for you at the side entrance. I congratulate you – wouldn't mind a tumble with her myself!" And off he went, chuckling as usual. I was determined to appear casual in front of the men I was talking to at the time. "I'd better go and see what this is about." They weren't fooled and their loud banter followed me outside.

There, standing beside a huge clay pot planted with herbs, was Salvia. She spoke in the melodious accent of her Syrian homeland. "I'm glad you've come. I feel very conspicuous standing here. I'm not sure what people will think."

"I'm sincerely sorry to have put you in that position. But I'm delighted to see you."

"I have a message from Lucius Servius Celer – and some documents," she managed to tell me before we were disturbed by whistling and shouting as several comrades piled out of the side entrance to watch what was going on. Pretty visitors to the barracks were not a common occurrence.

"Come, let's go somewhere private so you can give me the message without being overheard." I made a shooing gesture at the men, grinning at the same time, knowing that if I were surly they'd only follow and carry on making fun of us. Gently I took her arm, and it was only then, as my blood turned to fire, that I realised this was the first time I had actually touched her. I kept my hand resting lightly under her arm and led her towards the little courtyard where I often went to study, entering it through a gateway half smothered in jasmine. I was relieved to see there were no workmen or gardeners there today – I wanted no potential spies or eavesdroppers.

"How lovely this is! So many flowers."

"I thought you'd like it. Come, let's sit on the bench over there." Reluctantly, I let go of her arm as we sat down.

She heaved a sigh of relief and smiled at me, not so shy now. "Thank you for rescuing me! I don't know what they must think."

"Don't worry, they won't think badly of you. They're bored young men delighted to see a pretty face."

"What will you tell them?"

I hadn't thought about that. "I'll tell them you had a message for me. No – perhaps not." Suddenly I was confiding in her. "I can't tell them about Lucius Celer – you see, he's acting as my teacher because my ambition is to become an architect one day. But I have to study secretly in my free time – until I've learnt enough to prove I can serve the King in another way. I can't just leave the army; it would be seen as disloyal to him. My father was a favourite of the King's and a friend of Nicolas of Damascus too, so *he* keeps a particular eye on me. Or that's how it feels – as if I'm being spied on."

I paused, surprised at my own openness but even more so to see that her eyes shone with undisguised admiration.

"That sounds wonderful! To be able to design buildings which will last after we're... well, which will be there for our children and our children's children – that's... that's such a gift!" She blushed, perhaps wondering if she'd said too much, but I was elated, realising that far from dismissing my dream as unrealistic or foolish, she was impressed.

"Thank you for the encouragement! May I call you Salvia? It's such a lovely name."

"Of course! What else would you call me? I'm not the daughter of a king, or a fine lady, you know!" She gave a little laugh of merriment, which turned something over inside me.

"You are to me." My tone was soft and serious, nothing other than a declaration of love. We looked at each other for the space of several heartbeats before I leant over and, breathing in a mild herbal fragrance from her hair, kissed her gently and chastely on the lips. That was all – I would have liked it to be so much more and it was so hard to stop, but I was conscious that I must show her respect, especially because her slave status could so easily be abused.

When she drew away, she busied herself with extricating the documents from her apron. To cover her confusion she started talking fast. "Lucius Servius Celer said to tell you that he's been unexpectedly recalled to Rome because his father is ill. But he wanted you to have these." Gingerly she handed me the scrolls of papyrus, looking at them with a reverence which even I might not have displayed. Despite my pleasure at seeing them, I was dismayed to hear that Celer had left Jerusalem.

"I'm so sorry. Is his father dangerously ill?"

"I think so. He left in a hurry last night. He said to tell you he doesn't know when he'll be back, but while he's away he'll try and get a translation done for you to keep. He has a cousin who could do it."

I shook my head in surprise, touched that Celer had been so thoughtful at a time of personal crisis. I looked down at the scrolls and ran my finger along one of them. "He's been extremely kind to me – far more than I could have expected." I felt genuine concern for him, but then sat back in alarm as a sudden thought struck me. He might not have had time to tell Alexander of Salome's advances.

"Did he... were there any other messages?"

"No, that was all. He was in a great hurry."

"Do they – your master and mistress – know you've come here today as his messenger?"

"Yes, I prefer to tell my mistress everything I do. I think it's safer that way – it means I can't be suspected of anything."

Wise girl, I thought, and I remembered Alexander's good opinion of her, though it was clear she'd been infected by the prevailing mood of fear and suspicion. "Are they good to you?"

She nodded. "Yes, I can't complain. My mistress – well, when there are quarrels in the family she gets upset and angry and then she shouts at me. But usually she's kind. Once she said she preferred to talk to an honest slave who knows her place in the world, than to relations by marriage who pretend to be what they're not. I haven't risked telling her I don't come from a slave family – that it was my father's bad fortune that brought me here. She'd probably think I too am pretending to be what I'm not and send me away!"

Wise indeed! I was delighted that she'd now shared a confidence of her own, and I wanted so badly to ask her a hundred more things about herself, to hold her, to drink in every little detail of her. Then we heard the trumpet call from the barracks announcing evening roll-call and I had to stifle an oath. Instead I said, "That's the worst thing about being a soldier. You have to follow rigid timetables, always other people's. There's no freedom."

Too late I realised how tactless that remark must have sounded to a slave, but she wasn't offended. I noticed for the first time a little birthmark at the corner of her right eye, which crinkled when she laughed. "It'll be different when you're an architect. Still, I did once hear Lucius Servius Celer say that he never has any time to himself. That's why he hardly ever goes hunting with my master."

As we got up to leave the courtyard, it came to me in a sudden panic that with Celer away, there would be no more pretexts for us to meet. Touching her lightly on her arm, I said, "Would you – could you – come here to meet me sometimes?" She looked up at me, and I wondered if the light in her eyes was merely amusement, or – as I hoped – something else. She didn't answer for what seemed an agonisingly long time, before whispering, "Yes, if you like."

"Oh, I do like. Please. I'm on early duty for the next week. So try and come… let's see… shortly before the third sundown, so we'll have a little time before it gets dark. I'll meet you here. You saw the way we came in?"

"Yes, but I don't want to be spotted as I pass the barracks. Perhaps I'll wear a hood. If I don't come, it'll be because they've given me tasks I can't avoid. I too have very little freedom."

The soldier and the slave, their lives so alike and yet so different, I thought, as I leant down and kissed her again, gently, where the dark silk of her hair met the smooth curve of her forehead. I was wondering whether to pluck one of the white lilies from its pot by the archway and slip it into her plait, when the second blast of the trumpet made me jump and before I knew it, she had slipped away without another word.

Chapter 16

"Meet me at the third sundown." Words muttered in haste, and I couldn't understand afterwards why I hadn't said 'the second sundown', or even the next one, for the intervening three days seemed the longest of my life. Whenever I tried to study, the edges of the diagrams would blur into sleek dark plaits, or the text dissolve and stare up at me with twinkling eyes. I missed Theo, who had had to join the escort to Antioch, as there was so much I now needed to tell him. I was on the receiving end of plenty of good-humoured teasing from the men who'd seen Salvia, but there was no one else I could confide in.

When the third evening eventually arrived, I was hurrying out of the building when I bumped into Ziper. "Are you coming with us tonight, Simon? Been talking to some workmen up at the Temple who know a really good joint. And we haven't yet made good that promise we made you!" It was an anxious moment but I mumbled an excuse about being late to meet someone I'd known in the Antonia, and for once Ziper didn't read anything more into it.

I arrived early and paced up and down the courtyard in delicious if anxious anticipation, not at all certain she'd be able to come. But when she did arrive it was a very different Salvia who appeared under the jasmine from the cheerful and positive young woman of three days before. Several long strands of hair had escaped from the combs meant to hold her plaits in place, her cheeks were flushed and her eyes reddened. As she came close I saw teardrops glistening in the curl of her lashes.

"Salvia! What's happened?" She looked over her shoulder as if afraid she'd been followed, then shook her head, unable to speak as she fought for breath. I led her to the stone bench where we'd sat before, now bathed in the golden rays of a descending sun, and sat quietly holding her hand, waiting patiently for her to disclose the dreadful thing that had upset her.

As she became calmer and her breathing more regular, I ventured, "Was it your mistress?"

"No, no, not at all." She shook her head. "No, she was happy to let me come. I think she likes the idea of one of her father-in-law's soldiers wanting to become an architect instead of a bodyguard – she's asked me questions about you." I was taken aback by that. I hadn't expected her to pass on information about me, but as I hadn't expressly asked her not to I made no comment and continued to probe.

"So who... what has upset you?"

She passed the back of her hand across her face, several thin gold bracelets on her wrist falling back as she did so. I wondered if they, like some of her dresses, had been a gift from her mistress. "Well, there's a visitor from Sparta staying in the palace. He's been spending a lot of time with my master and mistress. They both seem to like him, though he's much older than them, more the age of the King himself, I think – but I've noticed that he flatters my mistress a lot, like a younger man would."

"Yes, I've heard of him. He came bearing fabulous gifts, they say, and that he's a friend of Caesar's as well as of the King."

"I didn't know that and it only makes it worse. Anyway, as I was leaving to come to you now, he stopped me and asked me where I was going." For me this was bad news.

"Did you tell him?" I must have allowed my anxiety to show, because she looked up at me quickly.

"Ye-es… well, I said I'd arranged to meet a friend. I thought maybe he was accusing me of leaving without permission, so I assured him my mistress was happy for me to have some time off. I'm sorry if that was wrong."

"No, it wasn't wrong. You didn't have any choice. How did he react?"

"He said… he said, well… that a girl like me probably had lots of admirers and… er… he hoped that this was a nice one." Something about the hesitant way she related this suggested the stranger had expressed himself more crudely than she was admitting. I bristled.

"Indeed, what he said about you was true, though it was presumptuous of him to say so. But that in itself can't have caused your distress. What happened then?"

"He came out of the apartments with me. That's when he lowered his voice and said he was speaking to me on behalf of the King himself. He said he knows I have a special position in my mistress's household, and he needs me to tell him things that I observe about her and about my master – what they talk about, who visits them and all that sort of thing. At that point he was talking politely. Then," she gulped, "as we got further away from the apartments, his tone suddenly changed. He began to raise his voice and speak harshly. He said if I didn't do what he asked the King would be told that I wasn't a loyal subject, and did I know what happened to disloyal subjects? And then, then…"

To encourage her, I squeezed her hand which I hadn't relinquished during the account. "…then he said that he'd found out where my brother works, and if I didn't do what was asked of me, it would be the worse for him too." At this she broke into sobs, and it was the most natural thing in the world for me to draw her to me and whisper words of comfort. Those words came easily enough but I knew only too well that they were meaningless, because this was a situation in which there was no comfort. Suddenly she had become caught up, helpless, in the midst of a monstrous power struggle. I held her close as the sobs subsided, reflecting sadly that this was something I'd dreamed of many times, yet it had become reality only through distress and fear. Fear that was all too justified, as I thought of those screams of terror in the night. Lengthening shadows were warning me that time was slipping by, and reluctantly I drew back a little, my hands holding her arms.

"Have you told me everything?" I asked gently.

She swallowed and shook her head. "No. Before we parted, he told me not to worry about my mistress and master. 'I'm a friend of Glaphyra's dear father, King Archelaus,' he said, 'so I'm on their side. I need to persuade King Herod they aren't plotting against him and your evidence will be important, so you'll be helping them. But if you so much as breathe a word of what has passed between us to anyone, anyone at all, let alone your master and mistress, it will be the worse for you – and for that brother of yours out on the Mount of Olives.' That's word for word what he said to me. So he really does know where he is – my brother, I mean."

I felt my blood burn with a rage which was becoming familiar but remained silent, not sure how to respond. She started to cry again, but more quietly this time. "What am I going to do? I don't know whether he's telling the truth about being on their side. I don't trust him, so I can't – I won't – betray my mistress, but what about my poor brother? And I shouldn't have told you, it was silly and dangerous – if he knew I'd probably be on the rack already, but I couldn't keep it to myself. I couldn't. Please help me, Simon. I don't know what to do."

Neither did I, though I admit to a tiny thrill of pleasure at hearing her use my name for the first time. I thought of Father and how he had protected me from the intrigues of the royal household for as long as he could, and now I was discovering how wise that had been. On the one hand, the fact that Salvia had appealed to me in her distress, that she trusted me, was gratifying; on the other I recognised only too clearly that there was little or nothing I could do to protect her. For an all-too-brief while longer we sat close together in silence, my arm encircling her shoulders. The gentle splashing of water cascading from the jaws of the stone fish was the only sound, but it was not soothing as it had been before. I noticed how the roses in the pots beside the pool had wilted and faded, and decided they were a fitting image of what was happening to everything I held dear. The sinking sun had turned the water to liquid gold, and time was passing rapidly. I judged it better not to tell Salvia that Salome had asked me to spy on her master and mistress and on Celer as well. All I could offer was, "Dearest Salvia, I will think what we can do about this. But now I have to be back for roll-call, as our strictest officer is on duty. But I can come back part of the way with you – we'll take the longer route round, as the trumpet hasn't sounded yet."

She smiled a brave little smile, sniffing and again wiping her eyes and nose with the back of her hand. "And if we meet – you know – *him*?"

"We'll start laughing and talking as if we hadn't a care in the world. If we look serious he'll guess you've been confiding in me."

As we left the courtyard, she looked back with a wistful glance. "It's so pretty – I love it here. It feels so… well, safe." I loved it too, though perhaps for a different reason. We walked hand in hand along the paved path that threaded between lawns and flowerbeds and silvery olive trees shivering in the evening breeze. As we reached the central passage which bisected the whole compound, we heard a sudden gust of deep, male laughter. We froze in our tracks, like two hunted creatures in the instant before taking flight, my hand clamped around hers. There, walking some way ahead of us on the far side of a double row of olive trees, were two men, one much larger than the other.

"I think it's the King himself," I whispered. "And… yes, the other man is Nicolas of Damascus. Salvia, we mustn't be seen together."

Thinking at breakneck speed, I directed her, "Go back the way we came and take the other path past the barracks – turn right out of the courtyard instead of left." The two men were deep in conversation and clearly weren't aware of our proximity. "I'll carry on along the central path. If they see me on my own, there's no harm in that."

She was turning away when I realised with dismay that we hadn't fixed another meeting. "Come back at the same time in two days – I'll try and think of something by then," I breathed. "Please?" I added, not wanting it to sound like an order. She nodded agreement, then turned and ran quickly back in the direction of the little courtyard without a backward glance.

Trying to look composed, I continued on my way, knowing that I would almost definitely be spotted when I passed the junction with the path on which the King and Nicolas were talking. Sure enough a shout rang out, "Simon – what a coincidence. We were talking about you and your father earlier. Come here – you've not yet been presented to the King, which is an oversight on my part."

There was no avoiding this. Walking deferentially towards the two men, my knees feeling as liquid as they had on that first occasion in Caesarea, I bowed very low and wondered fearfully if my dress was adequate for the occasion. I had certainly not worn my helmet or cuirass to meet Salvia and was aware that her tears and hair oil had marked the front of my tunic.

"Well, well, let's have a look at you then." The King leant forward and peered at me from under slightly overhanging brows. "So – this is the son of Philip of Nîmes. Sad business, that accident of his. But yes, I caught a glimpse of you in Caesarea, I recall. I never forget a face." *That's ominous*, I thought. "You have your father's grey eyes, I see," continued the King with approval. Then he put his head on one side and said thoughtfully, "Ah, of course, this is the boy my sister was asking to have moved into her new guard attachment. Well, we can't have that, can we, Nicolas? Haha! See that he's brought to my apartments soon instead!"

Then he turned to me again. "Do you know anything about pigeons by any chance?"

Stunned by this turn of events, I managed to stutter, "N-no, Sire, I'm afraid not."

"No matter, not many people do. Not even the finest mind in the kingdom here." The King gave Nicolas a robust slap on the slight curvature of his back. "I returned from Antioch to find the ones in that cage over there have some strange malady, and we aren't sure what to do about it." I think I arranged my features to register profound concern for the state of the King's pet creatures but was at a loss to make a comment.

"So where have you been at this time? It must be almost the hour for roll-call?" asked Nicolas pleasantly enough, but I detected an implied threat.

"Oh... I, er, had an errand to run!" I stammered.

The King made me jump with another of his loud, hearty laughs. "Nicolas, the poor young man is blushing to the roots of his unhelmeted hair. It's quite obvious he's been having an amorous encounter in his off-duty time, and what's wrong with that?" Then to my utter astonishment, the mighty Herod, great military commander, King of all Judaea including Samaria, Galilee, Trachonitis, Batanea, Auranitis and Idumaea, friend of Caesar Augustus himself, raised those great eyebrows and curled his thin lips in what was clearly meant as a sign of amused approval. At that moment to my enormous relief the trumpet call sounded from the barracks, faint but distinct across the compound.

"Off you go, Simon," said Nicolas. "You'd better not be late – but if you are, tell the officer you were talking to the King. He'll beat you for lying, instead of absence!" And the two men broke into another gust of laughter, as I thanked them, bowed again and retreated, as quickly as was possible, to the main path.

*

When I got back to barracks, I was delighted to find that Theo had at last returned, a day or two after most of the party from Antioch. He was standing in the roll-call lines, rubbing his saddle-sore behind, and gave me a surreptitious wink by way of greeting. Afterwards it was clear that he was in high spirits, having had the chance to perform in front of the King more than once during the long journey there and back, and to a favourable reception.

"And how is that pretty maiden of yours?"

"If only she were mine! But, oh, Theo, I have so much to tell you." At last we went off for a kit-cleaning session, and I had the opportunity to tell him everything that had happened in his absence – the meeting with Salvia in Alexander's apartments, Salome's attempt to recruit me as a spy, Salvia's two visits to the courtyard near the barracks, her fear and distress because of the stranger from Sparta.

Theo listened attentively until I got to the bit about Salome referring to how much the King had valued Father's loyalty. "The vixen. They don't call her 'Salome the Sly' for nothing." But when I told him about the encounter with the King himself, he looked genuinely alarmed.

"Now see what you've done! You'll be taken up there to the King's chambers and you'll have no freedom at all! Thank the goddess of mercy they didn't see you with Salvia. Loyalties are liabilities, you know, and yours are leading you to play a dangerous game, Simon. I'm hearing things which make me think the situation is deteriorating again, for all old Archelaus's good work while he was here."

I knew Theo was not exaggerating. Salvia was not any old slave-girl; she was Princess Glaphyra's favourite and was seen often enough in her company for the King to recognise her. *I never forget a face.*

"So when are you seeing her again?"

"I've asked her to try and come back in two days." Theo sighed in exasperation.

"All right, so maybe it *is* risky, but what am I meant to do? Forget all about her?"

"Yes, in a word, if you value your life. I'm serious, Simon. You should know by now that to be linked with people who are suspected of conspiracy is to risk everything. Banishment, imprisonment, torture. Don't think you're safe because only slaves get tortured – not so in King Herod's Judaea. There is darkness in that royal heart, I tell you. And from what I heard only today, Alexander and his brother are very much under suspicion yet again. Take it from me."

"Oh, take it from you. That's what I always have to do, isn't it? You with the contacts, the behind-the-scenes superior knowledge all the time." I'm not sure where that eruption of rage came from; it just happened.

"Well, by Zeus himself, I was only trying to save your skin. I won't bother myself in future if that's how you feel." We were cleaning our sandals at the time, and Theo knocked the soles of his together with a vehement thud, sending a thick cloud of dust into the air.

We continued cleaning in a tense silence while anger and guilt at my overreaction wrestled with each other in my head. "All right, Theo, I'm sorry. I didn't mean that. But you must see how frustrating it is. Just when I get close to Salvia, I'm being pulled as far away from her as ever. And… and, well, to be quite frank, it does disturb me that you're so embedded in 'Antipater's camp', as you've put it sometimes."

"You wouldn't get to know half the things you do if I weren't," he retorted.

"All right, point taken. So, are you going to tell me what makes you so sure things are getting bad again?"

Theo's desire to tell overcame resentment. "Well, all right, as you've apologised. I've spent the last day or so with my brother, trying to get my shoulder and arse right after that cursed long ride to Antioch and back. They have ointments up there you can't get in the barracks. So I had my ear to the ground as usual. That man who threatened Salvia – the Spartan schemer, as I call him – is playing a double game, stirring things up again. He told Antipater that his half-brothers are after his blood, as well as the King's and are only waiting for the right moment to ambush him. He's got Antipater so shit scared that he's now openly accusing his brothers of holding secret meetings with two of the army commanders. They were racked last night – see what I mean about torturing anyone? – and they must have said something to convince the King that his sons really are plotting to murder him this time. There's talk of weapons and money being hidden under the floor in the stables – oh, and Alexander is meant to have written to the commander at Alexandreum asking for refuge after he and Aristobulus have killed their father."

"But what's in it for the Spartan?"

"I suppose he wants the King to be indebted to him."

"But why?"

"Money, power, riches – the usual."

"But everyone was talking about the fabulous gifts he brought for the King – he must be so wealthy already."

"Simon, I can't be angry with you for long – you're such a child. No one like that is ever wealthy or powerful enough. That's the way it is." He ran his hand through his prematurely thinning hair, feigning parental despair, enjoying as he often did the role of old man of the world. "Anyway, you may not believe me, but this time my information came from the slave who looks after my brother's uniform – and who knows what else." This with a suggestive cough. "He's a good source because he spends a lot of his time standing around listening and no one takes any notice of him."

I couldn't believe what I was hearing. A great tragedy was unfolding and all we could do was look on, helpless bystanders. Apart from the fact that Salvia belonged to the household, my own encounters with Alexander and the close friendship between Alexander and Celer left me in no doubt where my allegiance lay.

"The worst is to come, I'm afraid – the bit you're really not going to like, Simon. All the servants in Alexander's and Glaphyra's household are to be questioned, and in Aristobulus's too, starting tonight. The King believes that's the only way to discover whether they really are guilty."

My heart lurched. There was little doubt what 'questioned' meant. I'd already discovered enough about the court and its workings not to be lulled by the innocuous word. If Salvia was to be 'questioned', then she was in real danger. The mere thought of her being beaten and bruised and pulled about on the rack stopped my breath.

"Yes, you may well look three shades paler. It's what we do about it that's the real question." At that the summons sounded for the evening meal. We turned to go inside, though neither of us had any appetite.

*

Next morning as the men pushed and shoved in the usual rush to grab a crumb of the always limited goat's cheese with our morning bread ration, talk was buzzing about the latest developments.

"Every single one of the servants and slaves who work for the two princes and their wives. I bet they've seen a thing or two that'll be worth teasing out of them."

"Or pulling out, more likely," added another, chortling at his own flippant reference to the dreaded rack.

"What's going on?" I asked tentatively, as Ziper, who had spoken first, passed me.

"Oh, haven't you heard? Our unit's now on duty at Alexander's apartments – by special order of the King. We have to stand guard while his band of special thugs – sorry, interrogators – try to find out from the servants what's going on. He's convinced there's a conspiracy to murder him. Again." Ziper yawned and then nonchalantly took a huge mouthful out of his loaf, while my own bread turned to pulp in my clenched hand. When Ziper's mouthful allowed him to speak again he added casually, as if predicting the weather, "If you ask me, those young men are as good as dead already, whatever the poor bastard servants say in their defence. Strange way for a father to behave with his sons, I'd say, but this is no ordinary family."

"No, Ziper, you're talking out of your arse as usual. The King might punish his sons but he's not going to have them murdered." How I prayed to the gods that Ziper's big brother was right.

But I simply asked, "So… so what are our orders?" A tiny, forlorn hope flared that if I were on guard near her apartments I might – in some as-yet-inconceivable way – be able to protect Salvia.

"Make sure there are no escapes, I suppose. I imagine having the building surrounded by the King's special guard shows he means business." Ziper shrugged and downed the rest of his bread. I'd always liked the jovial Thracian, who was not a cruel man, but it was hard to comprehend his nonchalance in the face of such ugly developments. My anxiety must have shown, for Philo, standing next to me, whispered, "They're not being taken to the torture tower yet – it might not mean the rack." I gave him a grateful glance. Ever since the night when we first heard the screams – and there had been other occasions since – whenever the subject of interrogation came up we had exchanged a look of tacit understanding. Some of the men seemed to accept these things without question or even with a strange sort of relish.

As we were being allocated to different groups for deployment, Theo arrived, breathless and tousled, particles of sleep still in the corners of his eyes. "Simon, I've had an idea," he whispered, grabbing me by the arm. "I'll tell my brother that I'm involved with the girl myself and ask him to intercede with Antipater. Then he might tell the interrogators to go easy on her. How's that?"

Once again hope flared but quickly died. "Theo, that'll only draw attention to her. She'd get into trouble as a slave for having a relationship with any of us – you, me, it makes no difference. And anyway, she'd be labelled as a spy, with a foot in two camps because of your connection with Antipater. No, Theo, it wouldn't work."

Theo looked so crestfallen that I added gently, "Thanks, though, for the thought."

"Don't bother to mention it. It didn't suddenly occur to me, you know – I lay awake half the night working it all out." I understood this was Theo's way of demonstrating that his connection with the 'Antipater camp' did not spell disloyalty. Perhaps my outburst had made him wonder if, despite our friendship, I really trusted him.

"It was a generous idea. But you'd be putting yourself in danger too, and I can't risk losing a friend as well as… well, you know." Theo tilted his head enough for me to know I'd managed to mollify him.

"Are you two going to do us the honour of joining the patrol today – or is there something you'd like to share with us?" The duty officer glared at us, and we both stood to attention.

Soon after taking up our various positions, we saw three men being escorted towards Alexander's apartments by soldiers I didn't recognise, the little group advancing in a slow and purposeful march. Whispered word went round that these were the interrogators, men in a special unit recruited from the distant city of Hatra. There was something malign about their tall bronze helmets reaching right down to their eyebrows, the unusually broad leather-edged shoulder-pieces to their cuirasses somehow heavy with menace. They wore high riding boots instead of sandals and even the garish fringes to their *pteruges*[2] seemed to be little declarations of war.

After that nothing more was heard or seen of anyone inside the apartments for most of the day. The whole area was eerily quiet – normally there would be a coming and going of slaves, of tailors and carpenters and barbers and bakers and all the other artisans who play some part in the daily life of the royal household. Today there wasn't even a gardener to be seen. I would have been bored had I not been on tenterhooks as I marched up and down, up and down, beside the fruit trees lining my patrol patch, straining my ears to catch any cries inside the building. Birds of prey wheeling high in the blue vastness above embodied the sense of impending doom which hovered in the intense afternoon heat. The only possible consolation

---

2   Decorative skirts of leather or fabric strips worn around the waists of soldiers.

was that if Salome happened to see me in the vicinity of Alexander's apartments, I could make out I was taking the opportunity to glean information on her behalf and perhaps she'd leave me alone for a while. Towards evening a couple of male slaves emerged from the main entrance but made signs to the sentries that they were not permitted to discuss what had gone on. They seemed in cheerful enough spirits, and with the cooling of the temperature as well, I felt a little less tense.

Then on the second morning, Salvia herself appeared. I didn't notice her at first, as I was preoccupied with the sidepiece of my helmet which was causing me some discomfort, and it was only a low whistle from Theo stationed closer to the entrance which alerted me. She was hurrying, a blue shawl covering her head and shoulders, in the direction of the main gate. Her stride was purposeful rather than fearful and she looked straight ahead as she walked, her head held high. At first I hesitated to accost her, not wanting to alert anyone watching to the connection between us, but, quickly realising this was too important a chance to miss, I stepped out into her path.

"And where are you going in such a hurry, may I ask, young lady?" I asked loudly, for the benefit of one of the other men who was strutting by. I was taken aback by my own brusque tone.

"I have an urgent errand to run for the children of my mistress," she answered firmly, standing straight and surprisingly assured.

"And you have permission from the soldiers inside to do this?" Salvia's brow creased a little, puzzled by my tone; she took a step back and looked at me intently, silently trying to tell me something. When the other guard had passed she whispered under her breath, "The news is terrible. My master and his brother were taken away to prison late last night. My mistress is greatly distressed and is sending urgent word to her father which I have to deliver to a friend of my master's in the cavalry. She's fearful for her life and… and…" her voice wavered, "for her sons."

"Do the soldiers have any suspicion of where you're going?" I can confess here that my chief concern was for her safety, even over that of the two boys.

"They think I'm buying things for the children. Medicines and sweetmeats. They don't know about the note, which begs this friend to find a messenger to ride the long road to King Archelaus."

"And you, Salvia – have you been questioned?" I so badly wanted to hold out my arms and gather her into me for protection, though even if it had been possible, the bronze of my uniform cuirass would have crushed her painfully.

"No – only the men so far. And there's been no torture – or not yet, though plenty of threats of beatings and worse. We've been told the women servants won't be questioned until tomorrow, and maybe not even then if... if my master and or his brother confess in gaol." Then, loudly as the other guard turned round at the end of his patrol line and approached us on his way back, "Thank you, Sir. I have permission and will not be gone long." As so often a few strands of hair had come loose from one of her plaits, and she brushed it under her shawl in the gesture I found so appealing.

"Then be on your way! You know where to go for this nursery errand?"

"Yes, thank you, Sir – it's not the first time I've made these purchases for the children."

The other guard grinned at me as he passed. "A good one to choose to stop! Well done!" I responded carelessly enough, but my head buzzed with questions and anxieties, dark and disordered as a swarm of flies. The news about Alexander was indeed dreadful, but at least Salvia herself was safe for a little longer – and it was possible she might escape being questioned at all. But why had the King imprisoned his sons now, before everyone in the household had been interrogated? What more lies had that horrible man from Sparta been whispering into his ear? Or Salome, perhaps? Had further information come to light? Or had the King succumbed to fear and panic and simply lost all reason? And then something inside me seemed to turn upside down as it suddenly occurred to me that Salvia herself could well be caught and arrested while delivering Glaphyra's incriminating note.

It was as well I had to keep marching up and down as it was at least some relief to be moving. Everything I'd been taught to believe since boyhood, my recent if curtailed military training and my own hitherto acquiescent temperament made me want to be loyal to those in power, to those whom I had always seen as my superiors – ultimately to the King. Yet that was no longer possible. For among those very superiors I was witnessing at first hand the deadly consequences of fear, of lust for power, and, as Father had put it, of hate – and caught up in this tangle of intrigue was the girl I loved, as vulnerable as she was innocent. And I, Simon, though a symbol of martial power as I patrolled up and down in my rich and gleaming uniform outside a palace which had become a gaol, was in reality utterly powerless. My blood ran hot with a sensation which until recently I had never known. Anger. Rage. It was Nicolas who had first set it alight when he lied about Father's death. Reignited by Salome's menacing pursuit of me, followed so soon by the way the stranger from Sparta had threatened Salvia, it now started to smoulder again. An anger that was to be slow-burning but, in the end, life-threatening.

Chapter 17

My craving for more contact with Salvia was granted surprisingly soon – but in such a way that I would gladly have foregone the pleasure. In the fourth watch of the following night, while the skies were still untouched by dawn, I was roused by Walcaud shaking me. "Wake up, wake up, you've been summoned by the King himself. He has a special duty for you. You are to report to his private apartments. You'll be met at the entrance."

"But what... why... why me?" Immediately alert, I realised it had come, the moment I'd been dreading since that evening encounter by the pigeon cages.

"Don't ask me why you, I have no idea! Get your uniform on now, don't waste time! And don't forget to collect your sword as you leave."

"Do you know what the duty is?" I whispered, aware that the man on the next mat was stirring. I was already up and tidying mine, a flurry of moth wings unpleasant in my insides.

"Yes." In the dim light from his lamp Walcaud's face contracted into a sneer. "The King's son is to be questioned in the presence of his wife. A special escort is required to take him from the prison tower back to his apartments and to stand guard while it happens."

"But why me?" I repeated. "Surely the King has more experienced guards to do this?"

Walcaud ignored my tone of rising panic and hissed, "I told you not to ask that. Just do as you're told! And go now before you wake the others." As I gathered up my helmet and cloak, Walcaud gave me a sharp push in the small of my back to make me move faster. *Shame it wasn't Alberic*, I thought, missing the big German's gentler manners.

I hurried up through the compound in the grey light of dawn, meeting only one or two servants in the central avenue, to the grand entrance of the King's private apartments. Walcaud had said that I would be met but there was no one there to greet me, so I was afraid I had misunderstood the instruction, and that inner tremble of wings was making me nauseous. Then a small side door opened and I wasn't sure whether to be alarmed or relieved to see the rotund figure of Ptolemy coming towards me. With no salutation, he said curtly, "We have to wait for the other men now."

We didn't have long to wait. Very soon the sound of marching announced the approach of about a dozen soldiers through the external gate. Then the same door which Ptolemy had used swung open and who should appear but the King himself. He wore no diadem, and his dark hair was somewhat disordered. There was some sort of large stain between the purple stripes on the breast of his white tunic and the cross-laces on one of his boots were undone.

"Ptolemy," he said in a loud, agitated whisper, "with Nicolas out of town, don't forget…" He broke off as soon as he saw the approaching men and when they halted he gave them a long, searching look. Turning, he finally spotted me standing slightly apart.

"Good. I asked for you, Simon, son of Philip the Gaul. You will discharge your duties faithfully, I am sure, as your father always did." Then he gestured to Ptolemy to follow him inside to receive the rest of his instructions in private. When Ptolemy re-emerged, he commanded us to follow him and we set off towards the prison tower. I wished that one of my comrades were with me. One of Theo's caustic remarks or big Philo's good-natured grin would have helped relieve the dread of what we were about to find. Once at the tower, Ptolemy beckoned to two of the guards to accompany him inside, and I was relieved not to have been standing in the front. What was it Ziper had said? *If you ask me, those young men are as good as dead already whatever the poor bastard servants have to say in their defence.* Say 'Glaphyra' for 'poor bastard servants', and I was pretty sure that Ziper had accurately summed up the situation. In this nightmare I had been specifically singled out to help seal the fate of the friendly prisoner, who had even advanced my cause with Salvia by allowing us our first moments alone together. And that made me think of Celer. Oh, Celer! That was the worst of it. For above all it felt like betrayal of my mentor, the man who was doing so much to help me realise my dream, but who was also one of Alexander's closest friends.

After a tense wait they emerged, the two guards now bound at the wrist on either side of Alexander, who, to my great relief, still looked healthy and undamaged. He stood straight and tall and looked around, blinking as if sudden exposure to the now stronger morning light hurt his eyes after the gloom of the tower's interior. I would have liked to sink into the paving stones, afraid that Alexander would see me and assume me to be disloyal, or, horrifying thought, to suspect that I had betrayed him to Salome. But Alexander did not appear to notice me, and I fell in with the little posse behind him.

"So where are you taking me, revered treasurer?" Alexander asked Ptolemy with undisguised contempt. "Am I to be tried before the court already? Or does my father need to torture yet more witnesses to justify his treatment of me? And where have you taken Aristobulus?"

Ptolemy ignored the last question, but replied in his surprisingly reedy voice, "I am your father's servant, Alexander. I follow my orders, and those are to take you to your wife, who is to be questioned about your conduct in your presence. Nothing more, nothing less. No harm will come to her. There is no question of torture."

"And by Zeus, there had better not be. Never forget that besides being my wife, she is also of royal blood."

"I don't think that the King or anyone in his family will be allowed to forget that." Even from my position at the back of the group, the sarcasm in Ptolemy's tone cut sharp as a blade. We walked on in silence, the only sound the clinking caused by a loose end of the chain around the prisoner's ankle dragging on the ground. Even the doves in their cages under the olive trees were quiet as we passed. When we came to a halt outside his apartments, Alexander said, in milder tones, "I must ask you not to let my small sons see me bound in this way. Pray send ahead and ask the servants to keep them out of our way. Surely that is not too much to request?"

"No, indeed, it shall be done." Ptolemy looked around at the group and I knew an eye blink in advance that I would be the one singled out for the errand.

"Simon, son of Philip the Gaul, please go ahead of us and do as the King's son requests."

I made myself look Alexander in the eye and addressed my response to him, not to Ptolemy, desperate to convey my deep regret at having any part in the whole sorry affair.

"I will do as you request, and gladly, Sir!"

Alexander inclined his head in acknowledgement, but it was impossible to tell whether my real meaning had been communicated. Two other members of the escort ordered the guards at the door to make way for me, and once past them the first person I encountered was Salvia herself, hurrying through the first hall with some clothes over her arm. She stopped abruptly when she saw me, a look of pleased amazement spreading across her face.

"I've come from your master to ask that the children be kept out of the way. We've brought him here to be questioned together with your mistress and he would not have them see him bound as a common prisoner." I spoke formally, unsure who was listening. Salvia looked at me aghast, pleasure and colour both draining from her face. Her tone when she spoke was cold and accusing.

"*You* have brought the master here in bonds?"

"Salvia, I had no choice." My voice was now hoarse and low. I saw that servants were in earshot and Rufus, the male slave I recognised from his brief appearance at Celer's office, was looking at us curiously. But this much I had to say, if it cost me my life. "Believe me, it is the very last order I would have wanted and I would be glad if you could convey that to your mistress. I've known only kindness from your master and… and… oh, Salvia, don't look at me in that way." For the first time I wondered whether I should have refused the command and borne the consequences – whatever they might have been. I felt sure that was what she thought too, for there was ice in her terse reply. "I will need a brief while to make sure the boys are elsewhere. If I can pass on your message I will, but I can give no promise."

"Thank you." And that was all I could say before we turned away from each other. Never had I felt so despicable. I explained to the group outside in as steady a voice as I could that we were requested to wait while the Princess's maidservant removed the children. I made myself look at Alexander as I spoke. Only the most insensitive onlooker could have missed the apology in my tone and on my face, and no doubt it was not lost on Ptolemy, who stroked his beard and regarded me thoughtfully.

Presently he said, "I think we have allowed more than enough time now. Let us go inside. I trust that Princess Glaphyra is expecting us." This was a statement rather than a question aimed at one of the door guards, who drew aside to let us pass, his gaze directed at the floor so as to avoid looking into the face of his humiliated master.

"Good day, Joseph," said Alexander kindly. "You have no need to hang your head in shame. It is not you who have cast me into chains. And that," he added, looking around him, "applies to most of you." I understood immediately that this was my personal absolution, for I assumed I was the only one in the escort who had had personal contact with him. Yet despite feeling profound relief in one way, if anything his magnanimity increased my sense of shame.

Inside the apartments we were led through a reception area lined with stone pillars, past the beautiful room with the mosaic hunting scene on the floor, where I'd eaten with Celer and spoken with Salvia on that golden day only a few weeks before, and then down a passageway to the Princess's private rooms. She was waiting for us, dressed in a demure grey robe trimmed with white and seated alone on a couch, covered by contrast in some rich wine-dark fabric with two fur pelts draped over the back. She caught sight of Alexander between the two guards, his wrists in leather bonds, the chain still around one ankle. A livid weal showed where it had been drawn too tight. With a cry of anguish she leapt up from her seat, ran towards him and threw her arms around his neck. One of the guards, whose wrist was bound to Alexander's, leant outwards so as not to touch her, and raised his eyebrows enquiringly at Ptolemy, who nodded. "Yes, you may untie him."

I had previously only glimpsed Glaphyra in a state of almost haughty composure, so was all the more shocked by the sight of her distress. After shaking his hands free from the leather bonds which had constrained them, Alexander immediately enclosed her in his arms and then he too allowed himself to weep. There was silence in the room except for the muffled sobs. At that moment I foresaw with blinding clarity what the future held for this son of mighty King Herod and his murdered Queen Mariamme. I knew with intuitive certainty that any investigations which took place now would be no more than a piece of theatre, and I felt sick with rage at being forced to play a part in it so totally against my will.

Ptolemy broke the silence, his tone quiet and formal. "I think we should commence the investigation. Pray be seated." He gestured to the couch, though he himself remained standing. The irony of the visitor inviting the proprietors of the house to be seated was not lost on Alexander, who was no longer weeping and whose cheeks flushed dark with fury.

"And may *I* pray *you* to be seated, Sir!" Inclining his handsome head he indicated another couch, this one appropriately sporting the gaping jaws and bared teeth of a slain animal still attached to its fur pelt. I congratulated him inwardly on his spirited response. Then Alexander looked around the room, "You have my word that neither I nor my wife will attempt to escape, so why do we need such a garrison to hear what we have to say? Surely my position merits some degree of respect!"

Ptolemy looked around at us dozen or so guards, before countering firmly, "We will retain four. And my scribe here, of course. The rest may wait outside for further orders." He began to indicate the ones who could leave, which included me, but I was amazed when Alexander intervened quickly. "No, that one can stay. I like his face." He gestured with his head towards two or three others. "Send out instead the ruffians who fastened my straps too tight."

I held my breath for an instant, unsure whether Alexander would make reference to our previous meetings. Of course he didn't, protecting me by pretending he just liked the look of me, but when I breathed out in relief, it was as much because he clearly bore no grudge against me for being part of this whole humiliating scene.

"I must begin, Alexander, by asking you if in general your wife is aware of your actions and your intentions?"

"How could it be otherwise?" he cried. "I love her better than my own soul and we live peaceably together. She is the mother of my two beloved sons. How could she not be aware of anything I do?"

At this point, Glaphyra herself intervened in a clear, unfaltering voice. "My husband has no wicked designs whatsoever. I do not understand why he stands so accused, why he has been treated with such contempt, imprisoned like a common criminal."

"Worse, my love, worse. Most criminals are at least locked up together so they have some human companionship. My brother and I have been separated and must endure the hardship of solitary confinement. We communicate only…" Here he stopped, clearly not wishing to incriminate any third party, though I suspected he'd said too much already. It was not hard to imagine one of the gaolers taking pity on the desperate plight of the brothers.

"There is only one wickedness of which I may possibly be guilty, though I'm sure you, Ptolemy, will agree that it can scarcely be described as such. Because of the ridiculous suspicions which circulate constantly against Aristobulus and myself here in Jerusalem, we had planned to take refuge with my father-in-law, King Archelaus, and from there to Rome. That is all."

Glaphyra nodded in agreement. I noticed that she was much paler than when I'd seen her before and pronounced shadows had appeared under her eyes. "Yes, that and that alone. And it is hard to see how taking refuge with my dear father could be seen as treachery, when Alexander's own father, not to mention other members of his scheming family, make life here so unbearable for us. We have our children to consider too."

Silence descended once more on the room, the only sound being the stylus of Ptolemy's scribe scratching away in the corner. Ptolemy's face was impassive; it was impossible to decipher whether he felt contempt or compassion for the accused, not least because his little eyes were so deeply embedded in flesh that they gave nothing away. But, young and inexperienced as I was, even I could see that it was not so much the intention to flee to King Archelaus which would be deemed treacherous, but the plan for onward flight to Rome. Once there Alexander and his brother could use their past connections to influence Caesar against their father. Like most people in Jerusalem, I was well aware that the King of Judaea needed above all else to be a friend of Rome. Even before Glaphyra had been directly questioned, the couple had, with a curious lack of guile, incriminated themselves beyond rescue in one very short interview, and I had witnessed it all. I thought of the little boys, who would now almost certainly grow up fatherless, and wondered whether they would also be forcibly separated from their mother, these children of King Herod's lineage. It was more than likely he would insist that they stay in his household, and I shivered at the thought of Salome becoming their surrogate mother. And if Glaphyra returned to her homeland she would surely take her favourite maidservant with her.

Eventually the silence was broken by Alexander, who perhaps realised that too much had been given away. "Ptolemy, grant me one thing. I must see my sons, for this could be the last chance." At these words, Glaphyra put a hand to her mouth to stifle an involuntary cry.

"I thought you wanted to ensure they didn't see you shackled."

"I shall not demean myself by asking to have the chain removed, so will stay covered with a rug – if necessary I'll tell them I was injured in a fall from my horse and for the moment cannot walk."

"I note that untruths seem to come easy to your tongue, Sir." Before Alexander could utter a retort, he continued, "But granting this request can do no harm that I can see, so I concur." Then Ptolemy turned his great fleshy neck in my direction with a terse command.

"Simon, son of Philip the Gaul, who appears to be in favour, have the boys brought here."

Two members of the escort were standing guard just outside the chamber, which struck me as ridiculous – it was hardly likely that Alexander would attempt an escape, with one ankle trailing a chain and a veritable legion of his father's army in attendance outside. Further down the passageway, lurking in dappled shadow, I caught sight of a girl slave, scarcely more than a child herself. I called out to her in as gentle a voice as I could to summon the boys to their mother's rooms. She, looking terrified, scurried away to do as she was bidden. I waited in the familiar area at the end of the passageway, where harsh sunlight streaming in from a courtyard had all but set fire to the amber and crimson patterns in the floor. For once, however, I was in no mood to appreciate the beauty of my surroundings.

I waited, wondering if it would be Salvia who would come with the boys. As indeed it was. The little one, who was barely four years old, held her tightly by the hand and was asking where they were going. But it was the sight of the older Tigranes that brought me to the brink of unfamiliar tears. Standing beside Salvia, silent and serious, he was obviously aware that something important was afoot and was concentrating on being brave and grown-up for his eight years. Salvia made a point of not acknowledging me. I gestured for her to go on ahead of me with the boys, while I followed at a respectful distance, admiring the silky plait in the nape of her slender neck, wondering if I would ever have the chance of caressing it again.

I thought of Father as he had been that night on the inn roof in Caesarea, protective and troubled – all too justifiably, as it had turned out – by how the intrigues of the court might affect me. Ours had been an intermittent relationship, but Father had managed to maintain a certain bond with Chloe and me, for all his obligations to the restless King which kept him almost constantly on the road. Despite his untimely death, I'd enjoyed a privilege which would not be granted to little Alexander and Tigranes, unaware as they walked down the passageway that they were about to see their father for the last time. Strange that just as my father had witnessed the farewell scene between Queen Mariamme and her young sons, a generation later I myself was about to watch one of those sons take final leave of his own children. I felt my features crease into a private grimace of pity.

Chapter 18

When he entered the room and caught sight of his parents, young Alexander rushed straight at his father and tried to leap onto his lap, obviously used to rough-and-tumble play with him. The Prince made as if to get up, then remembered his ankles and sat back down, securing the rug across his knees.

"Steady, my son!" He laughed, clasping the child to him. "I've hurt my leg so I can't play with you like I usually do. Come, sit quietly on my knee." As he settled the little boy into a comfortable position, he reached out an arm to his firstborn, who stood close to him, biting his lip and glancing nervously round at the soldiers lining the room. "Don't be afraid, Tigranes, these men are not going to hurt you." He gathered the boy into him and leant across to give him a kiss on the side of his face. Glaphyra smiled briefly at her children and then looked down at her hands. She wasn't the only one who didn't watch what everyone knew must be a final farewell, for I noticed that even the inscrutable Ptolemy was leaning over his scribe's shoulder to study what he'd written. The other guards remaining in the room stared straight ahead, and it was impossible to tell whether any of them were affected. Salvia studied the floor and would not look in my direction.

After asking a few questions about what they'd been doing and receiving monosyllabic answers, Alexander told them in a firm, clear voice, "Boys, I have to go away and it may be a long while before we meet again. Be good for your mother and…" – here his voice wavered – "I want you always to remember that your father loved you better than his own life." At this Glaphyra broke down in sobs. Young Alexander wriggled across the couch to nestle into her and tried to pull her hands away from her face.

"But Father, if you love us why are you going away for so long where we can't see you?"

"Tigranes, that I can't explain but I can tell you it is your grandfather's will, not mine. When you are older you may come to understand." With the tenderest of gestures he brushed the child's cheek with the back of his hand. The boy nodded and frowned and bit his lip again, perhaps trying hard to understand now rather than later, and it was then that Salvia and I at last exchanged a glance of shared distress.

It was probably a relief for everyone when Ptolemy announced that the children would have to go, as it was time for Alexander to be escorted back. He did not spell out where he had to go back to, and he didn't rush Alexander in his farewell embraces. He could have been a much harsher gaoler, a fact Alexander himself acknowledged after Salvia had ushered the boys gently out of the room, one of them gripping her hand tightly in a flood of tears, the other pale-faced and wide-eyed. I imagined Alexander the father looking similarly forlorn as a little boy twenty-five years before and wondered whether some divine being had put a lingering curse on this family.

"Ptolemy, I appreciate the small mercy you have shown me."

Glaphyra shook her head. Perhaps she admired her husband's dignity in the face of such adversity; perhaps she thought him foolish to show any courtesy to his enemy's agent. Then, looking across at Ptolemy she uttered through clenched teeth, "The matter will not rest here, not when my father hears of the way his daughter has been treated. The boys are his grandsons too."

Ptolemy simply inclined his head and replied, "I do nothing more than my duty, my lady. Orders are orders." Then, to the soldiers, "Take the King's son back to his gaol."

Alexander raised a wrist in my direction, clearly indicating that he wanted me to be one of the two guards shackled to him. Sensing this to be in some grotesque way an honour, I submitted almost gladly as the senior guard bound us together rather more tightly, I suspected, than was strictly necessary. I was thus standing very close to him when Glaphyra approached and kissed her husband on the lips. "Go well, my love," she whispered. "I shall do what I can."

I soon discovered the reason behind Alexander's mute request to have me near him. Taking advantage of a moment when the guard on his other side was distracted by the man behind us, he urged me in an undertone I strained to hear, "Simon, you're Celer's student so I trust you. He was called home because of his father but may be back now. Tell him everything – I don't know how much time I have left, but he has influence in Rome, maybe even with Caesar. If our message hasn't reached my father-in-law, then Celer is our only chance."

"Oh, Sir, I haven't seen Celer for weeks. I don't know if he's back. I… I may not be able…" My voice trailed off for as soon as I'd uttered the words I realised how lame, even cowardly, they sounded. From his impossible position it must have seemed easy for me to meet or at least get a message to Celer. He shrugged helplessly. "I don't know what else…" At that moment the senior guard approached and growled at us to speed up. Then he marched alongside as we approached the dreaded tower.

How can I explain I couldn't make a vital promise I might not be able to keep? I asked myself frantically. *He'll think I don't want to try, am afraid for myself.* I'd almost given up hope of a chance to say a few more precious words, to explain myself, when the officer stopped and turned back to shout something to the men at the rear. I grabbed the moment. Rapidly I muttered, "I'll do my utmost to reach him. That I can promise. May the gods look—" But then the officer was back beside us. My reward was a small, sad nod of understanding that owed more to despair than to hope. A fleeting but vivid image of the moment when Alexander and Celer had left me alone with Salvia, grinning back at me in boyish, amused conspiracy, stung the back of my eyes.

*

Later that evening, Theo looked shocked to see the angry weal on my wrist. "How in the name of Apollo the healer did you get that? Does it hurt?"

"I was bound to Alexander, to prevent him from escaping. Ludicrous idea with half King Herod's army in attendance – or that's how it felt. And yes, it is quite sore as the bastards tied it too tight. But what worries me much, much more is how I'm going to get a frantic message from Alexander to Celer. He may be their last hope. Help me, Theo."

"Well, I do have news that might help. They've stopped interrogating the servants. People are saying that Alexander made some sort of confession today so we don't have to patrol outside his apartments anymore. And I've heard the duty rota for tomorrow – you and Philo and the others are up by the Temple. That'll be your chance to deliver the message!" I assumed this 'sort of confession' was Alexander's avowed intention to find refuge with his father-in-law and thence to Rome, as I was certain he wouldn't have confessed to anything else. Theo's news was some small relief but it didn't prevent the questions, *will it be in time? Will it be all my fault if...?* nagging at me incessantly during the night, although I knew in my bones that the message would, could, have no effect.

Tired and red-eyed after a nearly sleepless night, I perked up when I saw that Philo and I were to be stationed not far from Celer's office at the corner of the Outer Court. Walcaud was in charge but, preoccupied with painful toothache, he was much less vigilant than usual, and once in the area of our patrols he lost interest in our movements. As I was asking myself whether to take Philo into my confidence so that I could slip away to the architects' office, I felt a sharp tap on the shoulder.

"Excuse me – I'm not sure, under that helmet, but is it by any chance – yes, it is, I thought it was! Hallo, friend! Will you still acknowledge me in that fine red cloak of yours?"

I reeled around, to be faced with a man of about my age with honey-coloured eyes and protruding ears. He was leading a donkey, laden with panniers full to the brim with pottery vessels.

"Why, it's Zamaris! Greetings! Of course I'll acknowledge you! How are you after all this time?"

"Very well indeed, because I've left the army. I'm working with my father now in his business. Couldn't stand it a day longer."

"I know life was difficult for you. But how did you wangle it?" I was envious!

"I claimed my hearing had got suddenly worse. In the end that bastard of an officer couldn't face repeating everything four times, so when my father offered to buy me out he readily accepted!" He gestured to the donkey. "This is the fellow who dictates to me now. He doesn't walk a step further than he has to but at least he doesn't shriek and lash out at me!" He then became serious for a moment and looked up at Philo.

"This fellow here saved my life once. I was being punished for observing the Sabbath. Had to march for hours round the largest courtyard in the Antonia with a double load of equipment. Thought I was going to die in the sweltering heat – couldn't even reach my water skin, so Simon gave me some of his. Never more thankful, me."

Philo's big red face cracked into one of its slow grins. "He can behave well occasionally."

"I'm so glad to have bumped into you. You must come and see our shop – it's over there on the other side of the Enclosure. We sell gorgeous textiles, as well as ordinary stuff like this," and he gestured dismissively at the load of pottery in his donkey's panniers. "But what in the name of our God in heaven is the King up to now? Rumours have been even more shocking than usual. I gather those brothers are both in solitary confinement somewhere and lots of their allies were stoned to death in Jericho yesterday, including two cavalry commanders. The two princes will be next is what people are saying."

"Stoned to death? In Jericho?"

"That's what they're saying. And that the people wanted to stone Alexander and Aristobulus too, but were restrained by the King, who put them in solitary confinement for their own safety."

"Mmm." I recognised the unreliability of gossip, for I knew that the previous day Alexander had still been in prison in Jerusalem. Time enough to reach Jericho perhaps, but unlikely under the circumstances, especially given the notorious dangers of the route.

"Surely I haven't told you anything you didn't know already? Everyone's been talking about it since last night!" Zamaris took a step back in surprise at what must have been the alarm registering on my face, for a terrible thought had just occurred to me. What about Celer? He could very easily have been arrested at the port on his way back from Rome and taken to Jericho as a known friend of Alexander's. It was suddenly overwhelmingly urgent to call into the architects' office.

"I have to go and check on someone," I gabbled. "Philo, keep patrolling – don't let the others suspect anything unusual. If Walcaud asks, say I was taken ill or something. I'm sorry but I really do have to go, Zamaris – I'll find you at your shop one day soon." And with that I was gone, with a quick touch on Zamaris's shoulder to show that my haste was not meant to be unfriendly. I felt sure their gaze was following me – they must have been puzzled.

I arrived breathless at the door to the main office. It stood open, and the large table taking up much of the space was as untidy as before. I pulled impatiently at the bell rope and squinted into the dim interior, assuming someone must be there. Before long an older man with a lined face came to the doorway. I recognised him immediately as Tertius Sabinus, Celer's close associate. "Yes?"

I wasn't sure if Sabinus would remember me, so I dispensed with the civilities and went straight to the point. "Is Lucius Servius Celer available, please? It's urgent."

"No, he isn't. And pray, what might a soldier be needing to see him about?" The tone was distinctly frigid. If the man was afraid then he hid it well.

"No, no, I am here for private reasons, not on official duty. I am Simon, son of Philip of Nîmes, and Celer is helping me—"

"Ah, of course, I recognise you now. It wasn't easy to see your features under that great helmet, especially with the sun behind you. Come in, come in!"

I glanced furtively behind me, but Walcaud was nowhere to be seen, and in the distance Philo had joined up with two of the other men, so my absence would not be conspicuous for a while. I followed Sabinus into the office.

"I'm sorry, Simon, but sadly one has to be suspicious of everyone these days and to be frank, the sight of one of the King's soldiers asking for Celer struck fear into my bones."

"I can understand that. That's why I'm here – or partly." I hesitated. I was pretty sure from Celer's comments that Sabinus was completely dependable, yet something stopped me mentioning the message with which Alexander had so desperately entrusted me. Instead I blurted out, "I have just heard a rumour, that many of Alexander's friends and allies have been stoned to death in Jericho, and I-I—"

The older man nodded. "It is no rumour, I'm afraid. We have a team of couriers who take messages between us architects and engineers up and down the land, and one of our men came in late last night with the news. But you need not fear for Celer. We also heard yesterday that his father has died as expected. He was settling his mother with his sister and was to set sail from Rome in two days. He may already be at sea as we speak."

"And when he returns? He always thought he was safe because of the work he does here and because of his friends in Rome. Is that still true, do you think? I've heard it said that no one at all can be completely safe." I didn't spell out that this was from no less an authority than Nicolas of Damascus.

Sabinus looked grave. "If you want me to be quite honest with you, Simon, in my view Celer is too optimistic, unrealistic even. It's all too true that in today's Judaea no one is safe. No one at all. After all, Alexander himself has influential friends in Rome, so that can be no guarantee."

"Is it wise of Celer to come back then?"

"In my view, no, it isn't. But look at what he would be turning his back on." He gestured towards the door, through which a small slice of the Temple's Outer Court and a corner of one of the golden gates glittered in the morning sunshine. "This – and the other projects – are the meaning of his life. He would never lightly abandon them. But I fear he may in the end pay too dearly for them." He heaved a deep sigh. I remembered that he'd lost his only son to typhus the previous year, a son who had been destined to follow him into the profession. I knew then that I could and would trust him with Alexander's message, so in a fast, eager tumble of words, I confided in him all that had happened the previous day.

Sabinus shook his head in despair. "I fear there's nothing that Celer will be able to do, but I will ensure he receives the message as soon as he arrives. When that will be is in the lap of the gods – of Neptune especially! And Neptune has his mighty hands full, because I hear there are emissaries from King Herod about to sail to Rome. He wants Caesar's guidance – again – on what to do about his sons."

"But he's let the stoning go ahead already."

"Well, there are so many rumours and accusations flying around now that no one knows who or what to believe anymore, least of all the King himself. He's lost all shred of patience, they say, and has written to Caesar for guidance."

"I must get back to my patrol or I'll be in trouble. But please, will you send Celer word by courier so he gets it *as soon as* he reaches land? Just in case there's something he can still do?"

"Yes, I will. You have done what you can. And listen, young man, Celer has told me about you. If Celer isn't here and if I'm in the city,

I'll be pleased to teach you. I was getting used to being followed around by an apprentice, you see…"

"Yes, I am so sorry about your son – and thank you," I whispered, anxious now to get away but not wishing to appear unsympathetic. As I left the office, a couple of assistants whose accents I recognised as Athenian hurried in carrying tablets and discussing some point about drainage. They stopped abruptly when they saw me and regarded me warily. I greeted them politely, waiting to put my helmet back on outside, realising that my uniform might have led them to jump to false and frightening conclusions.

Chapter 19

Despite having delivered Alexander's message to the best of my ability, the nightmare continued. There was no sign of Salvia, no news of Celer's return, and rumours and counter-rumours proliferated about the fate of the King's sons. I was on constant tenterhooks that Salome would summon me again or that whenever outside the barracks my path would cross hers. Theo pointed out that as Alexander was already in prison, she'd be less interested in what I could discover, but I wasn't reassured.

Then came the news, gleaned from barrack gossip, that Caesar had sent word to King Herod that a committee of counsellors and regional governors should be convened in Berytus[3] to investigate the alleged conspiracy and reach a verdict. Caesar's judgment was that if the young men had merely intended to abscond to Rome, then a lenient penalty would suffice; if, on the other hand, the conspiracy charges were proved, they would have to be sentenced to death. The King had of course accepted the Emperor's advice but no one could answer my frantic enquiries about when the trial would take place. Not even Theo this time.

"Sorry, my usual source has dried up for the moment. Andreas went to Jericho with Antipater and they haven't come back. Gone on to Berytus most likely."

---

3   Modern Beirut.

"Jericho, did you say? Do you know what happened in Jericho recently?" Our off-duty times hadn't coincided for a couple of days.

"No, I don't. Why so sharp, Simon?"

It was clear from his frown and direct gaze that Theo was telling the truth, but I couldn't stop myself snapping at him. "Strange that you usually have so much information about everything that's going on, but you claim not to know anything about the stoning to death in Jericho of the brothers' allies!"

"Are you accusing me of hiding something from you – or worse? This is the second time you've implied I'm not to be trusted."

"I'm not accusing you of anything. But it is a shame that just when we need reliable information your sources seem to have dried up. And the question is, well…"

"Yes?"

"Well, what has your brother been doing in Jericho is the obvious question?"

"I don't know, but if he *was* involved then obeying orders is the obvious answer! And before you get all self-righteous about it, just spend a moment thinking about how you got those marks on your wrist." Theo's face reddened as he turned on his heel and stalked away.

The retort struck home like a spear thrust. It was true. I had been party to Alexander's unjust treatment. *I had no choice*, I'd said to Salvia, pleading for acceptance. *But isn't that the usual excuse?* I thought, remembering how the Temple guards had threatened to hurl their captive over the precipice to his death. Remembering Father, whose obedience had cost him his life. But a mass stoning! A prison escort wasn't exactly a massacre. The thought that Theo could defend his brother if he had joined in the Jericho killings, whether under orders or not, was repugnant, and I was not inclined to run after him to apologise. Still, the unsettling thought occurred to me that I couldn't afford to fall out with him. Theo knew a deal too much about my loyalties and alliances. *Loyalties are liabilities*, he himself had once said.

I would have to make sure we were reconciled soon, for different shifts might well separate us again.

I didn't have long to brood about it, because soon afterwards Philo – who'd been searching through the message box for something from his father – handed me a scrap of thin papyrus which had been loosely and hurriedly rolled.

Back from Rome. I have something for you so come to the office as soon as you can. Don't leave it too long. Celer.

Excellent news in one way, though no mention of Alexander's message. I struggled to think of a plausible reason for going across town to his office. "Is everything all right?" asked Philo, curious to know what had been in the message to produce such consternation.

"Yes, yes. I just need to think, that's all." Philo shrugged and turned away, probably disappointed that I didn't confide in him. It was Alberic who once more came unwittingly to my rescue, for when he read out the new rota I could have embraced him. Once again I was detailed to patrol up at the Temple Enclosure. The only snag was that this time my patrol partner was to be none other than Theo. I was saddened to think how only a few hours earlier I'd have been delighted to be paired up with him.

The following morning we marched as the last pair in a posse of six and were silent with one another. Knowing we would be on duty together I had put off making a conciliatory approach, so we hadn't spoken since our tense exchange. *It is understandable that Theo should defend his brother*, I kept telling myself, but I still didn't feel like apologising. Should we all meekly accept there was no alternative to going along with murder, and on such a scale? After all, this wasn't war. And yet, and yet, when I asked myself if I would have the courage to refuse an order I knew to be profoundly wrong, I couldn't answer with any conviction. Of course I couldn't. After all, not even Father had done so when ordered to penetrate King David's sepulchre, though you could argue that that was different because his motive had been concern for my future. A private obligation fulfilled at the expense of public responsibility. How confusing it all was.

So eventually I took a deep breath. "Theo, I don't want to fall out with you. You're my good friend and I want it to stay that way. I understand you have to defend Andreas. I just hate the idea that we soldiers make it possible for all these awful things to happen. But you're right – that's exactly what I was doing when I escorted Alexander from the prison." I saw again the ice-cold reproach of Salvia's glare. "So, well – I suppose it's not really for me to judge."

Theo was silent for a little while longer, and then, to my relief, conceded. "I know what you mean. I feel it too, which is probably why I was so angry. With Andreas as well as with you, if I'm honest. I love my brother, he's always tried to take care of me, but I don't like the man he seems to follow like a slave. Which, if I'm frank, is what he is. What we all are, come to that. I just want to go home and play music and forget about everything here. Trouble is, I don't have a home anymore. This is it. And, what's more – it's Antipater who holds my future as a musician in the palm of his pudgy hand. I'm stuck."

I had never heard my normally humorous, sceptical friend sound so defeated. Despite our previous tensions, I touched his arm in sympathy. But there was still something I needed to say.

"I did doubt you for a moment, Theo, and I'm sorry. But…"

"But what?"

"You once said to me yourself, loyalties are liabilities and… and I wondered…"

"…whether my loyalty as a brother was stronger than my loyalty as a friend? Which one was more of a liability? I can see what you were thinking. Oh, it's all too difficult, Simon. If only I could just stick to my nice, uncomplicated lyre!" Then he exclaimed, "But see who's coming towards us. If it isn't your friend Lucius Servius Celer – looking pretty upset, though!"

Sure enough, Celer was indeed hurrying in our direction, but it was a different Celer from the calm and controlled professional whom I had come to know and revere. Today he was the very picture of worry, his fine wide forehead puckered, his lips moving as if silently rehearsing a speech. As he drew nearer the beginnings of a dark gold stubble were visible on his normally clean-shaven chin and I thought he'd also lost weight in the weeks since I'd seen him.

"Celer – thank you, I only got your mess—"

"Oh, Simon! I'm afraid I can't stop and talk to you, not now. I fear the news from Berytus is very bad, very bad indeed. When I got Alexander's message – the one you sent via Sabinus – I sent an immediate supplication back to Caesar. But it won't have got to Rome in time. I'm on my way to Glaphyra now."

"I am so sorry, so sorry. Has there been a verdict?"

Celer shook his head. For a moment I thought he was indicating there was as yet no verdict; then I saw the glisten of tears and realised that he didn't trust himself to speak. Then, with obvious effort, he swallowed and a rush of words came out. "I wasn't sure if I'd see you so I've taken the books to your brother-in-law's workshop. Such a nice man – what a mercy your sister is one of the few Gentiles to marry into a Jewish family. My cousin excelled himself and translated almost the entire work while I was in Rome. No illustrations, of course, but never mind. Study carefully and come and see me when you can. If I'm still here, that is – nothing is certain anymore! If not, my assistant Sabinus will help you. He won't be as strict as me – he's rather too gentle – but he's very skilled and very experienced."

"I... I don't know how to thank you!" This was literally true, so taken aback was I by this extraordinary mark of favour, this long speech devoted entirely to me at a time of such tragedy. "But... but what has...?"

Celer shrugged and said, "I don't know very much, only what our messenger was able to bring us early this morning. There was a moon so he rode through the night at considerable risk. It seems both brothers have been sentenced to death. There were some judges like the Governor of Syria, who pleaded for leniency, but that bastard countryman of mine, the procurator Volumnius, was the one who swayed the mood of the court. Don't ask me what his motives were. I believe Salome was there too, no doubt adding her venom. Of course the brothers weren't allowed to appear in court to defend themselves – nothing as fair as that. The cursed King knows only too well that Alexander would win everyone over with his openness and honesty. At the moment they're still in gaol but I fear there is almost no hope. I really must go – Glaphyra will be in great distress." He included Theo in his brief valedictory wave and briefly touched my forearm as he passed.

At first Theo and I were both lost for words. *And I have to keep marching up and down on these bloody stupid useless patrols which help no one and achieve nothing, while all this is going on*, was all I could think of.

"We'd better catch the others up quickly. But at least thank the gods that you haven't been sent up to Berytus to do the King's dirty work for him. I wonder who will do it. I suppose they'll be strangled."

"I don't want to think about it." I pictured Alexander's small sons saying goodbye to their father and wondered what would become of them now. It was then only a heartbeat before my thoughts turned to Salvia, who seemed to have become the boys' nursemaid. What would become of her now? How could I find out? And was there anything, anything at all, that I could do to protect her? They were all questions which chased each other round and round my head as I made my way later to Leah's and David's house for some of my permitted hours of leave.

*

I had barely arrived when David burst into the house, flushed and agitated. "Leah, you'll never guess what's happened now!" Then he caught sight of me. "Oh, Simon, you may know more than me."

"I know only that the two brothers have been condemned to death but haven't been executed yet. I met Celer on his way to see Princess Glaphyra."

"Well, I do know more, and it is a grim story," said David, looking hesitantly at his wife. "My senior mason has a brother in the cavalry and he gets to know things before anyone else. The cavalry has its own fast messengers. Anyway, if there ever was any chance of reprieve for the brothers, it's definitely gone now."

"Definitely?" My last glimmer of hope faded.

"I'm afraid so. Apparently after the trial an old soldier called Tiro, who used to be loyal to the King, went to him and accused him of having lost his senses. To begin with he was respectful and apparently the King did seem to listen, but then Tiro suddenly overstepped the mark. Seems the old man completely lost control and yelled at the King, to his face if you can believe that, calling him an unhappy wretch and accusing him of turning against his two honest sons at the bidding of villains like his brother and sister. He said everyone could see they only want Antipater to inherit the kingdom because he's their puppet." David paused for breath and blew out his cheeks. "It's unbelievable that he can have said all that, but it seems he just went wild. So of course both he and his son – a close friend of Alexander's – were arrested immediately."

"That's courage!" breathed Leah.

"Well, I'm not sure. I doubt such an outburst could ever really have helped the brothers, but Tiro also claimed that the whole army was sorry for the youths and actually named officers who he said are openly cursing Herod. He really must have lost his wits to give so many people away like that. Of course they were all immediately arrested." Leah had gone pale and sat unsteadily down on a stool.

"And I'm afraid that's not all. The King has a barber, and it seems – remember this is just a third-hand report – that he came forward, though only our great God in heaven knows why, and claimed Tiro had instructed him to cut the King's throat when he was shaving him. He was told that Alexander would pay him well, and then…" David stopped in mid-flow as one of his sons appeared.

"What is it, Sami?"

"I'm hungry."

"All right, dearest. It won't be long," soothed Leah. "Here – take these figs and share them with your brothers. No, just one each." She shook her head after his retreating figure. "I really do not want them hearing any of this – it would terrify them. It terrifies me." I couldn't but agree, unhappily aware that a lot of soldiers were now under suspicion. It was all getting uncomfortably close.

As if reading my thoughts, David said, "This whole thing must be very distressing for you, Simon. You're closer to it all than we are – it's well known that Celer is an old friend of Alexander's. But I have to tell you the rest. Tiro was racked severely and his son – I've forgotten his name – tried to save his father by saying he'd tell the truth if his father was spared. So the son claimed it was indeed his friend Alexander who'd persuaded Tiro to ask the barber to cut the King's throat. Maybe he felt he had to save his father more agony, even at the cost of betraying his friend."

"So what happened to them?" I could hardly hear my own whisper.

"The King called a mass meeting where he accused the named soldiers of supporting the conspiracy. He handed them all over, Tiro and his son and the barber as well, to the mob to dispose of them. Apparently they…"

He must have seen from our faces that he didn't have to explain what the mob had done. We all three sat silent for a while, thinking of so many unfortunates who had ended their days in such a gruesome way. Not even the delighted shouts of the boys playing hoops with the neighbours' children outside could lighten the atmosphere.

When Leah muttered, "These are truly terrible times. I am fearful for the future of our sons. David, Simon – where will it all end?" I only wished I knew the answer. It was inevitable that my thoughts should turn then to Chloe and her unborn child.

Chapter 20

I was so troubled that I began to lose track of time. I had no appetite and my belt became noticeably looser; worse, I was too preoccupied to study the translated texts which Celer had so thoughtfully brought back from Rome and which I'd collected from David. There just didn't seem any point anymore. When outside the compound we overheard rumours and snatches of conversation, each more shocking than the last. According to one, the King intended to marry Glaphyra himself once Alexander was dead; to another – and this was a slingshot to the stomach – the brothers' entire households were to be put to death, including the seven children and all the servants. It was impossible to discover what was really happening.

The news, when it came, was every bit as grim as expected and it seemed that once again I was to be directly involved with the consequences. I was summoned to a private interview with Alberic, so I panicked that Salome had sent for me. My trepidation was not misplaced, but for a different reason.

"Simon, a courier has brought a message for you from Nicolas of Damascus. On his way back from Rome, he has joined up with the King near Sebaste, where the sentence of execution was to be carried out. In accordance with the trial verdict in Berytus." He didn't say that the sentence had actually been carried out but he relayed the information in his usual clipped style, and the lack of visible emotion made me wonder whether my liking for him had been misplaced. A current of the now familiar anger coursed its way up through my body, but of course I said nothing. And I didn't at all like the sound of a personal message from Nicolas of Damascus.

"What I am now going to tell you is not to be spoken of outside this room, Simon. I must remind you that you are already under oath not to repeat anything you hear or see in the King's court." I merely nodded my assent. What could be coming next?

"Nicolas is worried for the King, who is in deep distress after all that has happened." Thinking back to the farewell scene between Alexander and his sons as his distraught wife looked on, I was tempted to make a caustic comment.

"It seems like the state he was in after the first Queen Mariamme died." *After he had the first Mariamme murdered*, was how I wanted to correct him.

"Nicolas remembered that your father was a comfort to him at that time. He was one of the few soldiers the King would have near him in those weeks. So Nicolas has…"

I knew with dreadful certainty what was coming.

"…has reminded the King that he intended to bring you into more personal attendance. He suggested this would be a good moment to transfer you." I thought I might be about to vomit.

"The King apparently said something like, 'Ah, yes, the grey-eyed boy who had a tryst near the pigeon cages! He looks like his father. That's why I wanted him to escort Alexander from prison that day. Yes, we'll have him.' I didn't realise you had already met the King, Simon." Then came the next spear thrust. "So, Nicolas has sent an instruction. You are to be in attendance as soon as the King returns to Jerusalem."

"Surely there are many more experienced men than me who would be better? Men the King already knows and trusts?" I knew it was useless to protest but couldn't stop myself.

"More experienced, perhaps, Simon. But there are large parts of the army who were loyal to Alexander and his brother. The King is at a loss to know who he can trust."

I wondered at Alberic's loyalty, just as before I had wondered at Father's, but I emphatically didn't feel obliged to share it. *I cannot revere a man – despite all the power and pomp, he is just a man and by all accounts not even of royal blood – who murders first his wife and then two of his own sons. Not to mention countless soldiers. I don't care how many fine new cities he's built or how many military victories he's had, his actions are wicked and unnatural. Theo was right: there truly is darkness in that heart.* "And… and my duties?" I ventured.

Alberic gave a rare laugh. "Anyone would think you'd been diagnosed with typhus, Simon. This is an honour, a privilege. Your duties won't be very different. There will be patrols and searches, like now, and you'll have to stand guard when the King receives visitors. And you will take your orders from another officer. I don't know who yet." I pouted, meaning to convey that I was content enough with Alberic, but he ignored it and warmed to his theme.

"You may also get the chance to go hunting with the royal party. And when the King travels abroad you could be chosen to go with him. That will be interesting for you."

Give me boredom any day. I didn't realise how lucky I'd been.

I went back to join Theo, who was exchanging jokes with several of our comrades, and I suddenly realised how much I would miss them all. Only then did it hit me that once I was transferred to duties at the King's apartments it would be more difficult than ever to meet Salvia, let alone Celer, even if the two of them managed to survive the current turmoil, which was far from certain. Scarcely an hour went by in which I didn't think of Salvia, almost obsessively going over each of our brief encounters in minute detail. It was as if I was afraid that without this frequent repetition they would fade from my memory like stars at dawn.

Chapter 21

It was on a cool, grey November day that the King returned to Jerusalem with depleted ranks of soldiers and bodyguards. Many of his previous entourage, suspected of allegiance to his disgraced sons, had been either stoned to death by the mob or sent into exile. I stood next to a friendly guard I recognised from my days in the Antonia, and together we tried to identify the uniforms of the motley groups of soldiers. It was a welcome distraction, but we spoke under our breath, because a strange aura of near-silence surrounded the homecoming procession. The horses' hooves clattered eerily on the paving stones, almost the only sound, for totally absent were the shouted orders of the officers, the triumphant blasts of trumpets and the insistent throb of drumbeats that normally accompanied the royal arrival.

In the forefront were men from Hatra with their elaborate cuirasses made of bronze and leather and their strange helmets topped with a sinister sort of bird's beak; then came the archers, probably from Idumaea according to my acquaintance, in striking bright red and white-striped tunics and open-toed boots in a creamy white leather; they were followed by a group of Gauls also wearing bronze cuirasses but with dark red tunics and mantles like mine; then there were many whose provenance was difficult to guess. Following the infantry came a small knot of cavalrymen, crowding protectively around their monarch who rode, straight and solemn, his head turning neither to right nor left. As he passed, one of the horses shied slightly and gave us the chance to admire at close quarters the King's attire, which was magnificent, proclaiming power as well as wealth. His mantle was of richest purple fringed with gold; his cuirass, decorated with winged horses, was gilded; even his white leather *pteruges* and the thin bronze greaves[4] on his legs were gilded. His horse's harness was equally opulent, in red leather with golden discs. But despite the King's immobile posture astride his handsome bay mount, the ostrich feathers and white horsehair crest on his gilded helmet fluttered uncertainly in the chilly November breeze.

We watched the procession, together with other guards and a crowd of slaves, as it came through the great gateway and progressed towards the bottom of the steps leading up to the royal apartments. King Herod dismounted and, to my surprise, paused for a moment to pat his horse's imposing neck. A small figure, bent even smaller in a low bowing position, ran forward to grab the bridle and lead the creature away. I immediately recognised Saul, the young man I'd befriended in my early days as a recruit. I was glad to see him there, for I was sure he'd have been bullied back in the Antonia, and knew he'd be much happier working with his beloved horses in the royal stables.

On the steps stood a group of the King's wives, together with Salome, her hair as elaborately styled as ever, and their brother Pheroras. I felt a stab of disquiet as Salome came down the steps directly towards us, her arms outstretched, but it was soon clear she was making straight for the King. However, he put out a peremptory hand, warning her not to approach him. Then, raising an arm for the briefest of moments in the direction of the assembled company, he proceeded into the interior of the palace, followed by Nicolas of Damascus, who had been hidden behind the cavalrymen. Salome reeled backwards as if stunned by the rebuff, and I saw how her

---

4   Pieces of armour protecting the lower legs.

daughter Berenice, pallid widow of the murdered Aristobulus and mother of his five children, took her arm and supported her as they walked up the steps to go inside. I recalled how Salome had claimed her brother's safety to be her paramount concern and knew a fleeting moment of sympathy for this enigmatic woman, so hated by those I had come to love.

Now that the King had disappeared a hubbub of excited chatter broke the unnatural silence, and all around us cavalrymen were either dismounting or riding back to the stables, and infantrymen were dispersing in little groups. Slaves were running around with buckets to remove droppings from the paving stones, and gradually the royal wives also vanished into the interior of the palace. My new acquaintance, one of the Celtic contingent, was as much at a loss as I was to know what we should do. We hadn't yet been told who would be giving us our orders after the King's arrival.

"Let's go to the stables and have a look at the horses. I'm hoping to get transferred into the cavalry soon and everyone seems to have forgotten about us!" I was only too glad to follow his suggestion and let him lead the way. While he wandered up and down admiring the horses and getting under the feet of the grooms, I looked around for Saul. He soon appeared, dwarfed by the huge saddle from the King's horse which he was carrying over his two arms. His grin of recognition made clear his delight.

"Hallo, Simon! I expect you're surprised to see me here. Old Scarface isn't such a bad fellow – he could see I'd never be able to carry all the equipment you need on a campaign. Training me would be a waste of time, he said. But he knew I was good with horses, so had me transferred here. Not a bad swap!"

As my Celtic comrade reappeared I introduced him to Saul. "This is someone who knows his way around horses," I said, and was rewarded by Saul's flush of pleasure. He proudly showed us round the tack area, where an array of richly decorated harnesses hung on wooden hooks, and racks were piled high with all manner of saddles and weapons, including some of the unusually long swords used by the King's heavy cavalry.

Back in the compound we were dragging our feet towards the King's apartments, wondering what to do next, when I suddenly heard a familiar voice calling my name. Turning round, I was startled but delighted to see none other than Celer hurrying towards us.

"Oh, Celer – what a surprise! Greetings."

But Celer dispensed with the niceties. "Simon, I was on my way to find you. We need to talk. Urgently."

I could see immediately that he was tense and preoccupied. He looked around him to check we weren't being watched. There were the usual slaves bustling along with baskets of provisions or laundry, and sentries walking up and down near the main gate, but no one was taking any notice of us.

"I'll go and find out who our new officer is," volunteered my comrade tactfully.

We had sat down on a bench under some apricot trees and what was left of their tattered leaves, when I realised I hadn't yet offered Celer my condolences on the death of his father. I did so now, and he mumbled his thanks. Then he turned his blue gaze on me.

"Oh, Simon, they have carried out the sentence. I've come to give the King my resignation. I cannot work for him anymore, not now, not after what he's done to Alexander."

Although fully expected, the confirmation still came as a shock. That friendly, handsome young man smiled wistfully at me from the remote, inaccessible land of death and for some moments I could neither feel nor say anything.

Then Celer's intention struck home. "But… but Celer – you can't do that! What about all this vital work you're doing here? The Temple! You told me once yourself that you're safe because of that."

"Simon, I'm not doing this out of fear for myself. I'd have liked to think you had more respect for me than that. But I can't go on serving someone who puts two of his own sons to death in that merciless way, believing the word of people who want only power for themselves. I'd feel like that even if Alexander hadn't been my childhood friend. But he was, so I feel it all the more intensely. I can't go on here – I *won't* go on. There are plenty of other architects and engineers in Jerusalem and Quintus Marius Severus can bring more from Rome. Though I think Severus is disgusted too, so I don't know how much longer he will carry on here."

"None as gifted as you, I'm sure." My compliment was totally sincere, informed by Celer's reputation as well as my own observations, but I was also playing for time. I was devastated by this news, both for myself and for Celer, for I was well aware that his work on the Temple was the crowning glory of his career. *The meaning of his life*, Sabinus had said. There was also an uncomfortable question which slithered into my head. Should I myself have disobeyed the command to enter the King's close entourage at this time, have found a way to refuse, whatever the consequences?

"But… but won't the King fly into a rage when you tell him? Is this the right moment – when he's only just returned? I mean, it's not for *me* to advise *you*, but—"

"I need to do it now. If I delay, I'll get drawn into all manner of problems and queries which colleagues are already bringing me after my absence in Rome. It'll be hard enough to leave poor Tertius Sabinus alone in charge as it is. But I have to do this, Simon. I've just come from Sebaste – I gave the gaolers a hefty bribe to let me see Alexander and Aristobulus before they died. Believe me, they were the worst moments of my life. Including being at my father's deathbed."

Celer's mind was clearly made up, but I could tell from the almost apologetic way he looked at me that there was something else he wanted to say. "Simon, I really wanted to help you. I recognised in you something of myself ten, twelve years ago. When I was in Rome saying farewell to my father, I knew then what was all too likely to happen to Alexander at some point. So, when Caesar graciously sent words of condolence – for my father was an immensely loyal servant to Rome for thirty years – I took the precaution of sending back a request, via the royal messenger. I asked him for a letter that would guarantee me safe passage out of Judea – should it ever prove necessary. I think Caesar is well aware of the dangers of crossing King Herod, and he complied almost immediately. I have that document, and the King would not dare to ignore its contents signed by Caesar. Anyway, the reason for telling you all that is to ask – why don't you come with me? At this point you could leave safely under my protection. Come to Rome, Simon! You can be my apprentice and there will be plenty of opportunities for you – Jerusalem isn't the only place where building is going on, you know! Caesar is building many temples himself. What do you say?"

Celer's offer reminded me of the radiant glow of hope I'd felt when he first agreed to help me. At first it seemed to contain all I could wish for my future. I would escape the service of an unpredictable, violent ruler whose orders could be murderous; I would leave behind the boredom of repetitious patrols and watches; I would no longer be subject to the petty rules and regulations of a monotonous, communal existence, eating when the trumpet sounded, going to the baths only at the allotted time, always being at someone else's beck and call, subservient to petty tyrants like Walcaud. What I was being offered was the very difference between existence and life, for above all I would finally be able to devote myself to what truly inspired me and for which I knew, with intuitive certainty, I had been born.

All this raced through my mind. Then a little voice reminded me why I was in the army in the first place. It had been my father's dearest wish that I should follow him and become a loyal servant of his master the King. I thought too of Chloe, about to give birth to my first niece or nephew – the only family I had left. And, above all, there was Salvia. I didn't know what was happening to her or even where she was now that her master had been executed, but it certainly wasn't – and was never likely to be – anywhere near Rome. These thoughts crowded in on me, each one a weight to counterbalance the temptations.

"Well, you're certainly taking a long time to respond, Simon!"

"Celer, there's nothing in the world I would like more, believe me. And I am deeply, deeply honoured by your offer. But I can't. I just can't."

"And why not?" His tone told me that he would not find it easy to understand my reasons.

"It would… I don't know whether you'll understand this, but it would in some way dishonour my father to leave the King's service, especially just now when I've been singled out precisely because of who I am. It would feel like desertion. And… and…"

"Yes, and?"

"There's my only sister in Hebron. I can't abandon her."

"Even though she has a husband – and brother and sister-in-law here in Jerusalem who have three children and would no doubt welcome her visits? Hebron's not so very far away after all." Put like that, it did sound ridiculous to talk of abandonment. Especially as in military service I was unlikely to see much of Chloe anyway. Yet still I felt – knew – it would be wrong. If I left now with Celer, there would, could, be no coming back. It would be desertion for life.

"You don't think your reason has more to do with the slave-girl you're so attached to in Alexander's household?"

I met his gaze and shrugged helplessly, unable to deny it. I felt both horribly ungrateful and utterly miserable that the one door that was ever likely to give me access to my life's dream was about to clang shut in my face. Forever this time.

"Listen, Simon, only you can make the decision. It's a big one, I know, but this is an opportunity that may – no, *will* – never come again. And taking opportunities means making choices, hard choices – sacrificing things. I've recently lost my own father, as you know, so I respect your feelings about honouring yours. But if he was a good father, then what he would want most for his son would be for him to achieve success in the thing that makes him most happy. That's given to very few of us in this life. Think of all the thousands of slaves and soldiers and farmers and fishermen and shopkeepers and shepherds and goodness knows who else, all of whom eke out a living with no choice. Not even many of the stonemasons and craftsmen who work for us have a choice. But you do, Simon. Make it." I looked down at the multicoloured paving stones and wondered idly where they had been quarried. Funny how I often found myself thinking of irrelevant things at moments of crisis.

"And as for Salvia, I do have news of her, from one of Alexander's manservants, but I'm not sure I should tell you as it may strengthen your resolve to resist my offer."

"Please, Celer, please tell me." The breeze grew stronger and colder as if to presage what Celer was about to say; I shivered as a flurry of leaves dropped on us from a branch above. I thought fleetingly of my childhood farm, where they would probably be sowing the barley now and starting to prune the vines.

"I called at the apartments on my way here to bring poor Alexander's last message to his wife. Unsurprisingly she was indisposed and not taking visitors. However, I saw his favourite manservant, who himself is inconsolable – though personally I'm not sure how he's managed to survive. He told me that Glaphyra's to be sent back as soon as possible to her father, but King Herod has ordered her to leave the children here. She is, as you can imagine, distraught. Utterly. I'll try again to see her later today, though nothing I can say will make her feel better. But Salvia will remain with the boys, who are very attached to her – that's Glaphyra's wish because she thinks it'll make the separation more bearable for them." He heaved a deep sigh, weighed down by the burden of what he'd just told me.

"So now I suppose you'll be more determined than ever to stay? Not that your duties – or hers – will give you much chance to see each other, as you must realise." He waited, but the soft tapping of his foot on the ground told me that his patience, never his most obvious characteristic, was running out.

Finally I responded in a voice gruff with emotion. "Celer, I watched Alexander saying goodbye to his little boys, and now you tell me they're to be separated from their mother as well. I believe I actually hate the King for the pitiless things he has done. But my father always did what he saw as his duty, and I think I must do mine. It isn't – or I don't think it is – only because of Salvia but, Celer, I cannot come. As you know, I hope that one day I will be able to leave the army with honour, to join your profession. But for now I cannot come. I may regret it all my life long, but I cannot come."

Celer's shoulders drooped a little as he got up and his lips were slightly pursed, but he touched me gently on the upper arm. "I respect your decision, Simon. It's a brave one. Keep the master's texts safe and study hard. I doubt another chance will come but you never know and Sabinus is a good man. He will help you if he can."

As he turned to go, a massive lump in my throat prevented me from putting even a fraction of what I would have liked to say into words. I couldn't even thank him for all he had done, or for the wonderful translation which so far I'd been too distracted to study. So it was that Celer had the last word. "If you change your mind, I'll be sailing from Caesarea in a few days. And in Rome Caesar's architects will know where to find me. Farewell, young Simon. May the gods look kindly on you."

I stood and watched him walk away towards the royal apartments and the difficult, possibly dangerous, interview with the King, which he had bravely imposed upon himself. He didn't look back. Tears of anguish stood in my eyes, and I found myself wondering how Father would have reacted to the most difficult decision I had yet made in my life. "May the gods have mercy on me," I murmured, horrified by a hot rush of anger against the dead man.

Chapter 22

Desperate to find out what had transpired between Celer and the King, at first I looked out for a message to arrive, until I realised Celer wouldn't risk getting me into trouble in that way. It was some small relief to hear that our new officer at the King's apartments was to be none other than Cyrus Scarface, who, on account of his long and unimpeachable service, had been brought back to the palace from semi-retirement as a trainer in the Antonia Fortress. The first few days of the new arrangement passed without a glimpse of the King or any switch of accommodation, so I was almost lulled into thinking that nothing was going to change, when Cyrus gave me an order that made my heart miss a beat.

"I'm sending you over to Alexander's former apartments. The King has summoned all his grandchildren to an assembly in the Agrippeum with his counsellors and Companions of the Household, as he has an announcement to make. Even the very little ones have to be there." Cyrus raised his eyebrows and shrugged his shoulders, by which I understood how he felt about the order.

"You are to fetch the two boys and have them brought here with whoever is now in charge of them. I understand their mother has already departed for her homeland. I'm sending other men for the five children of Aristobulus." I could hardly believe my good fortune.

I was admitted into the apartments by a slave, dishevelled, shabbily dressed and barely polite. "Wait here – I'll fetch Salvia. She looks after the children now." He disappeared, leaving me alone in the reception area without inviting me to be seated. The retreating footsteps had a hollow ring, accentuating the new emptiness of the place which made all the opulence seem somehow exaggerated, grotesque even. I half-dreaded seeing Salvia again, for it would be the first time since the morning of the farewells and I wasn't sure how she would receive me. Then, suddenly, she was in front of me. She caught her breath when she saw me and I fancied her eyes lit up, before she narrowed them in puzzlement and put her head to one side in enquiry.

"Simon, what… why?" Then she added, "This time?"

"I've been ordered to collect the boys for an audience with the King." Seeing the alarm that immediately supplanted the other reactions, I was quick to reassure her. "It's all right – all the children have been summoned together with his counsellors. It's for some announcement but I don't think there's anything to fear for them. And you are ordered to accompany them, so they won't be alone." At that her frown of anxiety relaxed a little.

"But… but, you?"

"Why me? Well, I've been transferred to the unit which attends the King more closely. After… what has happened – he doesn't trust many of his former guardsmen, and… well, because of my father he seems to think he can trust me." I intended my selective emphasis and tone of voice to convey my true allegiance.

"And can he?"

"Salvia! You mustn't ask me that!" Two other servants walked by, heads lowered and talking in hushed tones. It dawned on me that the sullen attitude of the slave who'd admitted me had been one of mourning. "The other day – there was nothing—"

"Yes, I know." She nodded. "How much time do we have now?"

"Not long. I think the assembly is at noon, but as soon as possible were my orders."

"I need to see they are properly dressed. We won't be long," she affirmed with quiet authority as she turned away. I offered up a silent prayer of thanks for her small sign of reconciliation.

On the way to the assembly the boys ran off from Salvia's side to wade through drifts of dead leaves which had blown off the fruit trees in the previous night's storm. They laughed at the swishing sound as they tried kicking leaves at each other. Then Tigranes picked up a stick and vigorously whacked the trunks of the trees as he passed.

"That's the first time in days I've seen them smile, let alone laugh," she observed tenderly. "You know that my mistress has left for Cappadocia, don't you? That was so hard for them all – but she told them she was going to see their other grandfather and hoped that before long they'd be able to join her. If only that were true. We know who the grandfather with the real power is, don't we?"

I was so relieved to see that she was no longer angry with me. "Presumably they don't have any idea yet of what the King has done?"

"No, I don't think so, but there's so much rumour around they're bound to find out before long. Tigranes is nearly nine now and not slow in his understanding. Poor children. Tigri – don't do that or you'll make yourself all messy before we see the King.

"Come to that, I didn't have time to make myself look tidy," she sighed, putting wandering strands of hair behind her pretty ears and smoothing the long blue folds of her gown.

"Never mind, you look beautiful as always." She blushed and gave a little giggle. We had stopped, on the pretext of watching the boys enjoying their play. I wished the moment could last all day and longed to fold her in my arms. But instead I asked, "Salvia, do you know what happened to Celer? He was going to see the King to resign from his office and I know he intended to see your mistress before he – or she – left the city. Do you know if he managed to do that?"

"Yes. He brought my master's last message for her, I believe. Of course I wasn't present – it was a very private thing."

"Do you know what happened – between him and King Herod, I mean?"

"Not in detail but my mistress told me the King took the news surprisingly quietly. Celer thought he seemed hurt rather than angry. My mistress was very sad because she doesn't think she'll ever see Celer again and he's been a good friend to her and my master." She paused, trying to recall everything. "Yes, she also said she was surprised the King doesn't suspect Celer of being a conspirator, as he was so close to Alexander."

*

As we were ushered into the hall – named after the famous Roman statesman and architect Marcus Agrippa, who had been King Herod's friend – we were confronted by rows of advisers and people the King called his 'Companions of the Household'. My task was to show Salvia and her two charges to a group of couches, where several of the other children were already sitting, which meant walking right across the wide space in front of the assembled company. For once I was grateful for the partial cover of my helmet. If we'd arrived a bit earlier we would have spared ourselves this embarrassment, but then we wouldn't have had those precious moments together outside. I walked straight-backed and stiff, mindful of Cyrus's whispered words as we'd entered. "Be careful to do everything exactly as may be asked of you – the King is very unpredictable at the moment."

Across the room I caught sight of Nicolas, seated next to his brother Ptolemy. Rather to my surprise he acknowledged me with a nod, so I gave a small bow in return, hoping it was suitably deferential in front of so many important people. After returning self-consciously to my position at the rear of the hall with the other guards, I was just in time to see Salvia bending down and gently removing young Alexander's hand from hers, before taking her place behind the couches with the other servants. The little boy immediately sought his brother's hand instead, seeking protection in the awed hush which reigned in the room.

When the King came in, he was dressed in his usual purple mantle and I noticed that even the leggings inside his sandals were dyed with costly purple. His tunic was dazzlingly white, edged with more purple, and on his head he wore a gold diadem. He inclined his head to the assembly, who had risen at his entry, and bade them be seated. He looked at the couches where his grandchildren sat in silent, wide-eyed awe and began speaking in emotional tones. "Cruel circumstances have taken the fathers of these children from me; now they are orphans they are commended to my care by the ties of family," he began. His was usually a deep, resonant voice, but today it was softer and at the back of the large, high-ceilinged hall I had to strain to catch every word. The King went on to say that although he had been doomed as a father – at that point there was a perceptible break in his voice and a hand went up to his eye – he would endeavour to be a loving and dedicated grandfather. When the time came he wanted to leave this life in the knowledge that his grandchildren were safe with the people closest to him. I couldn't resist turning my head to look across the crowded hall at Salvia and was delighted to see she was looking in my direction. She was too distant to be sure, but I guessed she would be reacting in the same way as me to the King's tears.

Then King Herod rose dramatically to his feet, one hand on his stomach as if it were hurting him, and addressed his brother. "So, Pheroras – I engage your daughter to Tigranes, Alexander's older son. Thus will you become his guardian."

Then he turned to Antipater, whom I noticed for the first time sitting on a couch next to his mother. "Antipater, to your son I commit Mariamme, Aristobulus's daughter. In this way you will in effect replace her father. Her little sister Herodias, still an infant, will be engaged to my own son Herod Philip."

I looked across at the wives and thought I spotted a stir of consternation in their ranks.

Then I turned my attention to Antipater, but, although his couch was a little closer it was impossible to see his face, for he was studiously looking down at his hands and fiddling with his many rings. Gaunt, grim-faced Two Times Doris touched her son's shoulder with her own bejewelled fingers, a gesture that was not lost on me. I couldn't work out all the implications of what was being announced, but I sensed they were highly significant and hoped I'd get a chance to see Theo later, who would surely enlighten me. I assumed the general gist was that Antipater's hopes of becoming heir to the kingdom were now in jeopardy, with so much honour being bestowed on the heirs of his executed half-brothers.

King Herod went on, looking pointedly across to his wives and his brother and sister, his voice booming much louder now and with an edge of menace, "I command that these my wishes be fulfilled, with no dissent from anyone who cares for me." After a pause, when one could have heard a needle drop, he walked over to where the children sat staring up at him, wide-eyed and still as if under a spell. "And I beseech God to confirm these bonds for the benefit of my kingdom and my heirs, and to look more kindly on these children than he did on their fathers."

Bending down, he joined the hands of the four older children who had been so unexpectedly betrothed and tenderly embraced each one. Then he turned back to the assembly, wiping tears which were now coursing down his cheeks, and dismissed it formally. As he turned on his heel to leave the hall, Nicolas got up to follow him and I thought it strange that Antipater did not do the same, as the only remaining son of adult age. I looked back at the children, who were still sitting transfixed. Tigranes was biting his lip and frowning, and as the crowd began to get up to leave, I saw how Salvia came round from behind the couch to take her two charges by the hand and whisper a few words in their ears. How gentle she was with the children. How I... *No*, I told myself, *I mustn't think like that, not now, not yet, perhaps not ever.*

As everyone dispersed, I made myself inconspicuous behind

a couple of my taller comrades as I waited for Salvia to join me, studiously avoiding Cyrus's eye in case he were minded to issue fresh orders. But no one tried to stop me as I left the hall and accompanied Salvia back towards the far end of the palace compound.

"You don't really need to escort us now. The important business is surely over." I wondered if this were a way of telling me she no longer desired my company, but her little sideways glance was the most encouraging she had ever given me, and I was reassured. As we walked, the boys ran ahead to play in the leaves again, pleased to be freed from the oppressive atmosphere of the meeting.

"Salvia, perhaps now there'll be no reason why we shouldn't see each other openly. All the same, suspicions linger and the King's moods are unpredictable so who knows where his orders will take me next. I want you to know how you can contact me if either you or I have to move away."

"Simon, I won't be moving away. Not unless the children are sent out of the city, and then I would go with them – or make every effort to. They've had enough leave-takings in their short lives." A shadow of sadness crossed her face and I wondered about her own leave-takings. But I also understood what her words were firmly telling me: she would never of her own accord abandon the boys, not even for me, whatever I asked of her.

"I understand that, Salvia – and I respect you for it. But the future is uncharted territory and who knows what lies in wait, so please, take these directions for how to reach my sister's relatives – I've been fortunate that she made such an unusual marriage. I'm not of their faith, but they are true friends and I know David would act as intermediary. You can trust him completely."

We'd reached the apartments and a couple of the servants' children were playing around on the terrace outside. One of them called out, "Come and see our new hoops, Tigranes!"

"I'll have to go – the King's grandsons are not supposed to play with the servants' children."

"Don't you want these directions? Doesn't it matter to you if we lose contact?"

She stopped. "Simon, of course it does." She looked up at me with her sweet smile, and I felt my petulant frown melt away like wax under a flame. "It's just that I'm sure you're worrying without cause. You'll be able to see me more often now, now that, well – everything has changed."

"I hope so, I hope so with all my soul. But everything is so uncertain. So please, to be sure, put this in a safe place where you won't lose it," and I reached into my tunic for the little map I'd prepared for her. Tigranes had now joined the other children with little Alexander in hot pursuit, and they were all chasing hoops with metal pieces attached that rang like bells as they gathered speed. "They're enjoying themselves. If I were you I'd pretend not to have seen who they're playing with for a while – what harm can come of it?"

"Simon!" she tutted, but her chuckle told me she was inclined to agree. She walked briskly away, but not before she had blown me a kiss which I pretended to catch and hold against my cuirass. I watched as she caught one of the hoops that came spiralling towards her out of control, and with a pretty little wrist movement that stopped my breath, sent it spinning back to the boy who had shouted to Tigranes.

"I'll see you soon," she called back over her shoulder. I raised my hand, wishing I could be so sure.

Chapter 23

King Herod had become so frightened of conspiracy that he now wanted his armed soldiers to stand guard when he received visitors; in the past that duty had fallen to slaves. Thus my orders the day after the assembly were to station myself outside the chamber where he was expecting to receive several deputations. The King himself would enter from private rooms which opened into it from the back, so I was spared the ordeal of any sort of exchange with him.

The sight of the first visitor, accompanied to the outer door by a trusted old chamberlain, brought a welcome shock of recognition, for it was none other than Quintus Marius Severus. He hurried in with a preoccupied air so did not notice me at first. When I stepped forward and asked politely if I could search him, according to my instructions, Severus still didn't recognise me, perhaps because of my helmet. It was only when I said quietly, "I trust you are in good health, Sir," that he peered into my face and exclaimed, "Why, it's young Simon! Oh, Simon – what a calamity this all is. But perhaps you don't know – about Celer, I mean?" I looked round at the doors, desperate for them not to open and reveal the King before I had had a chance to find out what had happened. The other guard was looking at us curiously.

"I saw him just before he went to the King with his resignation," I whispered. "Is he… is he… has he left the city?"

"Yes, he is on his way to Caesarea as we speak. But I have been summoned so I must go in now." He sighed and shook his head, and it was clear that even this highly regarded and influential man was worried. He tugged at the little bell rope appended to the door frame, and at the bark of acknowledgement which came from inside, my comrade and I pulled the great bronze handles, fashioned in the shape of lions' heads, and admitted the visitor. The King was seated, studying some scrolls at a table, and did not get up to greet his chief architect. My comrade and I bowed, and left the room.

To begin with I despaired of hearing any of the crucial interview inside the chamber. Then, with a start of surprise, I realised that my companion, having sidled up to the bronze handle on his side of the double doors, was first gesturing to get my attention and then pointing at the aperture which served as a gaping mouth in the sculpted lion's face. I understood immediately. He presumably had nothing like the same investment in overhearing the interview but was obviously relishing the opportunity, and grinned toothlessly back. I put my ear as close to the lion's jaws on my door as I dared.

I'd missed the opening remarks and the first thing I heard was the King, speaking in a more high-pitched tone than usual and with obvious distress, plaintively almost. "…his talents. I listened to his advice, followed his plans, changed some of my own ideas if they didn't agree with his. Young though he was, his flair and his expertise rivalled even yours, Severus."

Severus murmured something that I didn't catch, except for the word 'prized'.

"And now look what he has done, how he has repaid my trust! Is there no one in this city who is loyal to me? Can I count on no one's love?"

I glanced sideways at my comrade, who was gaping in amazement.

"Sire, Celer has not been disloyal to you. But as you know he was a childhood friend of your son Alexander, and they spent a lot of time together in Rome. He loved him and feels he owes him a posthumous debt of loyalty. But he would never deceive you. If he stayed, he says he would be doing so under false pretences. That is why he has taken the action he has."

"Bah! Can you do nothing to bring him back, to persuade him? You who were his teacher, his mentor, without whom he would never have come to Jerusalem in the first place?"

"Sire, it is true that I was once his teacher and could still be his mentor, though he now has much to teach me. But this... this is not a professional matter. This is... this is a matter of principle. Of honour. Celer's mind is..."

There was a silence, except for the sound of a chair scraping against the stone floor. The King had evidently got to his feet. "How dare you talk to me, the King, of principle, of honour. At such a time, when my own sons were guilty of conspiring to bring about my death – not just once but several times. What honour did *they* have, they to whom your precious Celer seems so devoted? What about me, what about showing loyalty to me? I don't understand what I have done to deserve such hatred not only among my own subjects but among my own family – and now, it seems, among my architects, of all people. It is not to be borne."

The other guard made a mocking face, pretending he was about to weep. But despite everything that had happened, I found a small space within me to pity this man who, for all his terrifying power, was feeling so lonely, so sinned against.

"I am sorry if I have offended you, Sire." Severus's voice was quiet but firm. "But it is because I speak my mind and give you honest answers that you can trust me as your servant. The fact is I cannot... no, let me even say, Sire, at the risk of your anger, I *will* not dissuade Celer from taking the action he has – much as it grieves me, for it is an immense sacrifice he is making. There is no more important architectural project in the Roman Empire at this time than the rebuilding of the Temple, and your palaces come a close second."

Another silence. Then the King said, "I, who have bequeathed to my people and to the rest of the world a legacy that will last forever, that will make Judaea the pride of the whole world, am undermined by my own architects – the very people I have raised up above all men. And you say I can trust you! By the great God of the Jews, if you didn't have the personal protection of Caesar himself, I would throw you into a pit in chains, you and the whole lot of you. And that includes that young good-for-nothing, whom once I loved and who calls himself my son's friend! Now go! Go! Out of my sight!"

His voice grew progressively louder during this tirade until it became a bellow, and we only just managed to dart back into our official positions before the doors were flung open and Severus appeared, flushed but with his head held high. I had always admired the man for what he had accomplished, but now I found a new respect, bordering on reverence, for the courage and dignity with which he had conducted himself.

Inside the chamber there was quiet at first, and then, clearly now through the doors which Severus had left slightly open in his haste, a barely audible but definite whimper, almost a sob. We two guards looked at each other in amazement, unable to believe what we were hearing. Then, footsteps and a voice speaking in a tone of gentle concern. "Sire, you are not well? You wanted to see me about those administrative matters, but they can wait if you are indisposed. And… and your son wishes to speak to you – he stopped me on my way here and asked me to request an audience with you."

"My son! My son! I have no sons anymore – or not adult ones anyway. My young boys would not be asking to see me."

"Sire, your son Antipater."

"Ah yes, Antipater. I knew it wouldn't be long before *he* asked to see me. He'll not be pleased with yesterday's betrothals. He thinks only of himself. Oh, Nicolas, what have I done to deserve such a family? And you know about Lucius Servius Celer?"

"Celer? The Roman architect?"

"Ah, you hadn't heard! He has been impudent, disloyal, ungrateful enough to resign from my service – from one of the most prestigious positions in the entire world!"

I heard Nicolas, usually so in control, utter incredulously, "Resigned! But... but he was central to so much of what's going on here, the construction work, the Temple, the... oh, Sire. I know he was a friend of Alexander's, but he was surely no conspirator!"

"No, in truth I cannot accuse him of that, though I would like to. He himself had nothing to fear from me and nothing to gain from this action. That's what is so hard to understand. Severus, who's just been here, seems to support him too. I'd have expected him to feel as angry, as betrayed, as I do. But he just talks of honour, of principle. Bah!"

"Sire, you do not look well. Let me help you to your bedchamber for some rest, and I'll arrange to postpone those other interviews. I'll let Antipater know you are indisposed. Come." There was more scraping of furniture on stone and then, "In truth, Nicolas, I do not feel at all well. Lend me your arm."

"Maybe you should have support on the other side too. Let me call one of the guards." Almost immediately there was Nicolas standing in the doorway and, unlike Severus, he recognised me immediately as he had done in the crowded Agrippeum.

"Ah, it's Simon, this is fortuitous. Come, please, the King is not feeling well and requires some help to take him to rest." And so I followed Nicolas into the royal presence. As I timidly approached the King, he removed his diadem and ran his hand repeatedly through his thick, dark hair. He was still seated and looked up, wild-eyed, showing no sign of recognition.

"Sire, if you remember, we arranged for the son of Philip the Gaul to be in closer attendance. This is he, Simon!" The King seemed to focus then, and, miraculously, his thin lips stretched into a tiny smile. "Ah yes, I remember. Poor Philip. But still, he seems to have had better fortune with his children than I have." I'm sure I blushed.

Then the King held out an arm to be supported and I placed my hand underneath it, applying a little pressure to help him rise from his seat, surprised by the royal weight. The three of us then made our way to the door at the back of the chamber, a much more modest affair than the exterior one through which we'd been eavesdropping. It was then a question of leading him along a couple of passageways, across a small internal courtyard and into another suite of rooms until we reached the door of his bedchamber. One or two servants looked at me curiously and bowed as we passed before melting away into the shadows, but no one came forward to relieve me.

"You can leave me now. Nicolas, have Malthace called. She is kinder to me than the rest of them – or she was. I'm not sure how she feels about the betrothals as I didn't include her two boys." He looked at me as he disengaged his arm. "Your father showed understanding at another terrible time. I don't forget."

I bowed but thought ruefully, *no, that is my misfortune.*

Nicolas led me out of the apartments by a shorter route. "Simon, do not mention anything about the King's indisposition to anyone," he commanded as we parted company. "I am glad it was you who were on duty today," he added, inclining his head briefly, and then he was gone. I watched his slightly bent figure striding purposefully away into the pale light of early winter, puzzled as I always was by the man, unsure despite our past connections whether he was friend or foe.

My duty at the palace over for the day, I walked slowly back to barracks reflecting on the extraordinary scenes I'd witnessed and hoping – in vain, of course – to catch a glimpse of Salvia. But when I reached the dormitory, some news awaited me which pushed everything else out of my mind, at least for a few hours. I had taken off my helmet and was shaking my head in relief at the removal of its itchy weight, when I was met by Theo, out of uniform and dressed in a simple belted tunic.

"Ah, there you are, Simon! You just missed one of the messengers from the main gates. He said it was important so I took the liberty of taking the message for you. Here!"

Immediately assuming the message would contain bad news, when I put out my hand I saw that it was trembling slightly. "I think I've had enough shocks for one day!" Putting down my helmet, I opened the little cloth container with a thumping in my chest.

"Simon, whatever is it? I've seen you in most moods by now, but I've never seen you in tears before!" With a whoop of joy, I dropped the message and leapt towards him, enclosing him in a vice-like embrace.

"Help, you're killing me. Your cuirass is a bloody rockface!"

I drew back, wiping my tears with the back of my hand and laughing at the same time. "I'm sorry, I'm sorry! But Chloe has been delivered of a baby boy. It was a difficult birth but both are doing well. Oh, Theo!"

"That's wonderful! I'm really happy for you – Uncle Simon!" Theo clapped me heartily on the back. "A boy too – a real cause for celebration! Even worth a broken rib or two to add to my sore ass!" He rubbed his side with an expression of exaggerated pain, but I was already looking back at the message.

"The message is from Leah – they heard last night and sent word immediately. Chloe's doing well, but it was a long birth and she was very tired." Theo inclined his head obligingly, though thinking back I appreciate those details can have been of little interest to him!

"Oh, how I wish... well..."

"Yes, I know," he said gently. And I think he did. For there was sadness in the midst of joy for me and there would be for Chloe as well.

Chapter 24

Despite my euphoria at Chloe's news, once I had scribbled a return message for Leah and David to pass on I felt a new sense of emptiness, with the executions now confirmed and Celer's departure from the city. The only consolation was the rumour that Salome had left Jerusalem to pursue a love affair with an enemy of her brother's – hard to believe at first but then corroborated when the men who'd been guarding her apartments were pulled off that watch. In any case my usefulness to her had presumably disappeared with the death of her two nephews. Not a day went by when I didn't think wistfully of Celer's urgent offer on that breezy day in November. I did try and study the Vitruvius in what free time I had, but it was hard to concentrate as I never knew when Scarface would have me undertake some new duty for the King or order me to change my billet to the palace itself. More than anything I yearned for contact with Salvia, but the new routine made it harder than ever to meet her.

Then one morning I was overjoyed to see her approaching me outside one of the entrances to the King's apartments. The boys had been summoned to an audience with their grandfather, and she had been instructed to wait for them. Although it provided an opportunity for the private talk I had longed for, it was immediately obvious that Salvia was distressed and my pleasure at seeing her was quickly dispelled by the news she brought. She had been informed that the boys would soon be moved into rooms nearer not only to their grandfather but also to the King's brother Pheroras, now their official guardian. They would then share the same servants as Pheroras's own children. Salvia had always feared that she herself would be tainted by her close association with Glaphyra and Alexander, and the messenger had confirmed she would not be permitted to stay on to care for her beloved charges. She had not yet broken the news to the boys, who were very attached to her. Tears stood in her eyes as she gave me the tidings. I felt a wave of compassion for the boys, about to be torn away from yet another adult whom they loved, but I also confess to a sharp stab of alarm for myself.

"But where will you go? What will happen to you?" *What about us?* was what I meant.

"I don't know. It's possible my brother will be able to buy my freedom. If not, perhaps he'll find a way to send me to my mistress in Cappadocia. Or even back to our parents." *To the parents who sold you into slavery.* "Nothing is certain."

"But... oh, Salvia. That's no future for you!" We were standing in the covered entrance to a doorway; beside us a huge stone pot of lilies, which had withered in the colder weather and not yet been removed, reflected our sombre mood. Without thinking, I leant forward and clasped her to me. She recoiled, reacting to the hard surface of my cuirass and the front edge of my helmet which had pressed into the top of her head, and I released her immediately.

"I'm so sorry, Salvia. I keep forgetting about it. Theo accused me of nearly crushing him to death the other day." She looked taken aback at that, so I hastened to explain, "I embraced him at the news that my sister Chloe had given birth!"

Despite the circumstances we managed to laugh. She brushed away a few residual tears with the back of her hand. "Your sister! Oh, that's wonderful. What did she have?"

"A little boy."

"I'm so pleased," she sniffed. We stood looking at each other, Chloe's happiness contrasting starkly with our own bleak future. Celer's siren words rang again in my ears. *Why don't you come with me? At this point you could leave safely. Come to Rome, Simon!* And now it seemed that I could have taken Salvia with me. What had I done? What had I thrown away?

We did not have the luxury of being alone together for long, because soon an older woman appeared with the two boys. Alexander's cheeks were wet, and Tigranes's complexion was paler than ever. "I've told them they'll be coming here to live tomorrow," said the woman briskly. She patted the younger boy on the head. "He's a bit upset but he'll get over it." To the child she added, "We're not unkind here, you know – and we probably have better toys for you to play with. And other children, too." The little boy wrenched his hand away from the woman's and ran to Salvia, who held his head close into her skirts.

"I will talk to them. Leave this to me," she said with dignity, and she shot the other servant a look of such hostility that I wanted to shout out a cheer. As the woman disappeared inside with a pointed sigh, I caught sight of Cyrus approaching. I just had time to whisper to Salvia, "Don't forget – keep in contact via David and Leah." I watched her walk away, knowing that it could, possibly, be forever. I yearned to follow her, to watch over and protect her from all that might lie ahead, yet I hadn't even wished her good fortune or the favour of the gods. I simply stood there in mute despair, like a bird with a broken wing.

"Simon – if I can drag your attention away from the young lady, pretty though she is – I need you to change duty urgently. Can you go to the antechamber? There's an important visitor expected and we're short of men – this stomach sickness has laid a lot of you low."

The important visitor turned out to be Volumnius, the Roman procurator who had enthusiastically advocated the death penalty in the trial of the two brothers. I had glimpsed him once before and knew him by reputation. He was brought over from the gate with several other senior figures, and I had the task of searching them all single-handed. It was not a pleasant duty for they, and Volumnius in particular, did not take kindly to this treatment by a guard of such obviously junior rank. When I courteously asked him to leave his sword in the anteroom, he let out a loud snort of derision. "Who are you to disarm me, you impudent young fellow?"

But the exclamation was loud enough to be overheard on the other side of the doors, which I had cause to know were not soundproof. In a moment, one of them opened and there stood the King, resplendent in purple and gold.

"Ah, friends, you have arrived. Welcome! But I heard a cry. Is there a problem?"

"Er, no, Sire, not really," replied Volumnius, his hand on the bronze pommel of his sword. "This young guard asked me to remove my sword and I was expressing surprise at his impudence, that is all. As if I could ever be a threat to your safety, armed or not."

"Young Simon is following his orders, and I am glad to see that he has done so faithfully." The King did not smile at his visitors but inclined his head in my direction in a very slight gesture of approval.

"Of course, of course, I understand, Sire," muttered the procurator, turning away so as to draw his weapon unthreateningly from its leather scabbard and lay it on the floor. The other officials followed suit. The King appeared immediately mollified, and, with one of those sudden reverses of mood which I had now witnessed more than once, clapped his chief visitor amicably on the back.

"Come in, come in. I will have wine brought. How was your ride?" The two turned and led the small group of men into the chamber, but not before Volumnius had darted a glance of pure, narrow-eyed dislike at me. *I pray I won't need to have anything to do with him again*, I thought with a shiver of apprehension.

The close of this distressing day brought an unexpected and welcome surprise, which for a while dispelled the deep gloom into which Salvia's news had plunged me. A letter from Chloe herself, written in the brief, breathless sentences which reflected her speech patterns, made me smile with the – admittedly patronising – affection with which I'd always treated her efforts at reading and writing.

> *Our little boy is a joy. Feeding well and thriving. We have called him Joshua, after Silas's father. I was very worried about the circumcision, but all went well, had good phisican. I expect I've written that wrong. We invited our friends and naybours from here. I wish you could of come. And David and Leah and the boys. I miss you all. Simon, when my days of puritey are finished, I want to come to Jerusalem and sacrifice some young doves in thanks for my little boy, and Silas will redeem him then too. He may be the only child we will have, for his birth was dificult. Silas says on the way we must go to Bethlehem for the census, so it will all fit well. And then I can show you Joshua. You will love him. That is the longest letter I have ever written so be proud! I must stop and feed your nephew, MY SON!!*
>
> *Your loving sister,*
> *Chloe (and I hope God is blessing you.)*

As I rolled up the letter, I reflected on the wholehearted enthusiasm with which my sister had embraced the practices and traditions of her adopted religion. She had always been drawn to Judaism ever since she'd become a close childhood friend of the daughter of a Jewish neighbour. Our foster father had tried to discourage the friendship, unsure what Father would have to say about it. But, in her usual open and guileless way, Chloe had introduced her friend to Father on one of his visits. "Why should I object? After all, I owe my livelihood to the King of the Jews!" he'd said, looking down at her in the way that always gave me a pang of something I couldn't name.

*

It wasn't long before I was required to accompany the royal hunt outside the city. It was the first time King Herod had gone out hunting since the death of his sons, an activity they had often shared, so Cyrus Scarface warned us to be especially careful and courteous in any exchange we might have with him. I was permitted to choose my own mount the evening before and was relieved to find Saul at the stables, who, loyal as ever, made sure that I took one of the more docile animals.

"You'll have to kick her hard to get her to gallop. The other grooms unkindly call her 'Pegasus' even though she's a mare. But the worst that'll happen is you might get left behind and be in trouble for that! Would you like some spurs?"

I thanked him but declined. The iron spurs looked fearsome and I knew I'd be afraid the horse would bolt if I used them. But Saul's prediction turned out to be accurate, and with consequences that neither of us could ever have dreamt of.

Early in the ride my knees suddenly lost their grip on the horse's flanks when the King actually reigned in beside me and asked if I'd ever been hunting before. I admitted this was my first time, and that I'd therefore requested the stable grooms to give me a docile mount. The King seemed to find that amusing and one of his booming laughs made me jump. "Ah, that's not the way to learn. And they should have given you spurs!" I didn't confess that I had declined the offer but bowed in courteous agreement.

"Still, young Simon, son of Philip the Gaul, we'll soon have you up there with the best of us! It's a great sport – there's nothing like the taste of a gazelle or a boar you've speared yourself." Again I bowed, at a loss to know how else to respond, acutely aware that the King had not only singled me out yet again but was also addressing me by name. We were cantering quite fast at the time, and I wasn't sure whether to keep my face turned to the King's for the sake of deference or to my horse's neck for the sake of survival. The resonant royal laugh sounded again in my ear as I opted for the latter.

"Haha! I can see you need practice. I'm going up to the front now. I'll see you at the first kill." And with that he urged his fine bay mount into a gallop, and to my unutterable relief was way ahead in no time. I hoped that wasn't meant as an order, for the King did not see me at the first kill, nor at any of the others for that matter. Instead Pegasus had me lagging behind most of the way, only just managing to keep the rest of the group in sight and hoping I wouldn't be missed in all the excitement. On the homeward journey, as the light showed signs of fading, she grew ever more reluctant, so I drew alongside a comrade who had kindly slowed down to keep me company.

"Thanks for staying back, but could you get up there with the King and his Companions? If he notices I'm not there – he might as he acknowledged me at the start – can you explain that my mount is, I don't know, tell him she's lame or something and I've had to drop behind! Make sure he knows it's not my fault. That I wanted to be in at the kills."

"All right, if that's what you want – see you later!" With a quick pressure on his spurs he was off and away, leaving me to trot gently along through the grey-green dusty scrub. The hunting party was becoming ever more distant and after a few minutes I realised I was enjoying the unusual solitude and the silent, empty landscape. Looking up I gasped at the glorious state of the skies, whose pale winter blue had earlier been strewn with pile upon pile of grey fluffy cloud. Now, as if ignited by the setting sun, those great cushions erupted into flames of rosy gold, stretching away over the bleached barren hills as far as the eye could see, leaving only narrow channels of purest turquoise in between. I had never seen such a spectacular sunset and I reined in the mare, who needed no second bidding, to stand still and watch. I sensed a curious stirring in my blood, as if the fire in the heavens was meant personally for me, burning away the sorrows and fears of recent days and giving me notice of some imminent and momentous change.

But when I tried to get going again, the wingless Pegasus refused to budge. I dismounted to inspect her legs and hooves, not at all sure I'd be able to diagnose lameness anyway. She seemed fit enough, so I decided it was just obstinacy and briefly cursed Saul's excessive caution. Shivering slightly as the breeze quickened and the light faded further, I looked about me and realised that darkness would fall before I'd had a chance to reach the gates of the city, whose outline crowning its hilltop in the distance had become blurred in the dusk. At walking pace it was still around two hours away. I had no overnight provisions or equipment with me, and no way of sending word to Cyrus or anyone else about what had happened. For the first time I felt a prickle of fear. Thieves were common in the countryside at night, and wild animals, and I was alone and almost undefended. I did have my sword and a dagger, of course, but I'd only ever used them on dummies in training and did not at all like the idea of one-to-one – or, a frightening thought, one-to-several – combat, with a real and hostile adversary. And escape by galloping away was clearly not an option.

"You're letting your imagination run away with you!" I told myself severely. "Just lead this wretched animal quietly along and look for a farmstead or cottage somewhere near the path. These hills may look deserted but there must be people around. Shepherds for a start." But I knew my breathing was faster than usual and I spoke out loud for reassurance.

As I walked on, the horse meekly allowing herself to be led, darkness fell quickly and smothered the land. I realised that I'd be lucky to spot an isolated cottage now, unless it was well lit with lamps and its windows had no covering. I hoped that at least it wouldn't rain, as I had nothing to cover myself with. I was beginning to wonder where I should settle myself down for the night, when a faint flicker of light caught my eye just before the path dipped over the brow of a low hill. There was a scattering of shadowy olive trees nearby, leading me to think I must be approaching some sort of smallholding. I drew nearer cautiously, a new thumping in my chest warning me that the light could on the other hand mark a bandit camp. The mare's hooves seemed suddenly too loud on the stony path. I tugged the bridle back to halt her, giving myself time to consider whether to advance further. The earlier celestial fires extinguished, a ghost of the moon now appeared between dark piles of cloud as they sailed raggedly westwards to reveal a high vault of stars. Suddenly the horse gave a snort and shied away from me, almost pulling me over. Startled, I regained my balance and peered around anxiously for the cause of such unusual alarm in the phlegmatic creature. It was then that I spotted two huge shapes moving silently on the low hill. Their long necks were stretched towards the ground, the mounds of their backs massive in dark, spectral distortion. Camels! Emboldened by the sight, for it was unlikely that brigands would have camels, I whispered soothing words to the horse and pulled on her bridle to urge her forward.

"Come on, old girl, these must be merchants, probably bringing spices for the Temple on their camels. Perhaps they'll spare us something to eat." I was suddenly aware of pangs of hunger, for I'd eaten only a crust of bread and the few dates and dried figs in my saddle bag since early morning.

"Who there?" snapped an anxious voice as I reached the little encampment, which consisted of several tents arranged in a circle around a fire.

"I'm a lone soldier and wish you no harm. My horse was lame and I got left behind by the royal hunt. I am seeking shelter for the night." Immediately the words left my mouth, I regretted being so honest about being alone. But the sentry made no sign of hostile intent or attempt to search me before calling out to his masters, who were sitting around the fire from which a tantalising aroma of roasting meat – I thought probably goat – was rising. I hesitated on the edge of the encampment, swallowing my saliva, unsure what to do next. One of the men by the fire got slowly to his feet and walked rather unsteadily towards me.

"Welcome, stranger, if you come in peace. Old Darius will look after your horse – he is with us to care for our animals, but he serves as an extra guard at night. We are but few in number!" He nodded at the man who had accosted me and gestured for him to take Pegasus away. "Come and sit with us in the warm."

I needed no second invitation and followed him with relief, removing my helmet to show that I indeed came in a spirit of peace. The first man took my arm and gestured towards the other two seated on rugs on the ground.

"Let me introduce ourselves. I am Melchior, this is Balthasar and… and this is my old friend Caspar, who unfortunately is hard of hearing, so he doesn't talk very much. What will you take as refreshment? We can offer you good wine which we've brought all the way from home, and soon the meat will be ready – when our cook, who seems to have disappeared, returns!" The other two men looked up, and I could make out friendly gestures in the flickering firelight. The men wore long robes and differing headdresses – the one worn by the man called Caspar was tall and turban-like, fastened by a brooch whose colour was unidentifiable in the deep shadow. They exchanged a few words between themselves in a language I didn't recognise, Caspar leaning close to his friend and clearly straining to hear, before he looked back at me, smiled and patted the rug beside him in welcome.

I felt it was time to introduce myself and explain how I came to be loitering in the countryside, alone and at night. I ended up by confessing, "I can't see any cause for lameness in my horse, so I'm afraid the only other explanation is my own poor horsemanship!" Melchior, who seemed to be the spokesman for the little party, chuckled sympathetically.

"I well understand, young man. I myself prefer camels – an uncomfortable ride until you become accustomed to them, but steady and reliable, no sudden changes of mood. We'll have Darius examine her for you at first light. If anyone can find out what's wrong, he will. But I am curious – you say you are one of King Herod's soldiers?"

I indicated my assent but said nothing more, remembering the strict instructions not to speak of the King outside the court.

"Our business is with the King himself. It is for his help that we come to Jerusalem. You see, we three are scholars, and we study the stars, which are an important part of our religion. For some time now, perhaps as long as two years, we've noticed that to the west of our homeland a special star shines more brightly than all its brothers and sisters. We have heard it said that, according to prophecy, it must be the star that stands over the place where a new King of the Jews is to be born. We've come to find that place so we can pay our respects to this new king born with such heavenly announcement. We believe that the famous Herod, present King of the Jews, is the person to help us find him."

I smiled inwardly at the quaint, formal manner of speech of this courteous visitor from the East, but I found the innocence of their trust in King Herod surprising in men who were clearly wise and learned. It seemed to me almost childlike. I seriously doubted that King Herod would be willing to help them as they hoped. After all, the King believed there were already too many contenders for his throne, as I knew only too well. But of course I voiced nothing of the sort.

While wondering what to say, I swallowed the juices which the smell of roasting meat had brought rushing to my mouth and was relieved when the cook arrived back in camp, breathless and apologetic for his absence, which he did not attempt to explain. Melchior, however, seemed to find it amusing.

"Poor Stipi – he sometimes eats too much of his own good food! But don't delay, Stipi – we have a visitor. He has been hunting all day and is very hungry. And we are too." I was impressed that Melchior was considerate enough to get up and help Stipi remove the laden spit from the fire, before they laid it down to cool a little on some skins spread out ready. We all watched as the young man – he wasn't much more than a boy – took out a sharp knife, its ornate silver handle glinting in the flames, and began cutting hunks of meat from the roasted animal. After he had handed round our portions, Melchior reminded him that Darius and the other servants also needed to have their share.

Melchior continued to do most of the talking, and it soon became apparent that his Greek was much more fluent than that of his companions. Caspar listened intently and every so often muttered something inaudible which seemed to indicate agreement. He was very attentive to me, helping me to some of the choicest pieces of meat and ladling out a sort of vegetable stew to accompany them. He kept putting more unleavened bread in front of me as soon as he saw my platter was empty, gesturing with friendly amusement that I could eat as much as I wanted. The bread tasted quite sweet and had a mild herby flavour. Even though eating outside in the wild, these men did not stint themselves, for there were bowls of almonds and pistachios and grapes, and after dealing with the meat, Stipi set about cutting up pomegranates. But even while eating, the one called Balthasar, who remained silent, kept gazing up into the night sky. Every so often he would put aside his food to note down what from my shadowy vantage point looked like squiggles and dots, on some sort of chart attached to a tablet on his knee. I was curious and intended to find out more, but not before I'd finished my generous helpings of food, for seldom had a meal tasted more delicious.

"Balthasar is the most hard-working of the three of us. He is very clever too," remarked Melchior, after a one-sided conversation in which he told me a little about the studies which he and his two friends were engaged upon, not that I could understand much of it. After a while he started to ask questions about the King and the recent execution of his sons, for rumours had reached them on their journey, but I was careful not to be drawn.

"I'm sorry – I wasn't there, and we in the army don't get told about what's going on, especially when it takes place outside Jerusalem," I said firmly, between mouthfuls.

Melchior studied my face with approval. "It is meet and right that you don't gossip. Not all kings have such loyal servants."

Suddenly, Balthasar gave a little cry of delight, and almost throwing down the remains of his meal, got clumsily to his feet and pointed up at the sky. "There she is – our guide star! See you, soldier?" And he looked across at me, eager to share the sight of this wondrous thing that had suddenly appeared, outshining its pale companions in the dark vastness above.

"Last night cloud, tonight more clear. Cloud almost go." He bent down and added something to his chart. "Come together Jupiter and Saturn in Pisces. This so rare, so rare, soldier! This mean big thing!" The elation of this obviously erudite foreign visitor was infectious, so I looked up at the place he was indicating, and sure enough there was an unusually bright light in the sky – like a beacon, or a double star.

"So tomorrow we must enter the city and make request to see the King. If hunting today, I think he will be in his palace tomorrow?" This was Melchior again, looking to me for affirmation. I thought the least I could do to repay the hospitality of these kind strangers was to advise them that on reaching the palace gates they should ask for Nicolas of Damascus, as that might speed up their access to the King. There were always so many people queuing to make petitions to him for a thousand reasons – in my short time as guard I'd already searched many of them as they passed through the anterooms. Melchior, again considerate, asked if they could mention to Nicolas of Damascus that I had sent them. My wary mistrust of the great scholar made me hesitate briefly before deciding that it wouldn't be a problem. I had simply been sheltered and fed by these strangers when lost in the dark and had done nothing wrong, except perhaps to get left behind in the first place. Nicolas might possibly give them some precedence as a result of their kindness.

I was asked if I would be prepared to share a tent with Stipi, which I was more than happy to do – the alternative being a shivery night with only the stars as cover. I was relieved when Stipi crawled into the tent carrying two thick blankets, for the night felt very cold now that the cooking fire outside had been allowed to die partly down. Before Spiti extinguished the little lamp, we grinned at each other amicably, having not one word of a common language, and then, warm and secure, I fell fast asleep almost as soon as I closed my eyes. It was the best night's sleep I had had for weeks.

At first light, as I waited for Darius to fetch my horse from her tether in the little grove of olive trees, I exchanged a greeting with Balthasar, who was sitting on a large stone and already busy studying his charts. Obviously keen to share something with me, he pointed to the one on his knee and repeated the word 'star, star' several times. Looking over his shoulder I could see lots of little symbols which of course meant nothing to me, but I tried to show my interest by nodding vigorously and pointing to the skies where the big star had sparkled the night before. When Darius brought the mare back, having checked her for lameness, I wasn't sure whether to be pleased or sorry when he spread his arms and shrugged his shoulders, indicating he could find nothing wrong. "She good, she good," he managed to say in Greek, smiling at me toothlessly.

"Definitely my horsemanship then!" I acknowledged as Melchior emerged last, rather stiffly, from the tents. I was touched that, despite still fumbling with the folds of his headdress, the old man – I could see now that he was quite lame and was certainly older than the other two – had made the effort to get up and bid me farewell. Caspar came forward with a little bag of dates and a piece of unidentified confectionery, patting his stomach and looking at mine, as if to convey that he knew I would be hungry again before long! In the morning light I could see how colourful they all were, this little band of scholars with their servants. The latter, shadowy presences the night before, were now busying themselves with dismantling the camp and leading camels down the slope to be loaded.

After warmly thanking each of my hosts for their hospitality, I donned my helmet, mounted and rode slowly away in the direction of the city, its ochre stones glowing in the early rays of the sun. Before long I came to a bend where the path dipped sharply downwards, joining the road from Jericho and Bethany, so I paused to look back before riding out of sight. Stipi and all three scholars were still standing there against the bare outline of the hills, apparently in no hurry to depart despite the protestations of the night before. They all, Stipi included, raised their arms in an endearing valediction and I reciprocated the gesture before turning to face the way ahead, the jangling of bells on a camel's harness receding gradually into the distance.

Chapter 25

I reached the gates of the city while the sun was still low in the sky, by which time griping pains in my stomach were reminding me of the sickness to which many of my comrades had succumbed over the past few days. Predictably, Cyrus was less than sympathetic.

"Well, don't expect me to be sorry for you. What do you expect if you dawdle around the hills wasting time with unknown foreigners? You got what you deserve." I was about to protest with righteous indignation, when I caught a flicker of amusement on the scar-puckered face, so I just lifted my arms as if to say, "Fair point!"

"Take the wretched horse back and get yourself into barracks! I obviously can't put you on duty anywhere near the King for a couple of days. Let's hope he doesn't ask for you personally again. My advice based on what the others went through is not to stray more than ten yards from the latrines." Cyrus might have found it all rather amusing, but by the time I reached the stables to return the horse, I was almost doubled up with stomach pains.

"You don't look too well. What happened to you after you got left behind?" Saul was cheerful as he took the reins.

"Well might you ask. Next time I'll thank you not to be so damned worried about my safety, and to give me a proper horse."

After a day or two confined to barracks, I was alarmed on

returning to the palace by the change that had taken place in my brief absence. There was even more coming and going than before, a flurry of constant and urgent activity. The various signs of sorrow, self-pity and even occasional tenderness in the King's moods, which I had had occasion to witness or overhear, had all vanished, leaving only agitation and rage. There were frequent outbursts of shouting, usually followed by the hurried exit of whoever had been in audience. I couldn't help cringing when this happened, aware that at any moment the King might appear and vent his fury on me personally for some small thing that displeased him. But nothing of the sort transpired. On the contrary. After one visit, the King did indeed burst out of the chamber in pursuit of three priests from the Temple and their scribes, who had just departed in a cloud of white linen.

"As if I didn't have enough to worry about, without these absurd prophecies that everyone seems to take so seriously. How can I trust all these priests? They mean me only harm!"

I bowed low and heard my own hoarse voice: "Should I call your visitors back, Sire?"

"Ah, Simon, son of Philip the Gaul. A friendlier Simon than the one who has just left." He hesitated for a moment. "No, no, there's no point. Let them go. Let them rot. The priests are all saying the same thing. Three scholars from the East have arrived here – important men in their own country, so they would have me believe. Wealthy too, for they brought me handsome gifts of spices and scented oils. They came to ask *me* where the child King of the Jews is to be born – some nonsense about a bright star having guided them all the way here to Judaea. They thought I would know – I who am already the King of the Jews." He clutched at his stomach as if in pain, and the shrillness of his sudden laugh made me physically flinch.

"No, go to Nicolas instead and have him bring those scholars to me here, Simon. They're lodged in quarters where they can be watched. Those priests are all telling me it is written by the prophet Micah, that this new king, this ruler," and I actually saw a thin trail of silver spittle sail out of the royal mouth at the words, "is to be born in the town of Bethlehem, small though it is, in our – my – land of Judaea."

He tilted his great dark head to one side for a few moments as if listening to a quiet voice. Then he said, more softly, "I will tell those men from the East to ride to Bethlehem and find him. And if it's true, I will go and pay homage to him myself, for a king that is announced by a star must be a *king* indeed." Then he turned on his heel and went back into the chamber, muttering something under his breath. I wasn't sure but thought I caught the words, "Child... David's throne... we shall see," before I heard the inner door being slammed shut. There it was again – that ancient prophecy which Father had suspected might have led the King to desecrate the royal sepulchre with its precious throne.

*

Nicolas looked up from his neatly piled desk and greeted me with, "Aha, the nocturnal wanderer returns! I heard what happened to you from our visitors!" The tone was genial enough but his little dark eyes were as sharp and searching as ever, and as always I was uncertain as to where I stood with this clever and powerful man. Immediately on the defensive, I explained how it had come about.

"You were lucky. What with wolves and robbers, it isn't safe to be alone so far out there in the hills at night, as you well know. But these men have an important mission – they told you about it, I assume?"

"Yes, Sir. And I have come at the King's command to bid you have them brought to him as soon as possible. He has consulted the senior priests again today and..." I wasn't sure whether I should go on.

"And?"

"Well, they say it was indeed prophesied that a... a King of the Jews would one day be born in Bethlehem. King Herod wishes the three men to continue their journey and to go there immediately to find him – the baby, that is."

Nicolas nodded. "Yes. I was present at the meeting with the High Priest and others yesterday. I feared today would bring only confirmation. The King is sorely vexed. I'll fetch the visitors myself. But Simon – it is better you keep away and don't speak to them again. They seem innocent enough but in Judaea today one cannot be too careful." Then his tone changed as he added ominously, "And it's best you don't make friends with any more of the King's enemies. Your continued contact with the disloyal architect was ill-considered and against my advice. I was your father's friend but my protection cannot be relied upon forever." Only then did I realise I must have been spied on as I talked to Celer under the apricot tree, and when I bowed in acquiescence, it was an outward show of respect which was very far from how I felt.

"Very well. Go now to the stables and give orders that their horses and camels be made ready as soon as possible."

The rich smell of horse enveloped me as I entered the stables. I looked around for Saul or one of the stable boys to pass on Nicolas's message, but I did so distractedly, because something was bothering me. I stopped outside one of the stalls and went over in my mind the recent exchange with the King. What was it he had said about the baby king who was rumoured to have been born in Bethlehem? Yes, that was it: *I will go and pay homage to him myself, for a king that is announced by a bright star must be a king indeed.*

I will go and pay homage to him myself. How absurd! After all that happened – after the execution of his own two sons, whom he suspected of wanting to rule the kingdom in his place; after the mass murder of so many army officers thought to be less than loyal to him; after all that careful planning for the political betrothals of his chosen grandchildren. After all that, was he really going to kneel down before an unknown infant, who some long-ago prophets had foretold would be born to be king in the land? However bright the star, however revered the ancient prophets, however rich and learned these travellers from the East – this avowed intention simply did not ring true. In a lightning flash it dawned on me that the King's intention was not to pay homage to the child but to destroy him.

I was thinking frantically how to act on this sudden realisation, when one of the stable boys appeared with two buckets of water suspended from a yoke across his shoulders. I asked if he knew where the visitors' grooms were, and the boy jerked his head towards the courtyard where the camels were tethered. On my way in I had seen the animals but hadn't noticed Darius, who must have been on their other side. He was bent double, checking all their feet, and he came into view as I left the building, straightening up with a grimace which revealed the toll of his years. Within the blink of an eye I was beside him, my mind made up. I spoke slowly and clearly, only too mindful of the Persian's lack of Greek.

"I am come to order the camels and horses to be made ready. The King wants your masters to depart very soon for Bethlehem." Then I added in a low and urgent whisper, "Darius, tell your masters, tell Melchior, not to come back to Jerusalem. The King has told them to return here but please warn them not to come back. No Jerusalem. You understand?" I made a pushing away gesture with my hands to emphasise the point.

Darius put his head on one side and looked me up and down. He was digesting what I'd said with agonising slowness. I tried again. "You must go straight home to the East, not come back Jerusalem. Jerusalem dangerous. Important, Darius." As I spoke, again pointing first at Darius, then at the camels, then in what I assumed was an easterly direction, then drawing a line across Darius's throat at the word Jerusalem, I realised I was issuing my own death warrant with these counter-orders. Yet for once I felt no fear, only an overwhelming desire to make my meaning clear. To my huge relief Darius began to nod, as his lined old face split into the near toothless grin I remembered from our earlier meeting.

"No Jerusalem." He pointed to himself. "Darius tell Melchior." I could have embraced him; instead, I pressed my finger meaningfully to my lips. Then as I walked round the camel towards the stable door and turned to leave, I repeated in a much louder voice the order to prepare the animals for immediate departure, assuming that at least one of the stable boys would be watching inquisitively from the entrance. Looking back over my shoulder, I saw that my hunch had been right.

*

It took me a while to realise the enormity of what I'd done, but instead of watery-kneed terror, a strange sort of intoxication took over. I almost ran back to the royal apartments, where I was pleased to find the next shift had arrived. In my new decisive mood and with a brief space of free daylight time, I knew I could wait no longer.

But as I approached the now-familiar entrance to Alexander's former apartments, my palms felt clammy and my sandals weighed heavy on my feet, not out of fear for myself but out of dread of what I might be about to hear. There were few attendants and no sentries around now, and the servant who eventually answered the door in answer to a second pull on the bell rope was the sulky one who had met me when I called for the boys to attend the King's assembly. This time his manner was more forthcoming, even unpleasantly familiar. He thrust his face close up to mine and I recoiled at the stale smell of wine on the man's breath.

"There's hardly any of us old lot left now. The master's favourites have been executed or sent away. The kids are up at the palace with the King's brother, the fat one. They say some of the King's wives are coming to live here with their children, but we don't know if we'll be kept on." I noticed with distaste the stains on his tunic and thought that his chances of being kept on by the royal wives were probably slight. Then the man's expression changed to a prurient leer.

"I expect you're here to see Salvia. Well, she's gone!" There was a note of something like triumph in his tone. I tried to hide my dismay, guessing it was what the man wanted.

"Gone?"

"Yea. She wanted to go with the boys, but they," – he jerked his head in the general direction of the King's quarters – "refused. So then she offers to work up there as a nurse to anyone who gets sick. Thought that way she could see the kids sometimes, but they just laughed at her." I imagined Salvia's anguish. *They have had enough leave-takings in their young lives.*

"They accused her of wanting access to the King, who's often sick these days by all accounts, so she can poison him. Because of what he's done to her master and mistress. So first they tell her to push off, then they change their minds and call her back. Even sent a messenger down here for her. Said she could work for Pheroras. So she agrees, expecting to be near the boys. But then Pheroras had to get out quickly as his new quarrel with the King got nasty."

"Pheroras? He's quarrelled with the King again? Why this time?"

The servant shrugged. "Oh, surely you've heard the rumours? More plots. The King suspects Pheroras but they say this time old Two Times is behind it, wanting of course to get her fat son into power. Ugly old battleaxe."

"And Salvia?" When would the fellow get round to telling me what I needed to know?

"Well, Pheroras takes his slave slut away up to Peraea in the Jordan Valley where he's tetrarch or something, whatever that means – left the boys here. So Salvia won't be near the boys and she won't be the only slave neither. She'll have the wife for company – two slaves together. Haha! Too bad for Salvia, though – tasty little bit, that." He made a lewd gesture and my fist itched to knock the smirk off the man's face, but I told myself to remain calm. I needed more information. "Anyway, as I say, Salvia's gone to the Jordan Valley. Sorry!" He didn't look very sorry.

"She… she didn't leave a message by any chance?" The enquiry did not come out as casually as I'd intended. The smirk reappeared as the man shook his head.

"No, not a word, not a mite. You're out of luck, I'm afraid, soldier."

Determined not to show my stinging disappointment, I muttered a curt thank-you and turned on my heel. So, Pheroras and the Jordan Valley. Not so very distant, perhaps, but at that moment it might as well have been the furthest end of the Roman Empire. Things were now hopeless indeed.

Chapter 26

For a day or two after the three scholars had departed for Bethlehem everything went strangely quiet for a while in the palace compound. The King remained in his inner chambers. While on guard I spotted Nicolas frequently hurrying to and fro, head down and shoulders hunched, as well as other Companions I now recognised, but I wasn't summoned for any special task.

That respite was not to last. One late afternoon I was ordered, for reasons that were not made clear, to attend the King while he was inspecting repairs in the sumptuous Augusteum, the hall named after Caesar and used only for feasting with important guests. I'd not been in it before, but as I made my way up the steps I had to close my eyes, momentarily blinded by the dazzle of gilded doors in the low winter sunshine. The King was in one of his rages. He was expecting guests from Rome and had planned an elaborate entertainment in the amphitheatre out to the west of the city, with lions and other wild beasts currently housed in pens under the amphitheatre floor. He'd just been brought the news that there were structural problems in the theatre itself which would make it difficult to bring the lions safely into the arena.

"First a problem with the roof in the hall here, then this news. Always something going wrong. Where are my architects? Where is

Quintus Severus? He'll know what to do. He was in charge of the original designs for the theatre."

Nicolas answered patiently, "Sire, you dismissed Severus a couple of weeks ago if you recall."

"No, I didn't. I was angry with him for supporting that young hothead Servius Lucius Celer, so aptly named, but I didn't dismiss him. If he's gone then it's rank disloyalty on his part – no, worse, it's treachery. Everyone betrays me, everyone leaves me. Can I trust no one anymore? Not even my architects, who have enjoyed every favour, every privilege during my entire reign."

I watched as Nicolas first bowed low, then kept his counsel for many moments, allowing the high-pitched tirade to peter out. "Sire, be assured that all those who surround you now are your loyal and admiring servants. And I will have Quintus Severus recalled to Jerusalem forthwith – he is I believe supervising work in Jericho at the moment."

"Ah – so I didn't dismiss him!"

"Sire, I felt it advisable that he should not leave the country at this time – in case you should unexpectedly have need of him!"

"By the God of the Jews, you're a cunning old schemer, Nicolas of Damascus!"

I looked quickly down at the gorgeous mosaic floor to hide an involuntary grin of agreement. I still didn't know why I'd been summoned.

"Perhaps, Sire, but if I scheme, it is only ever in your best interests."

"Yes, I do believe that, Nicolas. When *you* turn against me that will indeed be the end. But I think I must retire, for I am not feeling at all well. I don't know what is the matter with me these last days – ah, what is this? Yet more bad news, I suppose?" A messenger had just been shown in by one of my comrades. He was still out of breath and somewhat dishevelled, with one of the legs of his baggy trousers almost entirely out of its ankle boot, the upper part of his tunic pushed untidily into his belt.

"Sire, it concerns the three scholars who... who came here from the East. I am sent by the men who were keeping watch outside Bethlehem."

"Yes, yes, and where are they? Are they on their way back here to report to me? Did they find... this child, this infant, this so-called *king*?"

"I don't think so, Sire, for they were seen only at an ordinary small inn in the town." The messenger paused to gain breath. "And, no, they are not on their way here. At first they could not be located at all, b-but I am ordered to inform you, Sire, that... that... that they were last seen heading in a south-easterly direction, away from Jerusalem."

The King turned and I saw that his large, once-handsome face had drained of colour. The line of his lips, always thin, disappeared altogether. "This cannot be. Why were they not followed? Stopped? They were told to come back to Jerusalem to report on what they had seen."

"I... I believe they left unexpectedly under cover of dark, Sire. The local man who spotted them did not know of your orders so did not immediately pass on the information." The messenger gulped and stared wide-eyed, visibly terrified that he would receive the blame for instructions which had not been obeyed. Nicolas, aware that the King seemed suddenly unsteady on his feet, led him to the nearest couch and supported him as he sat down. As Herod put his head in his hands, Nicolas took the opportunity of dismissing the messenger.

"Thank you, young man. You may return to your duties." I was near enough to hear the young man exhale with intense relief as he backed away out of the gilded doors. I watched him go and well understood why he turned and bounded down the steps as soon as he was in the open air.

For a while there was silence. Nicolas stood by the King, his hand resting lightly on his shoulder. Was it my imagination or did he give me a searching, even an accusing, look? But no, he couldn't possibly have come near to guessing the part I had played in this – could he?

In the background we heard some women's voices raised in anger, and the sound of pottery being smashed. Nicolas looked away in the direction of the disturbance, and I and the two other comrades in the hall exchanged raised eyebrows, anxious as to what would come next. We didn't have long to find out. Staggering to his feet the King gave vent to a roar which made us all jump.

"This is yet another betrayal. I knew those men could not be trusted. Scholars indeed – magi, they called themselves. I should have had them followed more closely, sent guards with them. I don't know what I was thinking. Well, if *they* won't tell me where this so-called child king is hiding, then all the boy babies under two will pay the price. My grandchildren will not suffer because of some absurd prophecies. It is those men who have brought this about! They have left me no choice!" Then, to my utter horror, he took a few unsteady steps directly towards me.

"Simon, son of Philip the Gaul, one of the few I can trust. Go and find Volumnius. He'll be in the Antonia Fortress today. Tell him I want a hundred cavalrymen made ready to depart immediately for Bethlehem. This is the order – every single boy under two in or near the town of Bethlehem must be put to the sword!"

It was clear from his unusually widened eyes and blown out cheeks that even Nicolas was thunderstruck. There was a pause and then he said gently, "Sire, come and sit down again. You are not well. Would it not be better to delay the departure until first light tomorrow? It will soon be dark." I felt a new respect for Nicolas – it was obvious he was trying to calm things down, play for time. To have contradicted the King at that point would only have enraged him further. But the King would have none of it.

"No, Nicolas. I will not change my mind. There'll be enough of them not to be delayed by brigands on the road. If they leave tonight, they can do what needs doing tomorrow morning at first light. There cannot be many boys under two in or near Bethlehem – it will not take long. They can be back here by tomorrow night."

There was silence in the room as his words struck home like stones aimed from a sling. The King sank back onto the couch, dazed. Like everyone in the room – the other guards, the slaves, the workmen in charge of repairing the roof – I was paralysed. Another cry came from somewhere outside the hall, which seemed to give the King new urgency. Half rising to his feet, he shouted, "Go, Simon – what are you waiting for? Go now this instant and find Volumnius. If he is not to be found, go to his second-in-command. There is no time to lose. You are to go with them, but report back to me personally before you leave."

I will never know how I managed to bow and leave the royal presence that day without my legs buckling under me. Reactions swarmed into my mind like locusts, and like locusts they obscured my thinking. But not for long. Bethlehem. Chloe. Her letter. Her longed-for baby. *Silas says on the way we must go to Bethlehem for the census, so it will all fit well. And then I can show you Joshua.* This could not be. It simply could not be.

I knew then what I had to do. There was no choice. I ran down the steps and until I was well out of sight of the great doors, I succeeded in running fast and purposefully as if bound on the King's errand. When I left the main gate to the compound – nodding to my acquaintances there as if nothing out of the ordinary was happening – I did not turn left in the direction of the Antonia Fortress, where Volumnius was to be found. Instead, I made straight for the stables, praying to all the gods I could think of that Saul would be there. They must have been listening for my first prayer was answered.

"You look terrible, Simon. What's the matter?"

"Saul, I need your help – desperately. And fast. I cannot tell you why, because the less you know the better for you. But please, I need a horse – really good and reliable, but fast this time. I need it in one hour, at the latest. Can you take it through the first gate to the north of the Jaffa, and meet me on the slope where there's a group of man-sized boulders by a small cave. You'll see a stand of wild fig there – that and the boulders will give us a little cover. You know the place?"

Saul hesitated. I saw him swallow and understood his well-founded fear but pleaded, "Please, Saul, I wouldn't ask this of you, but it is *truly* a matter of life and death. If the sentries or anyone asks why you're taking one of the best horses outside the walls, say it's needed as a replacement by an officer out on training, or something – I don't know. Surely you can think of something. Please!"

To his eternal credit – for he had no idea of my reason – Saul's decision was swift. "I have the right horse. But he's fast – you'll need to be careful. In one hour then – I know the spot." And he gave a brave little nod of acquiescence.

"You're a hero, Saul." As I hurried away in the direction of the Temple, I knew that I was gambling with his life, yet there was no other way.

The viaduct was even more crowded than usual. Every vendor, water-carrier, workman and priest in the entire city seemed to have decided to take that route at that moment to the Temple compound. I kept having to stop to make way for traffic coming in the opposite direction, nearly screaming with frustration each time. I almost wished I'd made use of the underground passage, built specially for troops to get into the Enclosure in a crisis without being seen, but I hadn't done so for fear of meeting other soldiers or officers who might ask awkward questions. On finally reaching the busy area below the arches of the Royal Portico, I prayed again silently, "Please, great and mighty Zeus, please don't let me down. Please let Zamaris be there."

Once more the gods were on my side. Zamaris was delighted to see me again, at first greeting with hilarity my panicky request for a disguise. "Have you left the military for the theatre then, Simon?"

Frantically I gestured with my hands to indicate the need for quiet and whispered a hurried explanation into Zamaris's ear, remembering his deafness and fearful that the neighbouring shopkeepers would overhear. Zamaris was swift to comprehend the urgency of the situation. Amusement vanished from his face and he led me to the back of the little shop, where we were well concealed behind an array of hanging textiles. In several blinks of an eye he had assembled an outfit in which I could pass as a merchant.

"But Simon," he said, again rather too loudly, so that once more I had to flap my hands to get him to lower his voice, "it's a noble intention of yours, but how are you going to warn all the families in Bethlehem with small sons? Who knows how many there are?"

I suddenly realised this was something I hadn't even considered. Getting out of Jerusalem unrecognised and before my absence was noticed had been my sole preoccupation. I'd just assumed I'd find Chloe and somehow manage to warn the other families with small boys to flee before the soldiers arrived. I looked at Zamaris helplessly as I threw down my distinctive red mantle and undid the shoulder fastenings of the cuirass. Zamaris pursed his lips, sizing up the situation. He paced around the tiny space while I changed, rubbing his forehead with his hand as if that would aid his thinking.

Then, as I was picking up and looking at my sword, wondering whether to abandon it or somehow secrete it under my merchant's disguise, Zamaris suddenly said, "I've got it! There's an old priest there – I met him at my cousin's. Retired from the Temple here because he's now quite frail, but he's well known there as it's his hometown. Make your way to his house – that'll be easy to find, I'm sure, even in the dark, as anyone will direct you. *He'll* have to get word to the families. You must not stay in Bethlehem a moment longer than you have to or that will be the end of you – the soldiers won't be far behind. You must leave the warning with the priest. I am deadly serious, Simon."

The soldiers won't be far behind. If I were lucky it might be about two hours before my disobedience was discovered; then it might take another couple for Volumnius to muster the hundred troops and be on his way. But that gave me four hours' start at the very most. Volumnius! That powerful Roman commander glared at me again like a vengeful ghost. "But the census. There'll be visitors in the town, and the priest won't know them – like my sister. And I don't even know if she'll be there yet. She might arrive at the same time as… Oh, Zamaris!" The desperate danger of the situation now almost crushed me – the urgency with which I'd had to act so far had somehow shielded me from the true horror of what was about to unfold.

"You could ask the priest to alert the Roman officials carrying out the census. They won't care one way or the other whether Jewish infants are killed, frankly, but they might just be decent enough to alert the parents. Who knows? But Simon, I'm utterly serious – that's all you can do if you want to escape with your life. Bethlehem's not a big place – on reflection there won't be all that many families with boys under two."

I was fumbling nervously with the disguise and Zamaris wasn't sure I was taking in what he said. "Listen to me, Simon – I'm concerned about *you* and how you get out of all this alive. I'll come with you now to the city gate in case you get challenged, though I doubt they'll bother about two merchants with a donkey. And I'll need to discard all your stuff – there's bound to be a search for you and if anyone finds it here my father and I will be dead too. Just as well Father's out of the city at the moment." He scooped up the heavy pile of discarded uniform and wrapped it in a bundle of fine linen. I was becoming all too aware of the perilous risks both Zamaris and Saul were taking to help me, but by now there was no turning back, no changing my mind. I had already done more than enough to merit the summary execution of all three of us.

"This damned helmet is a giveaway. I'll just stuff it all at the bottom of the ass's pannier and get rid of it somehow on my way back. Let's go. Just talk away as if we hadn't anything to worry about. Two merchants on their way to – I don't know – look at some merchandise for sale." I was flooded with gratitude to him for rising so unquestioningly to the occasion and dreaded the moment when I'd have to leave his reassuring instructions. I couldn't thank him as my mouth had gone as dry as old bone.

As we walked along, Zamaris was thinking aloud. "Your safest option is to leave Bethlehem with merchants going up to one of the old ports so you can take a ship to Rome. I'd say Joppa, as it's nearest. Caesarea's too far and anyway will be full of the King's men. A camel train would be best, if you can manage to join one – they're nice and anonymous. What you must do is this. As you leave Bethlehem on the Jerusalem road, you'll see a group of three, maybe four, cedars, on the left of the road. There are some shops under the trees there, and I think it's the second one along which belongs to a cousin of ours – anyway, it's the only one which sells cloth. He lives upstairs with his wife and sister. You can trust him – well, I think you can, he's certainly loyal, but he might panic a bit – still, you have no option anyway – and he'll know where to direct you. He might even be able to hide you if you have to wait – of course I can't be certain of that, but tell him I sent you."

"I thought your cousin was a woman – one you wanted to avoid at all costs!" I'm not sure how I managed even that ghost of a joke at such a time.

"You can have more than one, you know. This is her brother. Actually, you can tell him that if he helps you I might consider taking his sister off his hands after all. And don't look so shocked – it's an old joke between us!"

We passed through the gate without incident, as predicted the sentries taking barely any notice of two merchants leaving the city with a laden donkey. Knowing that he was more likely to be searched on the way back into the city, Zamaris planned to conceal my clothes somewhere in the gardens below. After a while Saul came into view, lurking beside one of the huge boulders I had described and looking around him anxiously, for we had taken longer than I'd expected.

"By God in heaven, I think he's *trying* to look suspicious!" exclaimed Zamaris. Before we joined him, Zamaris pressed a little bag of coins into my hand. "You'll need these. And they're a gift, not a loan – I've not forgotten that you were kind to me at my lowest moment."

I embraced him gratefully and when we came level with Saul I leant down to do the same to him. Then I regarded with some trepidation the huge bay horse which Saul had brought for me. "He's all right, Simon – he goes like the wind, but he's obedient too. He'll serve you well. Just don't ride too fast where there are lots of loose stones." It struck me that such a fine beast would all too soon be missed in the cavalry stables, but that way lay hesitation, so I dismissed the thought.

"Come – stand on this to mount him." Saul went red in the face as he rolled over a large stone to place next to the horse so that I could mount easily. Tentatively I took up the reigns in one hand, and with the other felt the front and rear pommels of the saddle for reassurance, then leant down to check the girth and ensure the saddle bags were fastened. There was even a quiver with arrows poking out of one bag. As I settled myself into a comfortable position I forced some words out of an almost clamped throat. "Farewell, brave friends. Between you you've thought of everything. And so fast. If the babies of Bethlehem are saved, it will be your doing. A thousand blessings on you!" And then, as the great horse started to move, I added the forlorn supplication, "I pray to all my gods and to yours that you won't pay the price for helping me."

Then I pulled Zamaris's cape and hood more tightly round me and urged my obedient mount down the slope towards the south-west. As I passed the sign for the road to Bethlehem and Idumaea I looked back and raised my hand. The final poignant glimpse in the gathering dusk of my two friends was of Zamaris, who had never met Saul before, standing with his arm around the smaller man's shoulders. I hoped Zamaris would explain everything to him, for Saul had no idea as yet why he had been asked to put his life at such risk. It occurred to me then with a jab of alarm that made me inadvertently pull on the reins and check the horse's speed, that as Nicolas knew from Chloe about David and Leah, their home would be the first place the King's soldiers would search. So many people in mortal danger because of one hasty decision on my part. Would I take that decision again if I had had more time to consider the consequences? Perhaps it is a question I will never be able to answer. Or is it? For as I got to the top of the opposite slope and quickened the great bay's pace with a light touch of the spurs that Saul had remembered, that final conversation with Father sounded again in my ears, above the rhythmic drumming of hooves on stony ground.

So... have you ever tried... to refuse? If at the time the question had sounded to Father like an accusation, made in the self-righteous arrogance of youth, the patient answer came back to me across the months. *It's a good question, Simon. A very good question.* And then, *sometimes we're told to do things which we just should not do. Bad things. But to refuse takes courage, more courage than I have.* Father's words echoed insistently, accompanying me like a blessing on that desperate ride to Bethlehem.

Chapter 27

Once I was on my way, something strange happened. The panic that had threatened to overwhelm me in Zamaris's shop evaporated. A gust of something very like joy swept through me – I was doing what I knew to be right; I had risked everything to fight an order that was evil, wicked. It was true that I had betrayed the King, who had come to trust me, but I felt no guilt for I knew that I had sacrificed a private loyalty for a greater public good. For the first part of the ride there was none of the doubt and ambivalence that had dogged me ever since I arrived in Jerusalem, the uncertainty about where my duty really lay.

But if I had learnt one thing from all the events of the previous months, it was that moments of pure exhilaration never last. Before long I was worrying about what might lie in store for Zamaris and for Saul, then the desperate fear returned for Chloe and her husband, who, little suspecting the peril they were in, were probably at that moment preparing their baby son for sleep because it was now dark. Above me the stars had begun to glimmer. I should perhaps have been more worried about robbers who frequently hid out in the Judaean hills, but my overriding dread was that Volumnius and his soldiers would overtake me on their way to commit mass murder. I was listening so intently for the thud of hooves behind me, that when I almost collided with a solitary farmer coming towards me in his cart, his curses made me jump and one of my sandaled feet came out of its stirrup. It was tempting to keep up the initial gallop for the whole of the five-mile ride, but the terrain was hilly and I knew that we would make better time if I allowed the horse to slow to a trot or a canter for at least some of the way so as not to tire him, and as there was only a sliver of moon I was anxious to prevent him stumbling on the uneven ground.

As I approached the little town of Bethlehem I was thankful to locate the cedar trees and to make out dark forms of the shops Zamaris had described. Then my horse and I clattered into the first street and I became suddenly aware that the brilliant star, which had so excited the three friendly scholars from the East, had started to blaze overhead among its paler brethren. I wondered whether it was guiding or mocking me. Whatever the star signified, it was Zeus who again responded to my silent pleading, for although the streets were almost deserted I soon passed a couple of young men whose dress identified them as Roman officials. When I reined in beside them I saw they were rather the worse for wine, but they were civil and explained that they were in the town to help conduct the census. I was afraid that as strangers they wouldn't know where to direct me, but when I told them I had a vitally important message for the priest, they obligingly pointed me down a side street and described the house I was looking for – I would recognise it by the large fig tree outside. I could have embraced them, vinous breath and all!

The priest was initially less helpful. I was ushered into his presence by a timid young servant who opened the door a little way, clearly alarmed by loud night-time knocking and only slightly appeased when I explained I had an urgent message for the priest. Looking back, I can see why the priest was so suspicious of this odd merchant in ill-fitting clothes who gabbled an extraordinary story about all the boys in the area under two being in grave danger. He shook his head in confusion and disbelief, probably thinking I was a lunatic suffering from hallucinations. He was a kindly old man, however, and instead of ordering me to leave his house immediately suggested that I take a seat and get my breath back. He even offered me water. I then decided, at the expense of precious time, to explain the whole story, as otherwise he would have continued to disbelieve me. He watched me unblinkingly, and I could see him weighing up my words to test their truth. This time I began at the beginning, and as soon as I mentioned the three scholars he nodded knowingly and interrupted my flow. "Yes, you can't keep many things quiet in this town so I've heard of those three rich visitors on camels looking for a King of the Jews. But I didn't pay too much attention – it all sounded a bit fanciful and I wasn't sure who or what to believe."

When I came to the King's rage and his murderous order, he nodded more vigorously, for the King's vengeful moods were well known in the land. "Sir, we must hurry. There is literally no time at all to lose. The soldiers may well be on their way. The distance is not great and they have swift horses. Can you help me to warn the families who have male babies? And…" for me the most important point of all, though I didn't admit as much, "also any families here for the census. Please?"

I got up, unable to keep seated any longer. All I could think of was the approaching soldiers, desperately wondering where they had got to and if they would start their evil work while it was still dark. The priest stood up too and paced the room, rubbing his forehead in an eerie echo of Zamaris's gesture.

Then he exclaimed, "Right! I will go to the houses of two families I know who have small sons who live very close by – I can do that quickly. One of them has relatives on a farm not far from the town so they'll have to try and get word to them and anyone else in the vicinity with little boys. There's another who'll be more difficult – we've not been on good terms because of the way they observe the Sabbath, so they may suspect a trick. As for the strangers who've come for the census, they're mostly in the taverns. I'll go to the nearest one, but you will have to go to the two furthest – you have a horse and I'm lame so can't walk far or fast."

"Thank you, Sir. I know Bethlehem is not a big place but surely there must be more than three or four families with boys under two?"

"Yes, probably. But I'll have to rely on the first ones spreading the news. Now, come to the door and I'll explain how to reach the inns on the edges of the town. They're on opposite sides, I'm afraid, but don't ride back through the middle or you'll risk meeting the soldiers if they do come tonight. If there's no sign of them as you leave here, I think you can safely cut through town now – you'll be going in the opposite direction from the Jerusalem road. Go first to Rachel's place – she'll be helpful."

He had to repeat all the instructions twice, as I was so agitated I found it hard to take them in. As I went to untether my horse, which was drinking from a trough under the fig tree, he called softly, "It's a brave thing you're doing, young man. I don't even know your name, but I shall pray to God to deliver you safely." I thanked him warmly, and with some effort – without Saul's help this time – I mounted.

*

Despite the repeated directions, I did take one wrong turning and reached some steps at a dead end, which made the clenching in my entrails worse than ever. I expected any moment to hear the drumming of cavalry hooves, but mercifully when I turned back there was only one other way to go, and at a brisk trot we soon reached the first tavern. Once again I was forced to rouse the household with loud knocking on the sturdy wooden door, and then there was an unbearably slow wait before it opened. Eventually the landlady appeared, somewhat dishevelled and dressed for sleep, with a blanket thrown over her for warmth and a lamp in her hand. She showed more surprise than irritation at the sight of me, and as my words tumbled out her eyes widened still further.

"I bring terrible news from Jerusalem. King Herod has ordered that all the boys under two in the vicinity of Bethlehem should be put to the sword – because of a rumour that a child's been born here who'll become King of the Jews, according to ancient prophecies. Please, you must believe me – I left Jerusalem disguised like this but am in truth one of the King's bodyguards and I heard the command myself." There was little point in concealing my identity – if the cavalry caught up with me I was as good as dead already.

To my relief she did believe me and in a bitter tone responded, "Oh yes, I can believe you all right. My nephew was one of those stoned to death in Jericho by order of the King, so I know what he's capable of. Come in, come in – it's cold out there."

"No, madam – thank you, there's no time to lose. I must hurry to warn people in a tavern on the other side of town. But first – are there visitors lodging here with small boys?"

"No longer. We have had a few families here for the census, but the last one left early this morning." Fortunately she went on to elaborate despite the urgency. "Nice people with a dear little baby called Joshua. I always like the babies. They were travelling on to Jerusalem and the mother told me how excited she was about showing him off to her brother who's in the King's bod... oh, by God in heaven, that couldn't be you – could it?"

The tide of relief that surged through me almost made me knock the lamp out of her hand. Without a doubt this had been Chloe.

"Yes, that's me. I cannot thank you enough. They left this morning, you say – so they'll be safely in Jerusalem by now?"

"Certainly, barring accidents or robbers on the way – and if you've ridden from Jerusalem tonight you'd probably have seen evidence of that. They'd arranged to share a cart with another family, I believe."

"I cannot tell you how happy that news has made me. Thank you. Go back into the warm now." Then, as I walked towards my horse, I remembered to put aside my personal feelings and ask, "You're sure you don't have any other families lodging here with small children?"

"Quite sure. But hurry now – the tavern on the east side might well have some. May God speed you."

It took a lot longer than I'd expected to ride around the perimeter as advised by the priest, but the risk of running into any advance party of soldiers in the confines of the small town was too great to take. A lone merchant riding through Bethlehem late at night would be highly suspicious to them, and in any case they might well recognise my beautiful horse. Leaving the town when I had finished my mad mission of mercy was going to be dangerous enough, but if they did come in the night I had to pray I'd hear them approaching and have time to find a hiding place off the road until they'd passed.

The path, strewn with loose stones, was not as clearly marked as the Jerusalem road and there was only a crescent moon that night. Thanks to the radiant star I did have just enough light to find my way though only at a frustratingly careful pace, remembering Saul's warning. My terrible fear for Chloe now allayed, I started to worry about Salvia, picturing her exquisite but sorrowful face when she told me she was to be forcibly separated from the boys. I agonised about what would become of her now she'd been compelled to serve the King's brother, and about how she would be treated. Would she ever be permitted to see Alexander and Tigranes? Would she be allowed to maintain contact with her own brother? Would he be able to buy her freedom? And then the raw pain of the most crucial question of all – would I ever see her again?

I thought again about David and Leah and reprisals that might be taken against them because of their connection with me. I reassured myself by recalling how kind Nicolas of Damascus had been towards Chloe. If it were necessary, surely she would appeal to him to be lenient with her husband's family. If – and I knew it was a Goliath-sized 'if', but I had to believe in a future – I did manage to reach Celer in Rome, I would ask him to write to Sabinus for news of what had happened to all the people I cared about. Not only Chloe and David and Leah, but Zamaris and Saul and Theo too. And maybe, just maybe, with the help of Celer, there might be some way of bringing Salvia to Rome. But for the time being all that was a dream, and in the previous months I had learnt a lot about the fragility of dreams. Rome was a long, long way from Bethlehem.

This time the inn appeared deserted and for what seemed an eternity no one answered my urgent knocking. Eventually a man leant out of a window and asked in a surly voice what the noise was all about. I decided to curtail the story this time.

"I have come from Jerusalem with a dire warning. The King has issued an order that all boys under the age of two in and around Bethlehem are to be put to the sword. That includes visitors who've come for the census. Are any lodging with you?"

"No, I have a house full – but no small children. Go away now, or you'll disturb everyone and they'll refuse to pay me."

I was on the point of turning the horse round when his head appeared again. "Wait there. I'm coming down!" Of course I waited, though not pleased as I was anxious to be on my way to find Zamaris's cousin as soon as possible. My life depended on it.

The landlord emerged, and explained in a friendlier tone, "I almost forgot. There is a couple lodging in our stables – I didn't have room for them inside. They were desperate for a roof over their heads as the woman was about to give birth. She had the baby a few days ago. We'd better go and warn them – if what you say is true." He looked up at me quizzically in the light of his lamp. I could see he wasn't sure whether to believe me, so I dismounted and tied up my horse before he could change his mind. We had to warn those people to leave at once. He led the way to his stable and pushed at the door which stood ajar. Inside the stall was empty, except for one small ox munching something that looked like hay in the manger. In the centre of the clean-swept floor the embers of a fire still glowed red, and coins had been laid carefully on a narrow ledge containing tethering rings which ran along one wall.

The landlord spotted the money and exclaimed, "They've left

their rent, I'm pleased to see. They can't have been gone long – look at the fire." As he bent to pick up the coins, he discovered something else. "What's this?" He squinted at it in the light of his lamp and passed the little bottle to me with a puzzled look.

I removed the stopper and immediately inhaled the pungent fragrance of frankincense. I recognised it from my childhood, as my foster mother believed it could cure all manner of ills and, despite its great cost, had usually managed to have a little in the house. "I think this was their way of thanking you for giving them shelter when their baby was born," I suggested. "Even this small amount is very valuable."

*

I can't describe the wave of gratitude I felt for the old priest, who had been true to his word. In the brief time it had taken me to ride to the two taverns, one of the first families he'd warned close by his house must have reacted with astonishing speed to save their children, and they had obviously taken the trouble to warn others as they fled in this direction. I was light-headed with relief. My death-defying gamble had paid off – at least for some of the little boys.

"I hope they'll make good progress – they only had a donkey. Let's pray that the soldiers won't arrive here before morning to give them a good start." It was clear the landlord now fully accepted my story, and perhaps the rent they'd paid and the gift left behind had aroused his sympathy for the little family. Then his dark brows creased in bewilderment.

"They seemed so poor yet they had a lot of visitors. Shepherds the night their baby was born, and later three men on camels who said they'd come all the way from Persia to pay their respects to the child. They were certainly wealthy because I saw the lavish gifts they brought – I suppose that's where this oil comes from. Guided by a star, they said, or some such nonsense." He shook his head and raised his shoulders in perplexity. But he glanced up at the sky as he added,

"A mystery child indeed!"

Acknowledgements

I have consulted many books in the writing of this novel, in particular those by Josephus, a Jewish, later Roman, historian and military leader who lived in the 1st century CE. These were

- Flavius Josephus, *The Jewish War*, translated by G.A. Williamson, (Penguin Books, 1981) and
- *The Antiquities of the Jews*, translated by William Whiston, (Wilder Publications, USA, 2009).

More personally I would like to thank Dr Jonathan Kirkpatrick of Wycliffe Hall, University of Oxford, who kindly read an early draft of the manuscript, and made a number of helpful suggestions and corrections related to the place and period.

I am especially indebted to Martin Goodman, Professor of Jewish Studies, Faculty of Oriental Studies, University of Oxford, who most patiently answered my numerous and wide-ranging questions about Judaea in the 1st century BCE.

For writing and publishing news, or recommendations of new titles to read, sign up to the Book Guild newsletter: